OVER THE LINE

STEVE HOWELL

Steve Howell

QUAERO

Quaero Publishing

Published by Quaero Publishing
Quaero Publishing
River Cottage
Isca Road
Caerleon
Newport
Wales NP18 1QG

QuaeroPublishing@btinternet.com

ISBN: 978-0-9931607-0-7

Cover design: Peter Reynolds
Book design and lay-out: The Write Factor
Printed by TJ International Ltd, Padstow, Cornwall

"WHAT I KNOW MOST SURELY ABOUT MORALITY AND THE DUTY OF MAN I OWE TO SPORT."

Albert Camus

OVER THE LINE

1

THE TRIAL

ON MOST DAYS, THE CROWD at an athletics meeting would barely fill a bus. We huddle in half empty stands, at out of the way tracks, almost unnoticed. But this wasn't most days: access roads had been gridlocked for hours, the stadium was teeming with expectation, and I was struggling to find my seat somewhere in the section facing back down the home straight to the start.

As I edged my way along a row, people half-stood or wriggled sideways to let me shuffle through. I had a few nods of recognition – familiar faces I'd seen around the athletics scene over the years – but I was relieved that there was no one nearby I knew well. I was in no mood for small talk.

I had left Megan in the warm-up area. I don't crowd my

athletes on the day of a race. I'll watch them warming up for a few minutes, I'll check they're okay, but I don't give them last-minute advice. Not unless they ask for it. I reckon it's too late by then for me to make any difference – the work's been done, and it's all about execution. You have to let them get on with it. Trust them.

Megan had gone through her routine of stretching and striding. There was nothing especially abnormal about her manner, no obvious signs of tension or trouble. As usual, she kept her side of the conversation to one syllable at a time. She was feeling "good". The windy conditions were "a pain". And "yes", she had stretched her dodgy hamstring.

I squeezed into my seat and looked around the stadium. On the track, marshals checked the hurdles, making sure lines were straight and heights were right. On a platform beyond the finish line, photographers jostled for position, lining their lenses up like a firing squad. In the stands, all the aisles were peppered with people hurrying to their seats, clutching bags and bottles. This race had been hyped as the highlight of the day, and no one wanted to miss it.

To my left, a man heading for obesity was working his way through the contents of a giant lunchbox, elbowing me as he shovelled food into his mouth. Much to my relief, the woman to my right was leaner, but I still had to hunch my shoulders as I sat between them.

"It's Megan Tomos in this one," the lady announced in my general direction, with more than a hint of a Brummie accent.

I kept my reaction to a nod, not wanting to encourage her. I take my coaching seriously – my ex-wife would say too seriously – and, at that moment, with all I've worked for on the line in more ways than one, I didn't need any distractions. I wanted to watch Megan even more closely than usual.

"I've been looking forward to it," she said. Obviously, the

nod was too much encouragement. "I think she'll do well in Rio." She paused for a moment, gazing into the distance as if imagining Megan with a gold medal round her neck. "I saw her on TV a week ago," she continued, turning back to me, undeterred by my silence. "You know, the Diamond League in Rome? Wow! She won it comfortably – beat the Americans. Super run. Nice girl. They interviewed her afterwards, and she seemed so lovely. Oh, here they come."

The athletes were emerging from a tunnel and turning onto a pathway at the foot of the main stand, heading for the start area. Each athlete was paired with a steward clutching a bright yellow container for their kit. Megan was halfway back. She was the fastest qualifier for the final, and that put her in Lane 4. A wave of enthusiastic applause was following her.

I pulled my specs out. I'm still in denial about needing them, but this was no time for vanity. I squinted through the lenses at Megan's broad shoulders, checking again for warning signs. It was hard to tell, but she seemed rigid and tense, and she wasn't responding to the crowd or walking in her usual, half-skipping way.

I pulled my phone out, shoved my glasses onto my fore-head and flicked through the headlines. Nothing on the news pages about Megan. Nothing was good. I tapped the Twitter button and thumbed the tweets gushing in from fans, athletes, pundits and reporters. Endless mentions of #Megan, @Meg_Tomos and #Rio2016, but it all seemed harmless. That was also good.

The woman next to me suddenly seemed beside herself with excitement. "I used to do the hurdles," she said.

Oh no – I sensed a life story coming. This time, I didn't nod. I was trying to concentrate, watching Megan and her seven rivals arriving in the start area, peeling off tracksuits and checking their blocks. All of them began limbering up with trial starts, the momentum carrying them over the first couple of hurdles. Megan's hurdling was as smooth as ever, like the obstacles hardly existed.

"She'll win this easily," the woman said, undeterred by my silence. "Ten metres. I'd give her ten metres on everyone else. There's no one to touch her."

She was stating the obvious. Of course Megan *should* win. "But it's an Olympic trial – anything can happen," I said, trying to make it sound like the last word.

The woman nudged me. "She doesn't look very happy," she said, nodding towards the far end of the stadium.

My eyes darted up to a huge screen above the start. The athletes were lining up now, and the camera crew was in Megan's lane, zoomed-in on her grim face. The commentator was introducing her, babbling about her being the world leader and British record holder and "our big hope for Rio".

I discouraged my athletes from showing-off for the cameras, but Megan would normally have given the crowd a warm smile and a two-handed wave. But her arms remained fixed at her side. She was staring into the camera like she was oblivious to the frantic cheering around her. My unease was growing.

The starter told the athletes to take their marks. I knew him well. He was old school and very particular. He held them in the set position for far too long, until one of the athletes jumped the gun, and everyone followed her. The starter fired two shots in quick succession to call them back. Some pulled-up before the first hurdles, others clattered through them. Megan only took a couple of strides. The camera focused on her again as she walked back. She looked even grimmer now, shaking her head as the ground staff tidied up the hurdles.

The athletes settled into their blocks for the second time.

The re-start was clean. But Megan was slow to get away. She was last to rise at the first hurdle and still trailing at the second. My hands were clenched, sweat gathering in my palms. The woman next to me was rigid and, mercifully, silent. But Megan didn't panic. In that split second, the years of work shone through. She clicked into gear like a machine, perfectly balanced, immaculate technique. And by the sixth hurdle, she was surging past the others, making them look like the parents race at a school sports day.

The whole stadium was on its feet. Some fans were waving 'Leg it Meg' placards. The commentator screamed, "Megan Tomos – That Was Awesome!" The man to my left nearly choked on a sandwich. The woman next to me was beside herself, jumping up and down, looking alarmingly like she might hug me.

"Did you see that?" she screamed. "My God, that was fantastic. What a super run."

I smiled and nodded but only from politeness and a large dollop of relief. It was a good recovery, but not super or fantastic – not by Megan's standards.

Momentum had carried her twenty or thirty yards beyond the finish line now, and as usual, she was bent with her hands on her knees looking up at one of the screens. As the results came up confirming her victory, she straightened, turned and started walking briskly across the track.

The other athletes were offering hands, hugs, and nods of respect. But Megan brushed them away and marched off the track, head down, ignoring cheers and shouts from the crowd, sweeping past the photographers and TV interviewers. One of the photographers darted towards the entrance to the tunnel, blocking her way, trying to take a picture of her face. I felt a sickening pulse of anxiety shooting through me, a sense of helplessness, as he raised his lens and she lifted an arm across her face, and then he stepped closer, and she swept her arm towards him like she was swatting him away, knocking the camera from his hands.

The photographer fell forward trying to catch his camera, hitting the ground face first, as Megan stepped sideways over one of his splayed legs and disappeared into the darkness.

The crowd released a collective gasp, which hung in the air and then floated away, leaving an uncomfortable silence. People seemed frozen for several moments, unsure of what to make of what they'd seen, or how to react to it.

Gradually, disconnected murmuring grew into a buzz of animated conversation like an orchestra warming up. I was too stunned to take in anything that was being said around me. The lady next to me had slumped into her seat without a word, her excitement punctured, but I remained on my feet, staring at the tunnel entrance, my last glimpse of Megan's back disappearing into the darkness still fixed in my mind.

I started to leave, giving a polite nod to the lady, who now seemed like a rare friend in a crowd that, I could see, felt bewildered and let down. I edged along the row, even more thankful no one seemed to know I was Meg's coach. On reaching the exit, I took a final look across at the photographer. He was making a bit of a show of dusting himself down, lapping up the solidarity of the fellow snappers who'd gathered around him.

I checked my watch. Megan and I had a press conference in half an hour.

2

THE TWEET

IT WAS NEVER GOING TO be an easy week. The Olympic trials are like a trip-wire set in the path of the best athletes. Eager rivals love to bring down the big names, everyone wanting the automatic place set aside for the winner, everyone's nerves twitching. There were bound to be unexpected problems: the nasty surprises you know are possible – a late injury, a stomach bug, a stumble at a hurdle. But what had happened on Thursday, three days before the trials, was something not remotely on my radar, and it threatened Megan's Rio ambitions and everything and everyone revolving around them – me included.

I was in the library at Middlesex University marking exam papers. My day job is teaching sports science, but my employer cuts me some slack for coaching Megan, and that includes taking several calls a day from Mimi Jacobs. Mimi does the PR, and she's permanently on a mission to embroil me in building Meg's personal 'brand'. Give me a break.

I was toying with not answering this call. When the phone started vibrating and moving sideways across the desk, I stared at Mimi's name for a second, wondering if it was going to be about meeting for lunch. Lately, nothing was too unimportant to warrant a pow-wow at a coffee shop she'd adopted in Hendon Central. "It'll only take ten for me on the tube," she'd say, practically heading for Belsize Park with her Oyster card ready before I could answer.

I wanted to finish my marking, but it was too close to the trials to ignore a Mimi call.

"Liam!" she said urgently, when I answered. "Have you seen the tweet?"

"Hang on," I said, walking briskly towards the exit, sensing a few dozen exam-weary eyes glaring at me.

Mimi sighed impatiently. "Liam, are you listening?" she said. "There's a tweet you must read."

I nearly laughed out loud – or should I say LOL-ed. I'm not into Twitter. Not at all. All that self-obsession is very irritating – but it's become part of the job. I don't tweet myself, but I do follow all Megan's rivals to gather snippets about how they're doing, what their plans are, what they're boasting about. It's surprising how much they give away.

"What tweet?" I said, now outside and hunting for some shade.

"It's about Meg," she said, "and it could be really damaging."

I decided to head for The Quad, which had coffee and chairs as well as shade.

"Do I need to be sitting down for this?" I said, trying to sound ironic. Mimi is easy to wind up.

"Liam," she said. "This is serious. Meg has an old boyfriend who's connected in some way to the death of another boy. They all went to school together. And it was a drugs overdose – he *died* of a drugs overdose."

That got my attention. "What do you mean? Like heroin or something? Read it to me".

"I've emailed it," she said.

"Hang on." I was fumbling with my phone, trying to get into my emails without cutting Mimi off.

The top one was headed @Will2Play and a tweet was pasted in it saying 'Make all the crazy threats you like but leave Meg out of it.'

I was in The Quad now heading for a chair in the darkest corner, away from the glare coming through the glass roof. As I sat down, I read the tweet through again.

"Liam?" Mimi said, sounding not sure if I was still there.

"Leave Meg out of what?" I said in a whisper, conscious some of the people around were sports science students who knew I coached Meg and invested way too much time in sucking-up to me in the hope of getting an introduction. "I don't get it. What crazy threats?"

"I don't know," Mimi said. "It's something to do with the police re-opening an investigation into this boy's death."

"Death?" I said. "When did this happen?"

"About two-and-a-half years ago."

"Two-and-a-half years," I repeated, stunned that it must have been around the time Megan had turned up at Copthall Stadium, my local track in north London, a nervous nine-teen-year-old looking for a new coach and – I later found out – scared I might say 'no'.

I allowed myself an inward smile whenever that thought came to me. It seemed so ridiculous now, with Megan so close to achieving the ultimate prize in sport, but even then there was no way I would have turned her down. I did have a waiting list of sorts, but she was already being talked of as another Jessica Ennis and any coach's dream opportunity.

"How did you find this tweet?" I said. "Are you sure he's talking about our Meg?"

There was a pause, like Mimi was trying to summon the patience to explain the alphabet to a moron. "Liam, darling, he *is* talking about our Meg," she said. "Do you think I'd phone if I wasn't sure?"

"You've phoned me for less," I said, regretting it almost as the words were coming out. I sensed Mimi recoil at the other end of the line.

"Look, I've had a call from the Argus, the local rag in Newport." Mimi sounded hurt or annoyed, or both. "Stuff about Megan can't be put on Twitter without a journalist spotting it or someone tipping them off. The reporter was asking questions about Meg's relationship with Will and lacing it heavily with references to the other boy's death being drug related."

"What relationship though?" I said, feeling a rising sense of anxiety, knowing how the 'D-word' – regardless what type of drug – would send Megan's sponsors into a panic. "I mean, I've never heard of Will. Surely she'd have mentioned him if they were still in touch? It doesn't make sense. She barely has time for Tom, never mind another man."

"I know," Mimi said. "I can't get my head round it either, and the guy wasn't giving much away. But it sounds like Meg was dating this Will for ages. Childhood sweetheart. Back of the bicycle shed and all that… And now he's in some kind of trouble."

"How much trouble?" I said.

"It sounds like the parents of the boy who died – Matt he's called – won't let it go. They weren't happy with the original police investigation, and now it's been reopened and Meg's 'ex' is in the firing line. I'm not sure why. I was trying to fob the journalist off. I didn't want to sound that interested. But we're going to have to ask Meg what it's all about. The journalist wants a comment, and I need to get back to him with something."

"No you don't," I said, more abruptly than I intended. "No way. I don't want her being bothered just before the trials."

"But Liam..."

"Wait until Sunday's out of the way."

Mimi sighed. "Look," she said, "the media don't give a toss about Olympic trials. They have their own agenda, and the Argus could run a piece any day. Then the nationals will pick it up, and before you know it... Okay, I think this guy was just fishing, but I don't know for sure what he knows, or what it's all about, and I don't like not knowing. We need to talk to Megan."

I read the tweet again. What was @Will2Play up to? Why mention Meg's name if you want to keep her out of it?

"Liam?"

"Okay, I take your point," I said. "There's a possibility the journalist could run a story anyway. But why guarantee it by feeding him a comment? Let's sit tight. If he's got something, he'll run it. If Meg goes mad because we haven't warned her, you can blame me. I'll take a chance on it. Let's just keep a close eye on her. We know her well enough to know if there's something on her mind."

"We could talk to Tom?"

I sensed Mimi knew this was a stupid idea even as the words left her mouth. Tom – a moderately successful 800m runner – had been living with Megan for about three months, having followed her around like a groupie for the best part of a year. You could see why she might have succumbed to his

Viking-like looks, but it was hard to spot any other grounds for attraction.

"Sorry, Liam, forget that one."

"But there's Jackie," I said.

"She'll freak."

"Best to tell her though," I insisted, knowing it would be madness to keep it from Megan's agent.

"Okay," Mimi said. "I'll tell her you've vetoed doing anything until after the trial."

"Against your better judgment?"

"Yes, and if the journalist phones, he'll be a missed call."

3

FACING THE PRESS

THE NARROW CORRIDORS UNDERNEATH THE Alexander Stadium in Birmingham aren't the best place for a meeting, but we didn't have much choice. Other athletes were using the changing rooms, thousands of spectators were milling around outside, and the media was waiting for us in a room upstairs.

By the time I got there, Mimi was already giving Megan a hard time. "This is a fucking nightmare," she was saying. "Deep shit, Meg. Why the fuck did you flounce off like that? *And* knock a frigging photographer over? Don't you get it? If they didn't think there was anything in this 'Will' thing before, they're bound to start wondering after that performance."

Megan's formidable five-ten frame winced, like a dart

had landed in her chest. She looked along the corridor, right through me, to see if anyone was coming and then leaned forward to within an inch of Mimi's face. "And what the fuck's it got to do with you? What do you know about Will – or jack-shit for that matter?" she said, her voice menacing but brittle.

Mimi threw her arms in the air and turned to me with a theatrical throw of her head. "Who *doesn't* know about Will? What do you think Twitter is darling, a secret frigging society?"

Tom rolled up at this point, looking nervously from Megan to Mimi; probably anxious his winning lottery ticket might be at risk.

"Where's Jackie?" I said as a starter.

"God knows! Hobnobbing with some sponsors, I expect," said Mimi. I arched an eyebrow. "Okay, I know, it's her job to hobnob with sponsors."

"It pays the bills," I said.

I turned to Megan, who had taken half a step back, but who was still pumped up and glaring at Mimi. I was fuming about Megan's tantrum on the track as much as Mimi, but this was no place for a scene. I waited for her to calm down and make eye contact.

"Good recovery," I told her when she finally switched her gaze to me. The praise seemed to surprise her, and she relaxed her shoulders fractionally and threw me a smile – the first for days. "Mind you," I added, trying to sound cheery, "it was your worst start ever. You sprang up like a jack-in-a-box. I've never seen you do that before. You really had to stretch for the first hurdle, didn't you?"

Meg nodded, but Mimi was looking at me, bemused, like I was making small talk while our world was in turmoil.

"Still, you didn't panic," I pressed on. "Your hurdling was a bit untidy over the second and third, but then you got into a rhythm and looked fine. Very smooth."

"I don't want to do the press conference," Megan said.

Mimi threw her hands up again and turned away and then back again, shaking her head. I guessed it wasn't what she wanted to hear.

"I told you we should have spoken to her about this before today," she said to me. "Now we don't have time to work out our line."

"She's ill," I said. "That's our line." I nodded towards Tom. "Tom's going to take her home. She's under the weather. That's why she had a poor start. That's why she walked off and got annoyed with that photographer. No press conference. Simple."

"Annoyed with a photographer?" Mimi said. "Are you kidding? She practically knocked him flat. We can't act as if nothing's happened. 'Under the weather'? You're kidding, right?"

Not for the first time, I thought Mimi was more worried about pleasing the journalists than anything else, but what did I know? I'd never had an athlete who warranted her own PR adviser before.

Mimi sensed what I was thinking. "Liam, they're sitting up there waiting for Meg, and if she doesn't turn up, *that* will be the story. The headlines will be 'Meg does a runner'."

"Why not stick to 'Meg legs it?'" I laughed at my own joke, but no one joined me.

"Liam, shut up! If she doesn't turn up, they'll have a field day – they'll shred her reputation," Mimi said, with a terse nod in Megan's direction. "We may not like the paparazzi but that guy was one of their own. They'll close ranks."

Megan straightened up again, her spiky hair seeming spikier, her broad shoulders bulging inside her tracksuit. She was six inches taller than Mimi and at least twenty times stronger. Anything physical would be over in seconds. Mimi stepped back. She's feisty but not stupid.

"I'm telling you now," Megan said, her eyes narrowing and fixing on Mimi. "This is really pissing me off. I'm sick of people talking about me like I'm not here. And I don't give a shit about the media. They can say what they like. I don't have to answer to them."

"But that goes with..." Mimi started to say.

"Yes, yes, I know it goes with the territory, *darling*. But not today. Like Liam says, I'm ill." She looked at Tom, who was wearing his hangdog expression. "And we're going."

Tom reacted instantly, turning to go. If he raced like that, he might win more often. They were both already a couple of yards down the corridor before we could say anything.

Mimi looked at me, shrugging. "So, it looks like she isn't doing the press conference then."

"I will," I said.

* * *

"Liam who?" You could tell the journalists weren't impressed when they realised it was just me and a UK Athletics official sitting on the platform in the media centre.

I knew a few of them quite well – the ones who'd been on the circuit for years and the ex-athletes who were making a media career for themselves. But such was the soaring interest in Megan, most of the faces were not familiar at all. In less than 18 months, she'd gone from being a footnote on the sports pages to appearing on magazine covers, quiz panels and chat shows. Last year, in the build-up to the World Championships in Beijing, her fitness somehow became a national concern after one tabloid published a shot of her thighs from a bad angle and quoted a self-appointed expert saying 'Megan's leaden legs needed toning up'. I was fuming, but Mimi told me to keep my mouth shut. She said there was nothing I could say that wouldn't make matters worse. And she may have been right because I would have ranted about dumb journalists driving female athletes to anorexia yet ignoring the lard on the bellies of top class rugby players, which might have made me feel better, but wasn't going to help Meg. She kept a dignified silence and promptly ran the best time in the world that year.

So it was understandable that Mimi was white with anxiety as she stood at the back, Meg's reputation in my hands and me at the mercy of fifty or so journalists. She had taken the precaution of checking with a friendly media contact that the photographer wasn't hurt, but the image of him splayed on the ground was bound to be on everyone's minds, and all over Twitter.

I smiled and nodded ingratiatingly at the sea of faces as the press woman from UK Athletics introduced me. Sonia Kerslake was an old friend. We had been in the British team together way back, and it was reassuring having her sitting next to me at the top table.

"Megan's under the weather," she said to a ripple of groans and knowing laughs, "and her coach Liam McCarthy has kindly stepped-in to answer any questions you have."

The room fell silent and people wriggled in their seats. No one wanted to go first. I scanned the faces, wondering if the photographer had been stirring things and if anyone from Newport was there with a killer question about a dead friend of Meg. Some of the journalists were bowing their heads, making out they had a something to write in their notebook, like kids trying to avoid answering a teacher's question. There was a lot of doodling going on in that room. Mimi shot me a look as if to say 'wait for it'.

"They're a quiet lot today," Sonia said with a nervous chuckle.

"We're lost for words," one of the journalists said. "We weren't expecting any wrestling."

Sonia ignored him. "So Liam," she said, "you've spoken to Meg. How was she after the race – how did she feel about her performance?"

"Not so good and very good," I said, trying to lighten things a little. "Not so good because she's got a cold or a bug of some kind. Nothing serious, but the race took a lot out of her and I told her to go back to the hotel and get some rest. And very good, because she's done the job – she's qualified for the team. It takes talent to win comfortably when you're sick and you didn't get a good start."

"About the start," said a grey-haired man I vaguely recognised as one of the hard-core athletics specialists. "That's a recurring problem isn't it? Her start let her down in Beijing last year too."

This was comfortable territory for me. "Yes it did. It nearly cost her the race. When you make a poor start, the danger is you try too hard to catch up and then everything goes wrong. You're tense, you lose your technique, and it's a downward spiral. The good thing about today was she had a poor start but didn't lose her composure."

"Yes, but there was no real pressure," a female ex-athlete was quick to say.

"There's always pressure," I said. "But, I agree, her start is an area we need to work on. You don't want that to happen in the final in Rio."

The ball was rolling now. A few hands went up, and I had a run of questions about her preparations for Rio: who she saw as the main threat and whether or not she was going to run in the sprint relay. This last one was tricky from a coaching point of view. Megan was the fastest British woman over a flat 100m as well as the hurdles, but I didn't want her to be distracted by relay training. I wasn't going to say that though. I didn't want to annoy Sonia or make Meg look arrogant.

"If the selectors choose her, I'm sure she'll seriously consider it," I said, catching a reassuring nod from Mimi out of the corner of my eye.

"But she might have other things on her mind," a male voice said abruptly from the back. His face was almost completely hidden by the people in front, but I was pretty sure he wasn't one of the regular athletics reporters

About half the room looked round. I calculated, in that seemingly long moment, they were the ones who hadn't heard properly or were surprised by the tone of the question. The other half weren't curious because they already knew what he meant – or knew enough to guess.

"Not sure what you mean?" I said. My voice had an edge to it and each word seemed to echo. Mimi had told me beforehand not to sound jumpy if, or when, the question came. But I was pretty sure I sounded as shifty as hell. I definitely felt shifty. And yet, why should I be? After all, I still didn't really know what this was all about.

Sonia looked at the guy as if to say, 'come on, then'.

"Haven't you seen the Argus website today?" he said, holding up a printout. A few of the journalists smirked as if they saw a funny side in the assumption that my day might not be complete without reading the Argus.

I could just about read the headline: 'Police to question Olympic star'. I hadn't seen it before, and I looked across at Mimi helplessly wondering why the hell she hadn't checked their website again - before we walked into that room. I could tell she was wondering the same thing.

"I've had a busy day. I was going to catch up on all the papers later," I said.

That earned me a couple of laughs. Sonia was fidgeting. I wasn't sure what she had known in advance. She was obviously not at all comfortable now.

"Look," I said, thinking I should take the initiative. "I've come here to talk about athletics. That's personal, and I'm sure Megan will deal with it in the right way. The main thing is she shouldn't have any distractions in the final weeks before Rio."

As the words came out, I sensed the absurdity of them. Some people must have been thinking 'that's not the main thing at all'. Others must have thought 'you'll be lucky'.

"So Megan will be talking to the police, then?' said the Argus reporter.

"This is bound to be a distraction, isn't it?" another journalist added.

"Is this why she's under the weather?" sneered a third.

I turned to Sonia with a helpless, 'save me here – for old time's sake' look.

"I think Liam's made the position clear," she obliged. "He's here to answer questions on Megan athletics-wise. If there's nothing else on that, we'll leave it there."

As she stood up, everyone seems to surge forward, surrounding me – pens and notepads or microphones in hand. One said: "Liam, what's going on? You're her coach, you should know." But the other questions were scrambled together and sounded like a chant in which a handful of words kept recurring: *Megan, drugs, death, police*. It wasn't a great combination just a few weeks before what I was hoping would be the high point of Meg's career, not to mention mine.

I felt a hand grabbing at my forearm, pulling me through the crowd. I went with it, following Mimi's bobbing head as she burrowed her way through the scrum.

4

DOOR-STEPPED

"THAT WENT WELL," I SAID, feebly toying with humour again to hide how rattled I was. We were threading our way through the VIP car park, looking for Mimi's soft-top something-or-another. The wind had dropped and a relentless drizzle was soaking the cars and us.

"We need a plan," Mimi said.

"A few facts would be a start," I suggested.

"That always helps," a voice added from behind us; the body it came from bumping into us as we stopped to see who it was.

My fuse had burnt out in the press conference, and none of it was left to stop me exploding. I grabbed the Argus journalist by his jacket collar.

"Chris Williamson," he said brightly as if we were meeting for the first time at a dinner party.

I pulled him towards me so that my chest – which is fairly chiselled for a forty-something – was pushing up into his chin. I was ready to throw him across the nearest car bonnet, and he was looking strangely smug as if he was enjoying the whole thing. Mimi was quick to intervene.

"Chris, I'm Mimi. I think we spoke the other day," she said, holding out one hand to him and pulling me back with the other.

The adrenalin was still pumping, but my saner senses prevailed. Tempted though I was, I realised Meg's coach beating a journalist up would not help matters at this point. I released my grip and stepped back as he made a show of straightening his jacket.

"What's this all about then?" Mimi continued.

"I was hoping you were going to tell me."

Mimi shot him a look as if to say, 'do you think I was born yesterday?' And she wasn't. I've never asked but I'd put her in her mid-thirties. I'd gathered from her endless stock of outrageous stories – always prefaced by "you really mustn't tell anyone this" – that she'd worked not only with sports people but also with actors, comics, writers and celebrities for years, spending as much time keeping them out of the media as getting them in.

"You've seen the piece?" he asked.

Mimi shook her head. We'd headed straight for the car from the press conference and were planning to look at it back at the hotel.

"We're reporting that the police have reopened their investigation into the death of Matt Davies and that Megan will be part of their inquiry." He furrowed his brow slightly as if asking Mimi for a reaction, but she was unmoved, looking at him levelly as if to say 'so what?'

Williamson persevered. "Matt Davies died two years ago of a drugs overdose at a house party."

"We know this," I said, "so what's your point?"

"When the police arrived, the only person there was Will Driscoll, and he was Megan's boyfriend at the time – *that's* my point," he said, his mouth beginning to curl into a smirk.

I was conscious that I was still glaring at him like an intruder threatening my home. I tried to calm myself. He turned to Mimi.

"And Matt's mother is claiming that Driscoll was dishing out the drugs," he added.

"Right," Mimi said, irritably. "So, Megan should be more careful picking her boyfriends. But she dumped him. What's the story?"

"My police sources say they're going to question her," Williamson said.

"Why would they want to do that?" Mimi asked.

"That's where I thought you could enlighten me."

Mimi's deadpan face finally twitched, anger surfacing. "Look, I'm sure the police are just being thorough," she said. "But that's it. Megan's been living in London for the last two years. She has a partner. They're engaged. Will's yesterday's news as far as she's concerned."

Williamson's smirk morphed into a derisive laugh. "That's not what I hear," he said.

Mimi looked at me helplessly, wiping tiny drops of drizzle from her cheek with the back of her hand.

I had nothing to offer. I was still processing the implication of his last statement, my ignorance of what was going on in Megan's life becoming apparent.

I spotted Mimi's soft-top in the next row and began moving towards it.

"Let's go, Mimi," I said.

We turned our backs on Williamson and headed for the car.

"And there's one more thing," Williamson shouted. "Will's a rugby player. Or *was* a rugby player. Talented. A junior international. But it all came to a sorry end when he was done for drugs. Steroids. Tested positive."

I was pulling the car door open as he said the 'S' word. Things were bad enough. I hadn't imagined they could get worse. I stopped myself from turning round and ducked into the car. I didn't want him to have the pleasure of seeing the blood drain from my face.

* * *

We reached our hotel in the centre of Birmingham to find a posse of journalists on the doorstep. Luckily, Mimi saw them before they saw us and dragged me through a separate entrance taking us via a restaurant to the lifts. We headed straight for Mimi's room where Team Meg – as we cosily called ourselves – was due to meet for its weekly run through her schedule and decide who was doing what. Jackie and Megan would be arriving in half an hour.

Mimi pulled a laptop from her suitcase and sat at the desk. I felt shell shocked and stood watching as she logged-in and waited for it to boot-up.

"Make yourself useful," she said, nodding towards the kettle.

I turned my attention to the task of disentangling the lead and finding a socket. It was challenging, but better than the alternative of kicking the furniture around and berating myself for how little I knew about Megan's personal life. I could not believe she hadn't told me about something as sensitive in athletics as a connection with someone banned for steroids. I sensed Mimi watching me.

"You okay, Liam?" she asked.

"Never better," I replied, surprising myself at the bitterness of my tone.

"It was shit, hearing that from him. How could she not know that an ex-boyfriend being done for drugs wouldn't come out sooner or later? But, Liam, give her the benefit of the doubt for now. Let's assume she was being naïve, that she didn't think she needed to tell you, or that maybe she was scared how you might react."

I shrugged, struggling to find any words that would be productive. The kettle was boiling and I made tea for both of us. Mimi turned back to the laptop and began clicking and scrolling through page after page of stories about Megan.

"How's it looking?" I said.

"Put it this way, I don't think those hacks downstairs will be losing interest in this any time soon."

I put Mimi's tea down on the desk and squinted at the screen. Mimi clicked back through the stories for my benefit. Everyone was running something – from the Sun's 'Meg legs it after scrap with snapper' to the BBC's 'UK Athletics plays down controversy surrounding Olympic poster girl'. They all had photographs of Megan stepping over the floored photographer, and most mentioned her 'no-show' at the press conference. Some referred to the police inquiry and Meg's connection with Matt and Will. But no one was carrying the story that Will had been banned from rugby for using steroids.

Mimi refreshed the search, and a new Argus story appeared at the top of the list. Mimi clicked onto it. As it came up on the screen, our gasps could probably have been heard in the next room. The headline read: 'Drugs cheat is yesterday's news, claims Meg spokesperson'.

I was speechless. Coaches like me live in dread of being tainted by a drugs scandal. Even if it's an innocent mistake – an athlete missing a random test or using a dodgy supplement – it can wreck reputations and careers at a stroke. Seeing Meg's name and the words 'drugs cheat' in the same headline brought home how perilous our situation was. Even if the connection with Will was naïve and in the past, people would talk and most of them would presume she must have known – or worse.

"The little shit," said Mimi, sticking two fingers up at the screen. "The fucking creep stitched me up. He's well and truly off the Christmas card list."

Christmas felt a very long way away as I scrolled down the story, trying to keep calm:

> *A spokesman for Newport-born Megan Tomos says the Olympic gold medal hopeful should be more careful choosing her boyfriends.*

> *In an exclusive interview with the Argus, Mimi Jacobs admitted Tomos had dated steroids cheat Will Driscoll, who police have been questioning in connection with the drug-related death of Matt Davies in Newport two years ago.*

> *But she said the police interest in the 100m hurdles specialist was just 'thoroughness' and cast doubt on whether or not the athlete would be able to help the inquiry.*

> *"I'm sure the police are just being thorough, but Megan has been living in London for the last two years," Jacobs said. "Megan should be more careful*

choosing her boyfriends but she dumped Will and is engaged to her new partner. Will's yesterday's news as far as she's concerned."

The rest of the piece was mostly a rehash of what we already knew: Matt Davies had died of a drugs over-dose after a house party, Will had been banned from rugby for failing a drugs test, and Megan knew both of them.

Mimi was still shaking her head. "I can't believe I fell for that one," she said. "I should have known he'd run with any scraps I gave him. Sloppy. Really frigging sloppy."

"Well, yes," I said, finding myself beyond anger now. "Maybe Meg would have preferred announcing her engagement to Tom in a different way. And possibly she'd like to have done it herself. But that's likely to be the least of her worries right now." My irony didn't get any reaction from Mimi. "Look", I continued. "The Argus is several steps ahead of us. We need to take control somehow. For a start, we need to find out more about Will, about his drugs test, Matt's death, what's going on between him and Meg, if there is anything going on... It feels like we're completely in the dark and someone's throwing shit at us."

A double rap on the door came somewhere between 'dark' and 'shit'. I wanted to talk to Mimi about how we should approach Meg and the meeting, but it was too late. Mimi clicked minimise and jumped up to open the door. Unusually, Meg, Tom and Jackie had arrived on time and together.

"Hi guys – so it looks like our Meg has booked her plane ticket to Rio," Jackie said, a tad too breezily to sound natural.

Sports agents are normally either marketing people or lawyers. Jackie was a marketeer but not of the fluffy variety. Her hair – a steely grey – seemed to epitomise her style. She was about my age and oozed a confidence and worldliness I found daunting. You felt she'd been through more than a few battles and won most of them. And it showed in the way she assumed command in any room she was in.

Mimi was still hovering by the door and I could hardly believe it when she peered out and checked the corridor in both directions. It didn't go unnoticed.

"Paranoia creeping in?" Jackie said.

Mimi flushed. "You can't be too careful. We were nobbled in the car park," she said, nodding towards me.

"And?" Jackie said.

"The Argus door-stepping us, with more on the…"

Jackie stopped her with wave of a hand. "We'll come back to all that later," she said, sitting down in one of two armchairs. Meg took the other; I claimed the desk chair and Mimi perched on the edge of the bed. Poor Tom chose his natural home and sat cross-legged at Meg's feet.

"Let's get down to business everyone," said Jackie. "I know it's been a tough day, but we've got an even tougher week ahead and we need to stay focused. Mimi, do you want to talk us through the schedule?"

Mimi looked at me as if to say 'business as usual – is she serious?' But she had the sense not to test the point straight away. Pulling a notebook from her bag, she reeled off Meg's appointments from Monday morning's photo-shoot for a fashion magazine to Friday's Diamond League meeting at Crystal Palace, when Megan was due to face her main rivals from the US and Europe. Jackie interjected with some name-dropping and a few practicalities, and I managed to fend-off sponsor demands on Megan's time to ensure I had a slot with her on Tuesday afternoon to work on her start. But Megan herself sat sullenly fiddling with her smart phone, hardly looking up as we talked around, across and about her.

"Thursday is tricky," said Mimi, looking at Megan. "You've

got this honorary degree ceremony in Newport. I'll have to talk to the comms people at the uni, and brief them on how to handle the Argus. How are we going to handle the Argus?"

That did it. Business-as-usual had hit the buffers. Jackie seemed to sense Megan was about to erupt. She was good at spotting early signs of volcanic activity.

"Meg," she said, reaching out to pat the hand of our golden girl. "You need to tell everyone what we were talking about earlier."

Megan raised herself from her hunched, 'truculent teen-ager' pose, straightened her back and looked earnestly towards Mimi and me.

"I realise I owe you both an apology," she said, surprising me with a nervous quiver in her voice. "I'm sorry about, you know, walking off the track like that and what happened with the photographer. He was just getting too close to me. I know it must have looked dreadful but, honestly, I didn't touch him. It was just the camera. It was in my face and my hand caught it. It happened so fast, I didn't think…"

"Or stop," Mimi said. "Stopping would have helped."

Jackie raised a hand and nodded at Meg. "Go on," she said.

"I know, Mimi – I've seen the photographs. I'll apologise, whatever's best."

"Let's think about it," Mimi said. "But what about Will and this police inquiry?"

"Look, I'm in bits about all this," Meg said, fiddling with her phone again and avoiding eye contact with us, "and I know this Argus thing is causing you bother – but, to be honest, you should just accept it's personal. I'll sort it out. It's my business, no one else's."

"Not when it's on…" Mimi began, but Jackie held her hand up again, and Mimi was surprisingly compliant, looking worn down and defeated.

"Yes, we know Mimi," Jackie said. "Not when it's on every website – we've seen them, and Meg's assured me there's nothing in it, and she'll clear things up. And I think we should leave it there."

It was an unwritten rule in these meetings that I didn't step on Jackie's turf and she didn't step on mine. The trouble was, there was an ugly patch of ground between us that definitely needed weeding.

"Meg," I said, having decided I didn't care whose turf I was on. "This has all come out of the blue for us. Until a few days ago, we'd never heard of Will or Matt, or Matt dying…" I paused abruptly, not for effect but because those words brought it home to me that someone – someone's son – had died. I thought of my own son and, suddenly, I felt ashamed that all our calculations had been about the impact of this on Megan and ourselves – our reputations and careers. "Megan, look," I said, "you and I have worked together for two years. Two-and-a-half years." I corrected myself, precision about the timeline now seemed important. "We've been through a lot. But we've never talked about your past or why you left Newport. If there's anything we need to know, you should level with us. If there's anything we can do to help, just say so. Talk to us…"

"We can't help you if we keep getting taken by surprise," Mimi chipped in, slightly off key.

Megan didn't react. She was looking at her feet now. She'd changed into jeans and a white blouse with thin grey stripes. She was wearing mascara and wine coloured lipstick. I rarely saw Megan out of a tracksuit and didn't think of her as an attractive young woman with a life outside athletics. It was as if I was seeing everything through a new lens.

The room was silent apart from the hum of the air conditioning.

"I'll sort it out, Liam," Megan said finally, lifting her head towards me again. "There's nothing to worry about. If the police want to speak to me, that's fine. It's my problem."

"And what about Will?" I said.

Megan straightened her back again, tensing. "What about him?"

"He's bad news," I said, feeling this was definitely my turf. "I'm not talking about Matt's death. I don't know what happened, and it's not for me to judge. But Will – he's failed a drugs test. That's over the line. He's a cheat, and you don't need me to tell you how it looks if you have anything to do with him."

Megan was rigid and staring past me at a blank wall. "Okay, I know," she said finally, "but it's complicated."

I looked at her, half of me wanting to leave it to her judgement – wanting to believe in her – and the other half of me mulling over whether or not to ask why it was so complicated.

An athlete and their coach go through so much together. To reach the level that Megan's reached, the coach drives the athlete well beyond anything they would do if left to their own devices, testing their limits again and again. That's the whole point. If people could do it alone, they would. But an athlete needs the right coach and has to trust the coach – through all the long months of training – to deliver them to the start line in perfect shape to achieve their goal. And, on the way, the coach has to bear the brunt of all the athlete's pain, anger, doubt and frustration. Megan had put her trust in me. And, at that moment, what could I do but hope my trust in her wasn't misplaced?

* * *

Once back in my own hotel room however, the adrenalin that had kept me going all day drained away and my resilience to dark thoughts plummeted to zero. I sat in a deflated heap on a chair at the desk, looking into the mirror above it at the flecks of grey in my brown hair and the puffy dark skin around my bloodshot eyes. I felt exhausted. All day I had been suppressing memories of the sickening foolishness I'd felt the first time my trust had been betrayed over steroids, but now I couldn't fight them anymore.

My mind drifted back to an autumn evening at Copthall 28 years ago. I remembered it like I was there, feeling the cool breeze and watching the sun descending behind the main stand, casting long shadows across the infield. There were six of us in my training group, all in our late teens, overdosing on self-belief.

I was already in the British junior team. I'd even trained with the seniors, rubbed shoulders with big names who were, that very week, at the Olympics. The group was normally boisterous. We always had plenty to say for ourselves, and we should have been talking that night about how, three days earlier in Seoul, Ben Johnson had lowered the world record to 9.79 seconds in 'the greatest 100m final ever'. But we weren't. Johnson had failed a drugs test – and we all felt sick. We'd all believed Johnson's denials. We'd all disliked the arrogance of his accusers. But now we were left feeling stupid and betrayed. Johnson was stripped of his medal but still claimed someone had put a pill in his beer. For days, I watched everything, read everything, all the reports, like I had been bereaved and needed to know every morbid detail.

Then the following week I missed training, giving a hamstring niggle as an excuse. And missing training became a habit. My interest turned to other things. I'd been going to the track week in week out since I was eleven. But then, as my eighteenth birthday approached, it suddenly seemed too much effort. Why would you want to train until you vomit when there were girls, pubs, football, so many other ways to spend your time?

At first, my coach would phone me about my hamstring, offer to arrange a physio. In desperation, he even came round to my house to speak to my parents. But it was hopeless. I was written off – another teenager who'd lost the plot.

And in the background, the Johnson case trundled on. My memory of the details was hazy now. The Canadians set up an inquiry. It turned out Johnson had been on steroids for years. He'd used a drug intended for horses. His doctor was a vet.

Johnson's coach came out of it as the main villain, the 'bad apple'. It was a view I found comforting, but then it became obvious Johnson wasn't an isolated case, and I began to wonder about the system and the money and the manipulation of a sport built on honest endeavour.

But time mellowed me and I realised athletics was building its resilience to those forces, and I began to wonder how things were down at the track.

It was the Barcelona Olympics that won me back. I had just graduated and had plenty of time to watch it on TV. And, when I finally went down to Copthall again, I found the world hadn't stopped. The place was buzzing: new faces, old faces, kids messing around in the long-jump pit, a group of young sprinters every bit as cocky as we'd been.

I smiled at the memory of all that, but sitting in the darkness of my hotel room, I couldn't escape the thought that everything was at risk now. I believed Megan was innocent but feared that 'guilt by association' could irreparably damage her reputation. The sponsors would run a mile, and my coaching career would be over.

5

DOING A RUNNER

"SO LIAM, WHAT DID YOU make of last night – the new, humble Meg?" Mimi asked me whilst tucking into a mound of steaming scrambled eggs on toast. I couldn't help but admire her ability to multi-task and, for someone so petite, her remarkable appetite.

I stared at my plate of rubbery fried eggs and stuck-together bacon wondering why I kept doing this to my body. At my age, I needed to start thinking about muesli and fruit.

"Humble is good - I like humble," I said.

"Yep, but there's talking humble, and there's *being* humble," she said, lifting her head to check I appreciated the emphasis. "And I'm not sure which we were getting."

I poked my fork into a shiny piece of egg white, shook the

grease off it and decided not to put it in my mouth.

"There is that," I said, "but talking humble might be a step in the right direction."

Mimi didn't reply. We seemed to have exhausted the 'humble' topic, and she obviously had more appetite for her eggs than I did for mine. I watched her polish off them off, mulling over if I cared whether or not Megan had much humility as long as I could believe her.

"Right, Liam darling," Mimi said, swallowing the last lump of egg and wiping her mouth with a napkin. "Much as I love it here, I need to get back to London. Are you catching the train or hitching a ride with me?"

I didn't get a chance to answer that one because Tom had turned up at the table looking even more like a dog who'd been kicked than usual.

"What's up?" I forced myself to say fairly cheerfully.

"It's Meg," he mumbled, barely moving his lips as if struggling to keep a grip on himself. I frowned and reached across the table for his shirtsleeve, tugging gently to signal he needed to sit down. The restaurant was full of familiar faces – athletes, officials, supporters, and a table full of journalists I recognised from the press conference, sitting too close to earshot for comfort. Tom slumped into the empty seat next to Mimi.

"What the hell is it now?" she whispered.

Tom was shaking his head. "She's done a runner," he replied.

"What the fuck do you mean?" Mimi hissed. She didn't have any patience with Tom at the best of times, and this wasn't remotely one of those.

"I woke up, and she was on her way out the door."

Mimi was right in his face now, her eyebrows saying '*and?*'

"She's gone."

Mimi turned towards me with a despairing look.

"Did she say where?" I asked.

Tom was shaking his head again. "The cow! She just told me to move out, that's all."

Mimi rolled her eyes and made no attempt at sympathy.

"I'm sorry, Tom… So you've split up?" I said, just to be sure what he meant. "And she's gone back to London?"

Tom looked at me now like it was me who was being dull.

"No, Newport," he said.

* * *

And so I took Mimi up on her offer of a lift. But our destination wasn't London. After a ten-minute scramble to pack and check-out of the hotel, we found ourselves heading south on the M5 towards Wales, without much sense of what we were doing or why.

"If you'd asked me last week how I'd be spending today, it definitely wouldn't be like this," I said. I was having trouble recalling my original plan, but the general idea was to spend the day celebrating Megan booking her ticket – and mine – to Rio. It would probably have involved a walk-about on campus – I wasn't averse to milking the plaudits after years of barely suppressed yawns from colleagues when I talked about athletics. These days, with Megan becoming so successful, I was mentioned in university marketing material and given one of the best seats at academic events I hadn't previously known existed. Why not enjoy it? "I can't believe they're about to announce the team, and Megan's gone AWOL," I continued.

But Mimi was in no mood for chitchat and gave me a sideways, thanks-for-stating-the-obvious glance. We were somewhere near Worcester with the SatNav telling us it was sixty-six minutes to our destination.

Mimi was driving like someone was cardiac-arresting in the back seat; gripping the steering wheel so tightly I could see what was meant by a 'white-knuckle ride'. Occasionally, she would use her left hand to pick her mobile up and juggle with it just above the dashboard, trying to read the flood of emails pinging into her inbox.

"Fuck this thing," she said finally, tossing it into my lap. "Liam, can you have a look?"

I skimmed through the messages. It mostly seemed to be panicky emails from her staff, either about Megan or with queries about how to handle other needy clients.

"It looks like your office is getting a load of calls, and no one knows what to say," I said.

"Phone them will you," she said. "You know the number."

I keyed it in from memory and, as it started ringing, the hands-free kicked in.

"Mimi, thank God you've called back," a female voice said.

"What's up Sarah?" Mimi said.

"What isn't? We've had about twenty media calls about Megan, and then there's all the usual Monday crap, you know – and Mimi, you haven't forgotten we've got two book launches this week?"

"Shit! Yes, okay," Mimi said. "Get the others on the line, and we'll sort out who's doing what," Mimi said.

'The others' seemed to be about four new voices, all of them failing miserably to hide their excitement at the drama engulfing their most high-profile client. Mimi cut through the babble with scary efficiency, issuing instructions and allocating jobs like she was running a state of emergency. The media calls about Megan were all to be answered with a bland two-liner, news alerts were to be set up covering every Megan-related keyword imaginable, and Meg's Twitter feed should pump out tweets as planned about how 'thrilled' she is about Rio.

As for the book launches, she told Jo or Joe – I wasn't sure – to take care of everything and report to her later.

"Everyone okay with all that?" Mimi said finally to a chorus of "sure," and "leave it to us".

Mimi nodded in my direction and I tapped 'End Call'. The SatNav lady told us to take the slip road for the M50.

"That was impressive," I said, meaning it.

"Fuck off," Mimi said.

"How many staff you got?" I asked.

"Just the six of us, and if Megan's work goes down the pan, I'll have to let half of them go."

"Really?"

"Yes – really, Liam. I've recruited two people just to handle her sponsorship work. It's been manic, something nearly every day, a photo-shoot, an event. And then there's Twitter and Facebook. And the fans wanting stuff. And the media. I can't do it all myself anymore."

I had no idea. I'd never been to her office or asked how it all worked. Over the last eighteen months, the 'business' of Megan had grown into a slick commercial operation. But I'd mostly kept out of it, happy to start receiving generous expenses and concentrating on my three coaching sessions a week with Meg. I left the rest to Mimi and Jackie.

Jackie had come on the scene first, recommended by another athlete to help Megan negotiate terms with the first wave of sponsors. And Jackie brought Mimi in to handle the media and marketing, which I thought was over the top at first. But how naïve that seemed now with Megan having already banked more than a million pounds in endorsements and appearances, and with the experts saying her earnings would top two million annually if she wins gold in Rio.

I glanced across at Mimi, taking in her bold, angular profile and her eyes – dark chocolate irises on clear white – her thick, dark hair combed back into the nape of her neck, showing smooth copper skin. We'd had countless coffees together at an odd florist-cum-coffee-shop in Hendon, but our conversations were nearly always about Megan; wrestling over how to split her time between athlete and 'brand'. But there were occasional exceptions. Once, she'd announced she was about to go to Cape Town on holiday and mentioned her parents lived there, and I said something lame about the weather and the wine. Another time she ranted about Megan being a magnet for dull men, which must have been around the time Tom had turned up on the scene, sniffing around like he could smell the money. I said, "You're sounding jealous," and Mimi flushed, and we both sat in embarrassed silence for a moment.

"I should have quizzed her. I really should have quizzed her!" Mimi said now, shaking her head. "All that, 'I'll sort it – it's my problem' crap. I just assumed Jackie had it covered. I thought they must have talked before the meeting, and Jackie was cool with everything, and we didn't need to know the details. This is what you get for being frigging trusting."

I looked at my phone to see if there was a message from Megan. I'd tried her mobile a few times but only to hear her chirpy voice telling me she couldn't get to the phone and to leave a message. I eventually left one, stressing how worried we were and how much we wanted to help.

"Any news?" Mimi asked.

"Not a thing."

"We need a plan. Where do you think she's gone?"

"Not to her parents, for a start," I said. "They've moved somewhere west. Cardigan, I think. And I don't think she'll want them involved anyway – her father isn't well."

"Yeah, she told me. Banned me from mentioning them in any PR."

"So we need to find out where Will lives."

A juggernaut was starting to move into the fast lane, intending to overtake another, even slower lorry and following the well-known trucking principle 'manoeuvre and maybe signal'.

"Fuck you!" Mimi said, accelerating through the gap before the lorry could block our way. "I hate that! He had no idea I was even there."

I smiled and took a few deep breaths. "So, back to the plan," I said.

"She'd be stupid to go to Will's, wherever that is," Mimi said. "It'll be crawling with paparazzi."

The road was clear now, the lorries left far behind. Yellow fields of grass and grain stretched to the horizon on either side. Ahead, the terrain seemed to rise endlessly under a big, clear sky towards what I assumed were the Brecon Beacons.

"I've got a hunch she's at Celtic Manor," I said, not knowing quite where the thought came from. But it suddenly seemed obvious. Jackie had struck a deal with Newport's only big hotel. She could stay more or less any time she liked. All she had to do was show up a few times a year and look pretty next to the owner.

"Fuck, yes, that makes sense," Mimi said. "She wouldn't go to Will's – she's not *that* stupid. And I doubt anyone would think of Celtic Manor. We haven't announced that yet."

The SatNav was giving us only thirty minutes to our destination now. I pointed to the radio. "How do you turn this thing on?"

Mimi looked at her watch, knowing why I was asking. It was eleven and news of the Olympic team would be on the bulletins. She prodded and flicked the buttons and knobs until she found Five Live. A presenter was running through the main stories. The Olympic team was the third item:

> *"UK Athletics announced its team for Rio this morning amid confusion about the fitness of its strongest gold medal hope. Megan Tomos failed to appear at a press conference at the Olympic trials yesterday, her coach saying she was 'under the weather'. There are unconfirmed reports she is linked to a police inquiry into a drug-related death in Newport two years ago. But the selectors say she was an automatic choice for the team as winner of the one hundred metre hurdles at the trials in Birmingham. They also selected her for the sprint relay squad."*

Mimi hit the mute button as the presenter started to talk about other selection issues. On any other day, I might have stopped her.

"Shit, it sounds awful when you hear it out loud like that," Mimi said.

For a moment, I was too choked to speak.

6

THE DISAPPEARING GUEST

AS WE PULLED UP UNDER Celtic Manor's oversized portico, men in red and gold plus-fours swarmed around the car like we were visiting royalty, opening both doors simultaneously, one of them grabbing Mimi's keys before she could say 'pin high'.

We handed over the car, waved them away and linked arms to show our determination to get through the revolving doors without any further fuss.

We found ourselves in a vast, glass-domed atrium with six white, curving balconies towering above us like an over-the-top wedding cake. I felt about as far out of my comfort zone as a child starting school, but Mimi was already striding confidently towards a long, oak reception counter in the far corner.

"I've got a lunch meeting with Megan Tomos at midday. Could you give her a buzz and say Mimi's here?" she told a receptionist, as cool as anything.

If the young woman was ever trained in the dark arts of discretion, she was having an off day. Instead of pretending to check the system to see if there was such a person registered – which would have been the normal thing to do – she said, "Just a minute," and went into a whispering huddle with a colleague. I couldn't make out most of what they were saying but Megan was mentioned like they were on first name terms.

Turning back to us, the colleague – an older woman with a European accent I couldn't place – said firmly, "Megan Tomos is not staying here at this time."

This possibly wasn't strictly a lie, but I didn't see much point in getting into the nuances of what she meant by 'staying' or how precise she was being about time.

Mimi, on the other hand, seemed ready to tear them apart, which would have been entertaining but wasn't likely to get us very far.

I decided to step in with, "That's odd. We're due to meet her here, but maybe she hasn't checked-in yet. Could we leave her a note?"

The older receptionist wasn't having that either.

"No, we can't take a message, sir," she said. "I'm sure if you have a meeting with Miss Tomos, she will either turn up or you will have some other means of contacting her. You arranged the meeting, yes?" The question was obviously rhetorical but I gave her a nod to confirm I realised this conversation wasn't going anywhere.

Steering Mimi with me, I turned to head back across the

atrium with the thought we might sit on one of the plush settees in one of the many bars to take stock.

"Tossers!" Mimi said, en route.

"Well, they were helpful in as good as confirming she's here or she's been here," I said.

"Of course she has. That receptionist practically had a sign on her forehead. So what do we do? Hang here all day in the hope we bump into her ladyship?"

Hanging wasn't quite the word: we had just landed our backsides on one of the settees and were sinking so fast I thought we would need a crane to get out.

"We may as well have something to eat – I'm starving," I said, reaching with difficulty for a menu from the nearby coffee table.

The only other person in this space looked nearly as out of place as I felt. He was sitting in the next but one group of settees fiddling in turns with a smart phone and a small notepad. He wasn't wearing either the casual clothes of a golfer or a business suit. Maybe I was stereotyping the guests of a five-star golf resort, but his zipper-jacket, stripy blue shirt and grey trousers didn't look the part.

A waiter appeared and asked how he could "help us today". I was tempted to say, "as opposed to when?" but that was just me feeling grumpy and there was no point taking it out on the waiter. A quick glance at the menu reminded us we ought to watch the pennies until our expenses payments from Megan were more secure. We ordered two coffees.

The zipper-jacket man was, meanwhile, being chatted up deferentially by a man wearing a black jacket, grey trousers and white shirt with a tie in the same colours as the plus-fours. He had to be hotel management. Zipper-jacket man nodded in our direction and the hotel manager sat down and leaned towards him so that he was speaking directly into his left ear from only inches away. With another nod from zipper-jacket man, the hotel manager stood up and walked over to us.

"I'm sorry, you can't wait here," he said in slightly exaggerated home-counties English.

There was no stopping Mimi this time. "You're kidding me, right? You *are* kidding. What sort of hotel is this?"

The manager looked indignant. "We're the sort that doesn't allow journalists to 'door-step' its guests, whether they're here or not – that's the sort we are, Miss."

Mimi was on her feet now, which was quite an achievement given her sunken starting point. "I'm not your Miss, and we're not journalists, and we're certainly not 'door-stepping' anyone," she said.

"Who are you then?"

"That's actually no concern of yours, but just for the record, we work for the athlete Megan Tomos and we're waiting to meet her."

The hotel man smirked – I assumed to show he wasn't convinced, never mind impressed.

By this point, I had managed to push myself up into a standing position. For the second time in twenty-four hours, my dilemma was who had more to lose by making a scene? I doubted the hotel manager would get the men in plus-fours to drag us across the atrium, but I wasn't sure I wanted to risk reading headlines saying, 'Olympic coach thrown out of five-star hotel'.

"Okay. Look, I'm Megan's coach," I said. "My name's Liam McCarthy." The man was still smirking. "I don't really care whether or not you believe me, but I'll only leave here quietly if you give me your word you'll tell Meg. I need to speak to her as soon as possible. Tell her to call me or find me at The Priory."

"As you've been told, Miss Tomos isn't…"

Mimi and I had started to make our way out of the hotel. "Yes… got it – she isn't here," I said over my shoulder. "But, if she does suddenly appear, you'll tell her, won't you?"

The manager was already walking back to zipper-jacket man.

Mimi looked at me quizzically. "The Priory?"

"It's the only other hotel I know in Newport," I said. "It'll have to do because I'm definitely not leaving Newport now – not until I know what this is all about."

"But *The Priory*?" she said.

"No, not *that* Priory."

"But, Liam, it's an unfortunate choice in the circumstances, and something else for the tabloids to conjure with."

We pushed through the revolving doors to find one of the plus-fours men looking smug and hovering next to the Mimi's soft-top with the key in his hand. Mimi took it from him, jumped in the car and was accelerating past a convoy of buggies before my bum had hit the seat.

"Reckon that guy in the zipper-jacket was a copper?" she said.

"Yes, but maybe I watch too much TV," I replied.

* * *

I'd stayed at the Priory a few years earlier on my only previous visit to Newport for a coaching course – long before I'd even heard of Megan. All I could recall about the hotel was that it was in a village with a Roman connection. Signs with a silhouette of a Legionnaire helped. Following them took us over an old stone bridge into the cosy, narrow streets of a village called Caerleon.

The Priory was as I remembered it, a rambling stone building that lived up to its name. It felt like the monks hadn't long moved out. We booked two rooms for one night, still clinging to the hope this was just a 24-hour aberration.

"Unusual place," Mimi said, as we went back out to a row of cottage-style rooms opening directly onto the gardens behind the hotel.

Mimi followed me into my room and slumped into one of the armchairs. I paced around a bit – checking out the bathroom and the toiletries and the sachets of tea – for want of anything else to do.

"I hope this doesn't go on much longer – I'm running out of knickers," Mimi said.

This was information I didn't need. "There are shops in Wales, you know," I replied, suspecting she thought civilisation ended at Hampstead.

Mimi waved a dismissive hand and sighed. "This is beginning to feel like one of those dreams where you're falling and can't grab hold of anything," she said. "I just can't get my head round what's going on. There's the Megan we knew and loved a week ago, and now there's this Meg who's a complete mystery. What's going on?"

I had no answer, but I was thinking we needed to find out more about Will. Earlier, a desire to keep a lid on things had put me off getting in touch with any of my athletics contacts in Newport. But now, with Megan still AWOL, desperation was setting in.

"We need some local knowledge," I said, sitting in the other armchair opposite Mimi. "I think our best bet – maybe our only bet – is a coach I know, a guy called Terry Gibbons. He's been around Welsh athletics for as long as I can remember."

"And you trust him?"

I shrugged. "I don't know him that well – I wouldn't call him a mate – but what have we got to lose?"

Mimi had switched her phone on and was trawling through some texts. But she gave me a vacant half-nod that I took to mean 'yes'.

It took me the best part of an hour searching online to find an email address for Tony and send him a one liner asking him to call me.

Mimi, meanwhile, had been trawling through dozens of voice messages, emails and texts about Megan. The vast majority were from journalists chasing for a comment on the Olympic team announcement, with no sign that they had yet picked-up a whiff of Megan's latest disappearing act. But there were also five voicemails from Jackie ranting in ever more colourful language about Megan's treachery and irre- sponsibility and the panic that was emerging among sponsors.

"I can't face talking to Jackie right now," Mimi said. "I'm not a frigging therapist."

"I'll do it," I said, surprised at my chivalry.

Mimi was right. Jackie mainly needed therapy. She was handling the sponsors as best she could, sticking to the line that Megan was 'under the weather' and there was nothing to worry about. But she was fuming about Meg's no-show at the photo-shoot that morning. Under the weather or not, the sponsor wanted pictures of Britain's golden girl draped in their latest range of clothing, and they weren't going to get off Jackie's back until she'd delivered.

"What the hell's up with her?" Jackie was saying as another call came in. Thinking it could be Terry, I cut her off and took it. I was right. After pleasantries and dancing around the Megan situation, we arranged to meet that evening at a country pub a few miles from the village. He said it had a beer garden, and we'd be able to find a quiet spot, which reassured me he understood the sensitivities.

"Good – that's something," Mimi said with renewed enthusiasm. "Right, I need food and a bath, in no particular order."

I was developing an ever-greater admiration for Mimi's spirit but, beyond two sorry looking biscuits on the tea tray, I couldn't help her on the hunger front, and I assumed she wasn't suggesting we share my bathroom.

"Piss off to your own room," I was about to say as my phone started vibrating with another call, but I actually said, "Shit! It's Meg…" fumbling so badly I almost cut her off.

Within seconds, I was beginning to wish I had. "What the fuck do you think you're playing at?" was her opener. "Things are bad enough without you stalking me. I told you yesterday I was going to sort things out, and that's what I'm doing – in my own way – and I don't need your help. Got it? This is private. And that's it."

She paused for breath, and I jumped in, trying to sound calm. "Look, last night we agreed your schedule for the week and then the next thing we know, you've disappeared. What were we supposed to do?"

"Trust me, Liam. How about trying that?"

I didn't want to say anything to make it sound like I didn't. "I want to help, that's all," I said.

"Look, Liam – I don't want your help. Nothing personal, you're a great coach, but you know jack shit about my life. So don't meddle. Please. Don't meddle. I'm telling you, it's none of your business… Just go back to London. I'll call you. Okay? I'll call when I've sorted this. I'll call…"

Her voice tapered, like she was welling-up, and I thought she was going to break down. But the phone went dead, and Mimi and I were left staring at it as if we could somehow will her to call back.

7

COACH TO COACH

"I WAS HALF EXPECTING YOU to phone," Terry said in between sips from a frothy pint of shandy. "When I saw the Argus report, I thought we'd see you in Newport sooner or later."

I smiled nervously, not sure why he would so readily make that assumption, but not wanting to ask.

We were sitting in the pub garden at one of those picnic tables with built-in benches designed for contortionists. Mimi and I were on the side facing the pub. Terry, who'd put on a couple of stone since I last saw him, was spreading out on the other. Our table was in a V-shaped corner with hedges on two sides. A lawn separated us from a patio where more comfortable-looking chairs and tables were filling up with summer evening drinkers. My back was already protesting, but it was a price worth paying for not having anyone in earshot.

"What do you make of it all?" Mimi asked, by-passing any small talk.

I'd tried to put her off coming, thinking I would get more out of Terry coach-to-coach. But she wasn't in any mood to sit around in a hotel room while the men did the talking.

"Of the Will Driscoll/Matt Davies thing?" he said.

Mimi gave a single, firm nod like she was thinking 'why the hell else would I be in this pub?'

"It's been brewing for months," Terry continued, speaking ponderously, trying a little too hard to sound in the know. "Matt's mother blames his death on Will. I hear she thinks he led Matt astray; that it was all his fault things got out of control the night he died. You know the story – the boy collapsed after a party, and Will called the ambulance."

"But why re-open the case?" Mimi said. "The police need a reason. I don't get it."

Terry wriggled, and I wondered how much of an expert he really was.

"She's on a mission," he said, "and she seems to have the ear of people in high places. Or her solicitor does. I don't know what she hopes to achieve, but rumour has it she thinks he should be charged with manslaughter."

"Oh my God," Mimi said, under her breath, but clearly enough for all of us to hear.

Terry sucked at his shandy again, looking pleased with himself now. "So how's Megan doing?" he said.

I had no idea how much Terry knew over and above the media reports, or how much of a gossip he was. I definitely wasn't going to tell him she'd gone AWOL.

"It's unsettled her," I conceded. "But she ran well yesterday…"

Mimi seemed to sense my discomfort. "So tell us about Will. What's he like?"

Terry was still looking at me, waiting for more on Megan. But Mimi leaned forward expectantly, playing his ego. He was, after all, here to tell *us* stuff.

"Nice lad who's made some stupid mistakes," he said.

We waited for him to elaborate, but he was sipping his shandy again.

"Okay," Mimi said, sounding irritated. "So we know of two stupid mistakes: a) using steroids, and b) being there when Matt died."

Terry seemed to take the hint. "I know him quite well," he said. "He used to come down to the track when he was a kid. Ran for our juniors for a while, but then he got into rugby, and we only saw him occasionally. A great athlete though, a beast – well over six foot, built like a tank, and very fast – a sub-eleven sprinter without really trying."

"So what about the steroids?" I said.

Terry was getting the hang of it now – we ask the questions. "He was done about three years ago, just before Matt Davies died and Megan went to London. It was a random test, open and shut case. He was given a two-year ban. His excuse was he'd been injured, and used steroids only to speed up his comeback. He told his mates he thought he wouldn't get tested because he was injured."

Terry paused, staring down into his shandy, shaking his head. "The tragedy is, he didn't need them," he continued. "He was on the verge of making it: professional rugby, national squad. They were all sniffing around – he played for Wales at under eighteen. It was all there for him, and my guess is he panicked because of the injury. Took a short cut. It's so easy these days…"

"Steroids?" I said.

"You just have to know where to go, really," he replied.

"So he's bad news as far as Megan's concerned," I said.

Mimi laughed. "More like the kiss of death. 'Megan teams up with drug cheat who killed friend with fatal steroid dose'. Love it. Great. What's she frigging playing at?"

I nudged Mimi with my knee. We didn't *know* yet she had 'teamed up' with Will, and we definitely didn't want Terry to think that.

"I'm sure Meg just wants to do the right thing," I said.

"Or she still loves him," Terry added, with a mischievous grin. "They were inseparable for years."

"So Matt's parents blame Will?" I said, trying to shift the discussion back to what we needed to know.

Terry nodded. "Which is a bit rich when Matt was one of the biggest 'roiders going. It could have been either way round. Matt to Will, Will to Matt, what does it really matter?"

I was having trouble getting my head around this. Okay, I wasn't that naïve. I knew, in my own sport, Ben Johnson hadn't been an isolated case, and I'd seen reports of steroids being peddled in boxing gyms. But school kids using them and dying at parties? This was news to me.

"So what sport did Matt do?" I said.

Terry buried his head in his hands. "Where have you been, Liam? I think I need another drink."

"My round," Mimi said, picking up our empty glasses. "But wait for me. No more until I get back."

The garden was packed now, with every chair taken and people spilling onto the patchy yellow grass. A few children were playing on a slide near our table. As I watched them, I sensed someone's eyes lingering on me and looked up to see a man with a mop of ginger hair and a bright check shirt turning to walk towards the garden gate.

Terry was talking cheerfully about Rio – as if I cared at

this moment. "Only five weeks to go then Liam. You must be pretty excited?"

I nodded and forced myself to smile, but I couldn't muster any words that would sound convincing. I deflected him on to the Olympic team, knowing he'd happily join me in moaning about some of the selections. That kept us occupied until Mimi reappeared, struggling to balance three glasses. She set Tony's shandy in front of him with a nod to carry on.

"Do you have any kids, Liam?" he said.

This was a sore point, and of doubtful relevance. I may even have winced. My marriage had been about as short-lived as my international athletics career. I rarely saw my son.

"A boy – twelve," I said, and Mimi shot me a surprised look.

"Maybe if he was a few years older, you'd know more about all this. That's all. It could be different in London, but down here it's not the really sporty kids who get into steroids. Not many of them anyway because, if they're good, and not stupid like Will, they know they'll be tested. It's usually the losers – kids who lack self-confidence." Tony drank about a third of his shandy in one gulp, wiped his mouth and smiled. "Do you remember those Charles Atlas ads? You're probably too young."

Mimi shook her head.

"Vaguely," I admitted, showing my age. "The guy in the comics."

"They were all the same: skinny kid gets sand kicked in his face by a bully in front of girlfriend, sends off for a Charles Atlas body building book, and before you know it no one's kicking sand in his face anymore. Well, these days it's steroids, that's all. Same thing: there's money in teenage angst. Charles Atlas made a fortune. God knows who's creaming it from steroids. But there's thousands of kids using them and plenty of dough changing hands."

"As simple as that?" I said.

"Yep – it's only a Class C drug, and you can order them online, but it's probably easier to pop down to a gym, if you know the right ones; slip into the back room and get an injection. Just make sure you check where the needle's been." Terry laughed, and Mimi and I looked at each other and then at the two sorry glasses of mineral water in front of us. I wasn't sure what she was thinking, but I was feeling foolish for preaching to my students about the evils of drugs in sport without really knowing what was going on, probably on my doorstep.

"So Matt was the kid who got sand kicked in his face?" Mimi said.

Terry hesitated. "To be honest, I didn't really know him that well. But, from what I hear, he wasn't into any sport. He was a small kid, always on the sidelines watching Meg and Will at athletics meetings. Then he got into the steroids and body building, and, bingo, he had nice big pecs and a six-pack, a fake tan and tight polo shirts."

"And sod the consequences," Mimi said.

Terry shrugged. "You don't think about that when you're fifteen, do you? I didn't when I was downing a dozen pints and whisky chasers as a student. Not until I ended up in A&E."

He chuckled and shook his head as if he was remembering something. "I've got a doctor friend in Cardiff who spends half his time treating 'roiders with abscesses on their biceps – infected needles. Mostly he drains them and dishes out antibiotics. But he had one guy with massive biceps – he was boasting they were 18 inches – who had an abscess buried in the muscle. They had to cut it out, and he walked away with one arm half the size of the other."

Terry found that hilarious, but I cringed and folded

my arms, instinctively checking if my biceps were still in one piece.

"He was lucky to be alive," Mimi said.

"Definitely," Terry said. "They're saying now that hepatitis is a bigger problem with 'roiders than heroin addicts. Around here anyway."

We fell silent for a moment, watching Terry drain the last of his shandy. Mimi offered another one with a nod of her head.

"No, I'm okay thanks – driving," he said.

"So is athletics affected much?" I asked, still digesting it all. "Are the athletes doing it?"

"Ha!" he said. "Are you worried you've got a Marion Jones on your hands?"

I winced – I hoped not too noticeably – but I could see Terry was expecting an answer.

"Of course not," I said, but it came out croaky, too eager. "I'm her coach, I trust her. And, besides, I know how much work she's done…"

Terry gave me a look, like he'd heard the uncertainty in my voice. And I thought about Meg's tendency to flare up and wondered what 'roid rage was like.

"Marion Jones – she's the American, right?" Mimi said, unhelpfully.

"Yes, denied it to the bitter end," Terry said. "Wonderfully talented. A natural. She didn't need chemicals, but she kept bad company."

Terry spoke those final words slowly, gratuitously, knowing we knew he was talking about Will.

"Right," I said, trying to make it sound like the final word. "That's been really, you know, helpful. Good to have some local intel, as they say.

"It's nothing Megan couldn't have told you," he said, but

I felt he'd crossed a line – one innuendo too many – and wondered if he might know more than he was letting on about our troubles.

I shivered. The sun had slipped behind some trees now and phones were glowing like Chinese lanterns across the garden.

"We'd better make a move," I said, and started to wriggle into a position where I could lift my leg over the bench.

But Mimi wasn't finished. "So where are the hot spots?" she said. "Which gyms dish out the steroids?"

Terry laughed. "Which don't?"

"Come on," I said, struggling to hide a growing feeling he was bigging this whole thing up too much.

"Look, I'm talking about the places they call 'hard-core' gyms, where most of the users are on steroids, not the lifestyle gyms or the posh university gym you go to. You need to get out of your ivory tower, Liam. If you think I'm exaggerating, try a few for yourself."

Mimi had pulled her notebook out and was looking at him to give her some names. Terry frowned. I thought he was going to have trouble naming some, but then a he started reeling off a list of gyms in Newport and obscure locations around South Wales, faster than Mimi could take them down.

"Okay, okay," I said. "Point made. But which one does Will use?"

"That would be the one in Grange Road," he said, pointing to a name scribbled on Mimi's notepad.

"I'll check it out," I said. "I'm curious."

* * *

After waiting for Terry to drive off, we picked our way through the packed car park ourselves to find Mimi's soft-top. It was dark now, with only a thin line of orange above the black hills on the horizon. We stood, watching the glow fade.

"You didn't tell me you had a son," Mimi said.

"Not much to tell," I said.

"What's his name?"

"Danny."

Mimi laughed. "Liam and Danny-boy. How sweet. So why's this the first I've heard of him?"

"I don't know: I don't see him much; we don't talk about that kind of thing." And I wasn't keen to talk about Danny now, not with my head spinning about Megan, and Terry's dig about Marion Jones, but Mimi persisted.

"So why don't you see him much?"

I sighed, but I sensed Mimi wasn't going to be put off. "He lives down in Sussex. My ex – Kelli – has done well. She's from the US, a banker. We met when she was doing an MBA at Middlesex. She's remarried now, and I don't have a car, and I'm busy most weekends and… anyway, she thinks I'm useless." I stopped. "Do you really want to hear all this?"

Mimi didn't answer; the lingering, expectant look was enough.

"Shit!" I said. "I've just remembered, she's going to New York this week. I'm supposed to be having Danny. I can't remember what we arranged."

"Liam, for God's sake."

"I'll text her. Let's get back to the hotel."

* * *

The pub car park opened onto a narrow lane leading downhill to Caerleon. It was country dark, the kind of darkness that unsettles city people. Even the light from nearby cottages and farms was blocked by the trees and hedgerows.

Mimi drove cautiously, having difficulty judging the width of the car against encroaching branches that looked soft and benign in the headlights but periodically slapped the windscreen like Triffids attacking us.

"What did you make of Terry then?" she said.

"God knows," I said. "I'm not sure what to make of any of it."

I looked across at Mimi, who was leaning into the steering wheel focusing on the waves of foliage. I thought it was about time I said out loud the words that had been on my mind – and almost certainly hers – all day.

"At first I assumed Meg dumped Will because she was disgusted he was a drugs cheat – she ditched him on principle, but now I'm wondering…"

"I know," Mimi said, glancing across at me. "You mean, was it on principle or was it only for the sake of appearances?"

The car veered a few inches nearer the hedgerow, catching a branch. Mimi corrected her steering and looked into the mirror. Her face was lit up by the reflection of alternating blue and yellow rays. In my wing mirror, I could see a white car, so close we could have been towing it. Mimi put her foot on the brake a little too heavily and the car behind shunted us forward, our heads jerking like dolls with loose necks. We were going so slowly now it took only a few metres for the car to roll to a halt.

"Shit – what now?" Mimi said, as we sat completely still watching in the wing-mirrors a uniformed policeman walking towards us. Mimi lowered the window.

"You seem to be having difficulty, Miss," he said.

Mimi was rigid, as upright as you could be in a low-slung soft-top. "Not really."

"We observed you driving erratically."

"Your headlights didn't help," Mimi said.

This wasn't going well, but I didn't think I could help.

"I require you to provide me with a breath test, Miss." He sounded like a robot with a Welsh accent.

"You're kidding me, right? I've had a shandy and a mineral water."

I put a hand on Mimi's arm, hoping it would have a calming effect. But the officer continued to be annoying.

"We saw you leaving the pub and suspect you have been drinking," he said, like he'd memorised the police manual.

Mimi turned to me with a 'can-you-believe-this' look.

"Best get on with it," I said softly.

She climbed out and followed the officer back to his car. I decided to stretch my legs, though I nearly changed my mind half-way through negotiating the branches, brambles and nettles along the passenger side of car.

I hovered in the gap between the two cars, but not – I thought - provocatively close to the police. I was wrong. The passenger door of the police car was thrown open and a second man jumped out. He wasn't wearing a uniform. In the glow of car lights, his ginger hair stood out. Only the collar of his check shirt was showing over a black jacket. I felt like saying, "Hello again," but managed to stop myself.

"Any problem, Sir?" he said. There's something about the way police officers say 'Sir' in these situations that sounds anything but respectful.

I held a hand up. Another oddity: do we do that instinctively or are we imitating the movies? "Just getting some air," I said.

The officer – I presumed he wasn't just someone along

for the ride – walked towards me so that we were now both in the space between the cars. We were closer than I like to be with anyone, unless we're on intimate terms. I could smell alcohol on his breath. He was my height but about ten years younger, and his jacket was having trouble containing a well-conditioned upper body. I wouldn't try kicking sand in his face.

"You're not local are you?" he said. I assumed that question was rhetorical; that they must have checked the number plate, unless that was only in the movies too. "What are you doing down here?"

I couldn't see how this was any of his business, but I still felt surprisingly calm considering what a bad day I was having.

"We've been having a drink with an old friend of mine," I said.

He raised his eyebrows. "That isn't what I asked. You didn't come all this way just to have a drink with an old friend did you? So what brings you to Newport?"

My calmness didn't last long. "Since when do people have to explain their movements to the police?" I said.

He smirked. "Don't get clever, bud. Since I decided to ask – that's when. Since I thought you might be connected to the little crime wave we've been having around here."

He looked hard at me – standing even closer now – but I was struggling to think of an explanation for visiting Newport that didn't involve mentioning Megan.

"I'm an athletics coach," I said, hoping it might impress him. "I think some of your colleagues will know of me. Megan Tomos is one of my athletes."

"And where are you staying?" he said.

I felt my pulse quicken and was tempted to argue again, but Mimi was walking towards us looking relieved, a grin forming.

"All clear, not surprisingly," she said, brushing past the plain clothes man.

"The Priory," I told him. "You know, in…"

"I know it," he replied, distracted now by Mimi who'd reached the driver's door of the soft-top. He was looking her up and down like she was wrapped around a pole. "Now you drive carefully Miss," he said.

* * *

The hotel looked even more monastic by the time we got back. There was lighting near the reception desk and behind the bar, but the stone arches leading to the restaurant were hard to make out in the gloom. I was half expecting Richard III to pop out of the shadows with a speech about treachery. But the only person around was a barman washing glasses.

"Fancy a drink?" I said, feeling I wasn't ready to sit alone in a hotel room contemplating how my coaching career was sliding down the pan.

Mimi put her arms round my waist and buried her head in my shoulder. I wasn't expecting this. Her hair was nestling around my mouth, making it hard to say anything. But I had no idea what to say anyway. I felt a slight wetness through my shirt. She was crying. The sobs were so gentle I hadn't noticed them at first. I was conscious of the barman checking us out with sideways glances. After a few moments, Mimi pulled her head back and looked up at me with watery brown eyes.

"Oh, Liam, what a fucking mess!" she said slowly, a quiver in her voice. "And those coppers… Bastards. What was the point of that?"

I felt awkward. I hadn't held a woman for months, possibly

years – I'd lost track – and I certainly wasn't expecting this from Mimi. She was usually so brisk and business-like. I hadn't seen much beyond the hard, PR-savvy London girl before.

I edged back slightly, enough to leave a space between us while her hands could still rest on my waist.

"Let's forget the drink, Liam. I'm wiped out. We can discuss things in the morning."

I was disappointed and I'm not sure if it was just the prospect of being alone – I have a bit of a phobia about hotels after staying in too many over the years – but I also found myself surprised that I didn't want this moment with Mimi to end. I'd forgotten how nice being close to a woman could be.

"Okay," I said, running my fingers through her hair, with no real clue what I was doing.

She took both my hands firmly in hers and kissed me on the cheek, and we walked silently back outside to the path that led to the bedrooms.

My door arrived before Mimi's, and I started to unlock it, fumbling with the old fashioned key. Mimi stood there watching, enjoying my difficulty, and I wasn't sure if she was waiting for me to invite her in. But, as the door finally flew open, she laughed and turned away, giving me a wave as she walked on to the next room.

I watched her – she had no trouble unlocking the door. It was done with a single flick of her wrist, and she turned back, holding the key up with a cheeky grin, her eyes sparkling under the lights along the path. We nodded and smiled and went into our rooms.

8

A WORD TO THE WISE

"YOU'RE A FUCKING ASSHOLE."

This wasn't a good start to the day. It was just after seven, and Kelli was on the phone, responding to a text I'd sent the night before. And it was definitely 'asshole', the American way. Even after living here for fifteen years, she always sounded more Brooklyn than Brit when she was 'pissed' at me.

"Liam, you're the most unreliable son of a bitch on the planet. Jesus! I need to be at Gatwick by eleven and I was depending on you meeting Danny at Victoria. He was all set to take the train – he was looking forward to it."

When we first met at Middlesex, Kelli was a sublime runner. Her long black legs could carry her through a 400m with such elegance that everyone – definitely every male – was mesmerised, whether she won or not. It was a time when my own athletics career was having a second wind. I was running well and learning to coach, and she found my obsession with the sport charming. If I was late, tied up at an event, it was okay because I was this absent-minded Londoner of her dreams, a Hugh Grant-like character, who'd swept her off her feet. It didn't last.

Danny's birth brought us both down to earth. It was not long after she'd finished her MBA, when she was starting to race up the ladder at the bank. She bore the brunt of it: beaten-up by a difficult pregnancy and long labour, then sleep deprivation and trying to breast feed the hungry beast while pursuing a career. My charm was in tatters.

The breaking point came in 2006, the year of the Commonwealth Games in Melbourne. I was 34 and desperate to make one final effort to be selected for a major championship, thinking I had a chance because England has a separate Commonwealth team – so no Welsh or Scottish rivals to worry about.

Right through the winter and spring I trained twice a day – weights, circuits, hills, track – driving myself mad with lactic and exhaustion. But I still didn't make the team and I'd missed Danny's second birthday to run in the trials. And Kelli had had enough: a few weeks later, I came home to an empty flat and a terse note.

So I had form, and there didn't seem much point now in mentioning the Olympic trials or my troubles with Megan. She must have seen the newspapers and already decided they were no excuse.

"Sorry," I said. "I'm in Newport and, well, I just completely forgot."

"Hell, Liam! When are you going to think of anyone but yourself?"

I knew this was an argument I was never going to win. We'd been taking lumps out of each other for years.

"What are you going to do?" I said.

"Don't worry, the child-minder's on standby. I had a hunch this would happen. But that's not the point – Danny wants to see *you*, not a goddam child-minder."

I could hear Danny in the background saying something about Megan.

"Can I speak to him?" I said.

She sighed. "No, not now. We've got to go. You can see him Sunday. And don't forget this time."

* * *

Even before the call from Kelli, I had decided I needed a run to clear my head. As I jogged across the hotel car park, cajoling stiff and weary limbs, the air was so thick I seemed to have to inhale twice as much as normal just to keep going. There had been no rain for weeks, and the air was dry and still.

The receptionist had pointed me in the direction of a footpath just beyond the hotel gardens that, she said, would take me past the remains of a Roman barracks. It sounded like inflated tourism talk, but as I pounded along the path, there it was, neatly laid out like a stone maze stretching out across an area the size of a football pitch. On any other day I might have stopped for a closer look, but I had more pressing things on my mind.

It had been a bad night: I hadn't had any trouble getting to sleep. Mimi's kiss had left me with a warm glow, but when I woke, barely three hours later, it was too warm and the only glow was an irritating light on the DVD.

The thing really nagging at me was Terry's dig about Marion Jones. I'd handled it calmly at the time, but the more I dwelt on his words, the angrier and darker my mood became. I was boiling at his smugness. What did he really know about Megan and how hard she'd worked for the success that was coming her way? The idea that she could have taken a short cut – and deceived me – didn't square with my experience of her. I couldn't think of a single thing, until now, that made me suspicious, even with hindsight. But, equally, I couldn't escape the reality that Marion Jones had lied shamelessly for years before she was eventually cornered into confessing the truth. I couldn't escape the image of her in handcuffs, humiliated, her duplicity laid bare after she'd been caught – after she confessed she'd been a fraud all along.

Through much of the night, I'd been turning the Jones saga over and over in my mind, trying to piece together what had happened and when. I remembered the Sydney Olympics in 2000. I was there, called-up to help out with coaching the British team. And I'd seen Jones at close quarters warming-up for the 100m final. Watching her, I was enthralled. She seemed such a natural athlete, so powerful yet graceful. Her sparkling eyes and gummy smile charmed everyone. It didn't occur to me for a second that she might be chemically enhanced. Why would she need to be? She won that final so comfortably that one commentator said, "This is the Olympics – you're not supposed to win by that much".

But then the news broke about C J Hunter. A shot putter failing a drugs test was no longer a great surprise, but he was Jones's husband – *and* her coach. Rumours about them spread through Sydney like a forest fire in a drought.

The two of them gave a press conference. Both were tearful. I watched Jones weeping on a big screen in the athletes' village. Hunter blamed the failed test on a nutritional supplement and Jones said she supported him. But Hunter eventually admitted using steroids, and Jones disowned and divorced him – to save herself – still insisting she was clean.

A few years later, she hooked up with Tim Montgomery, another sprinter – the men's world record holder – but investigations, allegations and rumours continued to swirl around both of them. For a coach, it was soul destroying. At the time, it felt like everyone in the world of athletics was working under a thick and putrid cloud of suspicion that wouldn't go away.

But Jones persisted with her fraud. By Athens, she was a declining force on the track, and she knew she would have to pay back millions in prize money and sponsorship deals if her cheating was exposed. She threatened to sue her accusers. She even started legal action against one of them. Then it all imploded. Montgomery admitted using steroids. He was banned and stripped of his world record. He started pushing heroin to pay-off debts. Apparently, he roped Jones into laundering the money. And, seven years after Sydney, she was caught depositing a dodgy cheque into her own account and confessed everything. That picture of her in handcuffs going to jail was in my head now.

I had followed the path and run across a railway bridge and past a neat, modern housing estate. Ahead was a lush flat meadow dotted with poppies, glistening in the early sun. But still, I couldn't shake off the darkness. I felt empty and disheartened. Surely this wasn't happening again? Was history repeating itself, but with me right in the middle of it? Okay, Meg hadn't married Will, but they were lovers, or partners, and he was a proven drugs cheat. Did Terry have a point?

My running slowed to barely a brisk walk. The path had reached a river that wound around Caerleon, its wide muddy basin filling with a tide coming in. I stopped and watched the water surging upstream, its power carrying everything with it.

I checked the time. It was eight o'clock. I was probably no more than a mile from the hotel, but I had no enthusiasm for going any further. I turned and forced myself into a running stride again, trying to suppress the doubts and dark thoughts. It seemed a long way back to the hotel.

* * *

Mimi was sitting by glass doors that opened onto the garden when I arrived for breakfast. The sun was catching the side of her face, creating a glow around her profile. Seeing her gave me a boyish pulse of excitement. I couldn't help grinning foolishly.

"So here we are in Newport," I said, inanely, sitting down.

"Wonderful," she replied.

After ordering coffee and helping myself to cereal, I told her about my run and the Roman barracks and the lovely meadow and the river changing direction, as if we were on a romantic weekend break. I was trying to be cheery, but she seemed subdued and preoccupied.

Finally, she said, "Well, Liam – what's the plan? Because I have no idea where we frigging go from here?"

The truth was, I had no plan either – beyond trying again to make contact with Megan – and a vague idea I wanted to see the gym Terry had told us about.

"The official itinerary says Megan is supposed to be working on her start with me today," I said, still trying to keep it light.

Mimi threw her head back dismissively. Levity wasn't working.

"I'd like to see this gym, the one Terry mentioned in Newport; Grange Road," I continued.

Mimi looked disdainful. "What, just walk in?" she said, leaning forward, her voice almost a whisper, "and say 'Gimme the steroids?' Hey, why don't you just ask them if they supply Megan? Are you kidding? What's that going to achieve?"

Her anger took me back. "I've no idea," I said. "I suppose it's just curiosity, and the fact I don't want to spend the whole day waiting by a phone for her to ring."

"It's too risky. Megan's coach going to a gym that sells steroids. How's that going to look?"

"No worse than how everything else is looking. And it's not as if I'm going to give them my own name. I'll go there like any other punter looking for a workout. I'll say I'm in Newport, on business or something."

Mimi laughed, louder and longer than was polite. "Face it Liam, you don't look like a bodybuilder any more. If you ever did."

I looked down at my torso. Her comment seemed a tad harsh, but there were a few flabby folds there, and I straightened up to stretch them out.

"Okay," I said. "I'll say I'm trying to get back in shape, and at least I won't look like a novice..."

Mimi raised her eyebrows sceptically, but before I could respond my phone started to vibrate on the table, crawling towards the toast. I grabbed it and hit the answer button.

"Liam, she passed!" Jackie shrieked.

"Passed what?" I said.

"The test, you idiot. She passed the drugs test, at the trials. It all came back clear. I've just had a call from UK Athletics. They were fretting about it because of all the gossip. But she's clear."

I had completely forgotten about the automatic test she'd

have had after the final. They were so routine now you didn't give them a moment's thought.

"She passed," I said to Mimi.

Mimi was holding both hands out flat, palms down, motioning them up and down like a conductor who wants the orchestra to play more softly.

"I heard," she whispered, raising her eyebrows towards the dozen or so people still having breakfast. "And so did most of the frigging restaurant."

"Have you spoken to her?" I asked Jackie, making a point now of not mentioning Meg by name.

"Not a dickie-bird," said Jackie. "I've tried about four times this morning. I eventually gave up and left a message about the test."

"Hopefully some good news will help," I said.

Mimi looked at me sceptically and leaned forward to within a few inches of the phone, close enough for Jackie to hear.

"But why wouldn't she expect anything other than a clear test?" she said. "It's only us that should have reason to feel relieved. Isn't it?"

She had a point. Megan had no reason to be concerned about the test if she was clean. And maybe she wasn't concerned – maybe this was a non-event for her. But this wasn't a conversation I wanted to continue now.

"We're still having breakfast," I said to Jackie. "Best if we call you later."

Jackie hung-up. Mimi sat back in her chair, looking out through the double doors at the trees and yellow lawn stretching towards a field beyond where two horses were munching on the dry tufts of grass.

"I guess it's something though," she said, ruefully, as much to herself as me.

I sensed someone at my shoulder and looked up to see

first a navy zipper-jacket and then the face of a man in his forties with a pink complexion and thinning brown hair.

"Inspector Richards," he said, putting a business card down on the table. "Sorry to interrupt your little breakfast… Liam McCarthy?"

"Yes, that's me," I said. "I recognise you from Celtic Manor."

Richards smiled and sat down, uninvited, on the chair next to Mimi, facing me.

"Yes, I think we were looking for the same person. Any joy?

I shook my head. "You?"

He shook his.

"So you know we're not journalists, right?" Mimi said, pushing her plate away and sitting upright, arms folded, like she was waiting for an apology for being thrown out of Celtic Manor at his instigation. She was being optimistic.

"Yes, Miss Jacobs," he said. "You do the PR and he does the coaching."

"I guess your pals told you where we were staying," I said, but he looked puzzled. "The officers who stopped us last night…?"

"For what?"

"Apparently, Mimi was driving too slowly."

The inspector gave another little shake of his head. "That's news to me, I'm afraid," he said, sounding uncomfortable. "Must have been routine."

Mimi almost laughed out loud and shot him a 'don't-give-me-that-bullshit' look.

"Let's find somewhere to talk," he said.

I sensed Mimi was ready to object, but this was a conversation with a police officer I wanted to have. We might learn something. I stood up, leaving my cereal half-eaten.

"I'd really like to see the Roman amphitheatre while I'm here," I suggested.

We walked without speaking along the hotel drive, the gravel crunching noisily under our feet, and turned left onto a road that led to the amphitheatre. It was a proper arena, big enough for a tennis match. The centuries had reduced the stands to six grassy mounds held in place by the original stone walls, but you could easily imagine it crowded with spectators watching some gory Roman spectacle.

We stopped for a moment to read the potted history; how six thousand legionnaires had gathered there two thousand years earlier for their sport.

"Not quite the Olympic stadium in Rio," Richards said, "but I'm sure it had its moments."

There was nothing I could say to that, and I sensed Mimi flinching next to me.

"I'm sure you've seen the reports," he continued, speaking with almost theatrical intonation like he was imitating Richard Burton. "We've reopened the investigation into the death of Matt Davies, and I've been asked to lead it. And with all due respect to the Olympics, it's a very serious matter. I need Megan to help me with my inquiries."

Mimi was still prickly. "Why?" she said. "What's it got to do with her?"

"To be fair, I don't actually know. You might say that's the whole point. I need to find out, because I owe it to the family to leave no stone unturned. I'm revisiting everything. The family wasn't satisfied with the first inquiry, and my chief constable wants it all looked at again."

He stared intently at each of us in turn as if wanting to emphasise how serious this was, and how determined he was to get to the bottom of what happened.

"Megan was one of the boy's friends," he continued. "She may know something that could help. I don't know until I speak to her."

Mimi and I exchanged looks, not sure what to say. The truth seemed simplest.

"We appear to be in the same boat, inspector," I confessed. "We'd also like know what this is all about. But Meg seems determined to deal with it herself."

"So it seems," he said.

"How come you didn't see her at Celtic Manor?"

"She checked-out… well, to be honest, she didn't even check-out. She just disappeared. We understand she was with Driscoll, who we also want to interview again. And you don't need me to point out they are not doing themselves any favours by avoiding me."

He was right: I didn't need him to point that out.

"Mr McCarthy, Miss Jacobs," he said sternly. "A word to the wise. If you see Megan before I do, tell her to give me a call. You have my number now. The sooner I speak to her, the sooner we can clear this up and she can get back to winning a gold medal. I'm sure we'd all like to see her do that."

9

NO FRILLS GYM

GRANGE ROAD GYM LOOKED OUT of place in a residential backwater of well-kept, bay-windowed houses. It was based in a tatty converted warehouse, garishly decorated with banners advertising monthly weight lifting competitions and special offers for students. I pushed through a heavy plate-glass entrance door into a dark hallway leading to a reception area that was definitely at the no-frills end of the spectrum. There were no plush carpets, armchairs, marble fountains or beauty products. A small counter stood in front of makeshift shelves piled high with just-about legal products I'd seen many times before - protein powders, energy supplements and 'anabolic' muscle fuel – sold on overblown claims about the 'serious mass' they build.

A door next to the shelves opened and a man of about my age appeared. He looked like he was fresh from an army boot camp, with shaved head, a ring in his nostril and tattooed biceps bulging out of a sleeveless grey T-shirt.

It was a far cry from the gym I'd been using for years on campus, but that was as expected. What I was less certain about was what I was trying to achieve. Mimi had been insisting all morning that no good would come of my curiosity. She had even refused to offer me a lift, staying back at the hotel to catch up on emails. But I couldn't sit around waiting for Meg to phone any longer. I needed to do *something*.

"Alright buddy?" the boot-camp man said.

I took that as a question. "I'd like to do a work-out, if that's okay?" I said, self-consciously, the words echoing around the room. "I'm a visitor – only in town for a few days. How much is it?"

The man looked me up and down, like he was suspicious. Or maybe that was my paranoia. Why would he be suspicious?

"A friend recommended this place." I added, unnecessarily, inviting a question I didn't want to answer.

"A friend? Who was that then?"

This wasn't going well. "Oh, just a guy who lives in Newport. He isn't one of your members."

He squinted at me sideways for a moment, and I held his look, throwing in an ingratiating smile.

"Three quid mate," he said finally, pulling a clipboard from under the counter. "Sign this. Used this type of equipment before?"

I nodded, signed his form and gave him the cash, trying not to look surprised at how cheap it was.

"Changing rooms are over there," he said, pointing towards double doors on the far side of the gym.

I walked across, trying to take everything in without

looking too obviously like a snoop. The only other customers were two thick-set boys bench-pressing weights so heavy the bar was buckling above them. They looked like clones of the receptionist, but twenty years younger.

The gym was a vast windowless space, much bigger than it appeared from the outside. Dotted around were machines, old but well-polished, with exposed levers and chords connected to chunky tablets of iron. Free weights were piled high on racks. Where there weren't mirrors, the walls were covered with life-sized posters of men and women with freakish muscles. I stopped to admire a picture of someone called Eve, whose head seemed to be sinking into the mountainous tanned flesh of her shoulders. It was like something out of a freak show and not a look I could imagine Megan ever aspiring to. Not that she doesn't have to do some heavy lifting of course, but it's for building speed and not bulk for its own sake. And for the last two years, she's been working out it in the elite surroundings of the Lee Valley Centre of Excellence, with fellow athletes classed as having 'podium' potential. Somehow I couldn't see her here – or could I?

I pushed through the double doors and found myself in a gloomy square space with four doors leading off it. The two to my right went into the male and female changing rooms. To my left were doors marked 'Staff Only' and 'Treatment'.

No one was around. I listened at the door marked Staff and heard someone on the phone. I took a chance and tried the Treatment room, ready to plead poor eye sight. It was locked. As I turned to go into the changing room, I heard steps in the Staff room. I darted for the changing room door and was through it before anyone saw me.

What the fuck was I doing? Did I think they'd leave a stash of steroids on display in an unlocked room?

I was breathing heavily. Beads of sweat were forming

on my face. I threw my kit bag down, pulled out a towel, wiped my face and looked around. The changing room was as minimalist as everything else: metal lockers down one side, showers with plastic curtains along the other and benches in between. I changed as quickly as I could and went back into the gym, my pulse still racing. I didn't feel much like work-ing-out, but bailing-out would only draw attention to myself. I needed to spin the session out, look like a genuine punter.

I walked around, trying to be casual, checking out the equipment. The treadmills faced the wall mirrors. That would give me a good view of the whole room. I decided to run for twenty minutes, and then pump a few free weights. I could do those facing in any direction.

Once I got going on the treadmill, my pulse steadied and I began to feel calmer. I used the rhythm of the music from the local radio station to keep an easy pace.

On the far side, the two boys had started doing squats but were struggling with too much weight and sinking too low. I could hear their knees clicking and grinding above the music. But I wouldn't like to argue with them about it. One was six foot or more and lean but very athletic. The other was smaller but thicker set, his head sinking into his shoulders like Eve.

* * *

By the time I'd finished on the treadmill, the gym was filling up, mainly with young lads who looked like they'd come straight from school or college. In no time it was heaving with punters wearing Lycra vests, bulging with muscle-bound torsos.

The noise level rose with each new arrival, drowning the

radio in shouts, laughter and banter. You couldn't fault how hard they were working-out. But what did I expect? Of course they had to work hard. The steroids only boost the body-building. They don't do it for you.

I found a spare mat near a rack of weights and started doing a mini circuit of curls, sit-ups, squats and lunges, just for appearances. Once I'd done enough to work-up a sweat and look credible to anyone watching, I decided it was time to call it quits and confess the pointlessness of my snooping to Mimi.

As I bent down to pick-up my towel to head for the changing room, a voice behind me said slowly, "Well, well, well."

I straightened, a chill shooting up my spine.

"Just happened to be passing, did you?" It was the ginger police officer, still wearing the black jacket.

I nodded, struggling to recover some composure.

"Well, it's good to see someone of your stature supporting one of our local gyms. I hope they made you welcome."

"Very welcome," I said inanely.

He lingered for a moment like he had something else to say. Or maybe he was just toying with me, enjoying my discomfort. I didn't think saying, "What's your problem?" would help.

"Great place isn't it?" he said finally, with a theatrical swing of his arm.

"Yes. Yes, it is. Very impressive. You work out here do you?"

He pumped his chest out. "I like to keep in shape."

That was undeniable. His eyes lingered again, this time narrowing, his mouth stretching into a smirk.

"I'd better get changed," I said feebly.

"Yes, you better had," he said "Mustn't leave that lovely lady-friend of yours on her own."

I nodded and started towards the changing room, feeling

his sleazy tone had more than a hint of menace.

"Oh, and by the way, Liam, or should I say Jim?" he began.

I stopped and turned, struggling to hear him above the hubbub.

"It was Jim, wasn't it? The name you used, on the form you signed? Very original." He nodded across to the reception desk where boot-camp-man was giving me a chilling grin.

I was done, busted. I felt flustered and foolish like a child caught climbing into someone's garden.

"Anyway," he continued, like he was dismissing me. "When you do eventually find Megan, say 'hello' from Gary."

* * *

I was walking wearily towards the taxi rank at Newport railway station and somewhere deep in my kit bag my phone was ringing. I stopped and rummaged for it, squatting on the pavement. It was Megan. I hit 'Answer', fumbling so much I nearly dropped the thing.

"Meg!" I said, desperate to hear her voice again, but pathetically out of breath from jogging the mile or so from the gym after being spooked by Gary.

"Meg?" I repeated.

The silence was agonising, but the phone said we were still connected.

"Speak to me, Meg."

"Liam, it's me," she said.

"You okay?" I asked.

"What do you think." No question mark on that one. I needed to tread carefully. She sounded fragile. I waited for her to get to whatever it was she wanted to say.

"I don't want to talk now," she said almost in a whisper. "Can I see you later?"

"Sure, of course… where?"

"The Roman Barracks. You know it?

"Yes."

"Eight o'clock."

"But…"

She was gone. The phone now said 'Disconnected', and I felt like rolling-over and giving-up – then and there – on the pavement. I was exasperated and exhausted. These days my body was accustomed to a largely sedentary, stress-free lifestyle. The gym session; the stand-off with Gary; a draining two days of growing panic about Megan – all of it was taking its toll. And the oppressive heat wasn't helping. Every pore seemed to be leaking; rivulets of sweat were running down my forehead and chest, soaking my T-shirt.

I threw the phone back in the bag and pushed up from the squatting position I was in. My knees clicked in protest.

The taxis were only a few yards away. A train was roaring and clattering into the station. I looked around, wondering if anyone had been watching me. As I started walking towards the rank, I sensed a familiar face, larger than life, rising above the taxi rank. It was Megan, smiling radiantly at me from a billboard, trying to sell me car insurance.

* * *

The taxi dropped me on the gravel drive leading to The Priory. I tipped the driver, feeling guilty I'd snubbed his small talk about the freakishly hot weather, and headed towards Mimi's room.

She opened the door blinking at the sudden rush of sunlight.

"Liam, what the hell…?" she said.

I didn't know where to begin. Was it Gary giving me the creeps or Megan sounding lost and upset? Or was I just hot, tired and badly dehydrated?

Mimi stepped back as I stumbled into the room, dropped my bag and slumped into an armchair.

She was wearing a thin cotton dressing-gown and apparently nothing else. Her hair was damp and matted as if she had just stepped out of the shower.

"Have some of this," she said, grabbing a plastic bottle of water from the table and handing it to me. "I'll get dressed."

She scooped some clothes from the bed and went into the bathroom. I gulped the water down, emptying the small bottle in seconds, and sat like a zombie staring at the dust dancing in the shafts of light coming through the window.

Mimi emerged from the bathroom brushing her hair, dressed now, wearing jeans and a lemon V-neck top, and sat opposite me on the bed.

"You look awful," she said, laughing, but in a kind way. "Truly, truly dreadful. Your face is grey. That T-shirt looks like it's glued on. And, Liam, you smell rank."

"Thanks. I'm not at my best," I replied.

"So what big discoveries did you make at the gym?" She was teasing like she expected me to admit it was a waste of time.

"None, really," I said. "Except the creepy policeman was there."

That surprised her.

"Which creepy policeman?"

"The ginger one. He said his name's Gary. It turns out that's where he got his muscles… And he appears to know Megan."

Mimi raised her eyebrows just about as far as they could go. "Knows?"

"Mentioned her. Asked me to say 'hello' to her. And then, on my way back, Megan phoned."

Her eyebrows lifted a fraction further. "She phoned?"

"No, I'm kidding." That was feeble, but then I was feeling feeble. "Yes, and we're meeting her at eight o'clock, at those Roman Barracks up the path." I nodded roughly towards where I thought the path was, closed my eyes and pushed my head back, resting it on the back of the chair. I felt like sleeping, like I could slip into oblivion any minute.

Mimi came over and sat on the arm of the chair and ran her fingertips gently across my forehead and through my sweaty hair. With each stroke, the tension seemed to ease. My mind drifted through the images of the day, the faces and places. The inspector. Gary. The gym. The grubby upholstery of the taxi. It settled in the amphitheatre. I was watching Roman gladiators and legionnaires. The stands were packed with cheering crowds. There were people in golden carnival clothes waving Brazilian flags. Megan was unfurling a Union Jack. I was clapping. The legionnaires threw their helmets in the air…

* * *

I don't know how long I slept, but when I woke the sun was low and the curtains were half-closed. For a moment, I wasn't sure where I was. I stared through the gloom at Mimi, who was working on her laptop, head down, tapping out emails. She sensed me looking and turned, her lips curling into a smile.

"You're back, then?" she said.

"What happened?"

"You were telling me about how you met that nice ginger policeman in the gym and how he knows Megan."

I jumped up. "Megan! What time is it?"

"Relax, relax," Mimi said. "It's only seven. You said we're meeting her at eight."

Mimi picked up a plate of sandwiches that was sitting next to her laptop. "Have some of these, Liam, you need to eat something. "

I took a wedge of the neatly cut triangles and sat down again. "And your phone rang. Your son Daniel. I answered it. He said he was worried about you. He'd seen something about Megan on TV."

"What about Megan?"

"Nothing new – but you should call him."

"I will – later," I said, shoving one of the triangles into my mouth in one go.

While I was munching, Mimi gave me a rundown of the news. Jackie had been keeping the sponsors calm but she was worried about whether or not Megan would appear at the Diamond League at Crystal Palace on Friday. A few journalists had been sniffing around but the police haven't put out any more statements and no one has a fresh angle to run. The PR people at the University of South Wales are panicking about Thursday's honorary degree ceremony – will Megan show up, will the media be door-stepping it?

I finished munching. "Shit, I'd forgotten about that," I said.

"Forgotten what?"

"The uni-thing. Talk about bad timing."

"Yep, it's all bad timing. That's for sure. So let's not make it worse by missing Miss Tomos," Mimi said, on her feet now and holding out a hand out to pull me up. "Liam, you are changing, aren't you?"

I took her hand. As I reached full height, she stepped back, looking me up and down grimly. My T-shirt had dried out but was crumpled and turning yellow. I nearly said, "Meg's not going to care," but I was watching Mimi's face as she scrutinised me. It was caught in the rays coming through the narrow gap around the curtains. Her eyes were sparkling, intense and intelligent. I smiled and went to my room to smarten myself up.

10

THE PAIN BARRIER

"SO THIS WAS THE TOILET," Mimi said, reading the blurb and gesturing at a rectangle of two-foot high stone walls. "They sat on these, hung their arses over the back and dumped their load." She was looking down at a stone gully behind one of the walls that sloped towards a corner. "Pretty gross if you ask me. I thought the Romans were more sophisticated than that."

"This was for the legionnaires," I said. "I bet the generals had something posher. Probably with central heating."

We sat down. It seemed as good a place as any to wait for Megan, and we weren't sure anyway which direction she would come from. In fact, we were looking the wrong way when we heard her voice calling.

"Li…"

Megan could shorten names even when they couldn't get much shorter.

We both jumped up and saw her jogging towards us. There was no sign of Will, and I took comfort from seeing that Megan was wearing the same black tracksuit she'd used at the trials. Maybe this detour to Newport was as unplanned for her as it was for us.

"Hiya," she said in a making-an-effort tone, but looking tired, her features tight like she was holding herself in check.

We stood awkwardly at the entrance to the toilet for a moment and then shuffled towards one of the walls and parked our backsides like legionnaires on a comfort break, Megan sitting between Mimi and me.

"So what's going on?" Mimi said, her arm around Megan, who was leaning forward, elbows on her thighs, staring into the distance.

"We used to hang out here, after school," she said, nodding towards a rambling collection of buildings about a hundred metres away. "Me, Will, Matt, a few others – on summer's evenings like this. Nowhere to go. We were too young for pubs and clubbing. So we'd sit around here, or down at the amphi, drinking cider, smoking weed and snogging."

"And I thought you were a goody-two-shoes!" Mimi said.

Megan smiled. "I didn't do the cider or the weed," she said. "Well, not much."

We fell silent, all of us apparently reluctant to be first to talk about why we were really here.

Mimi was rubbing Megan's back in slow circular movements. I watched people passing on the footpath – strollers, joggers, dog-lovers and cyclists – a steady flow, soaking up the last of the day's sun.

"It's all so fucked-up," Meg said finally.

Mimi looked at me across Megan's back, raising both eyebrows.

"What is?" I said. "Tell us."

"Just about everything," she replied. "The police gunning for Will. Matt's mother stirring it, trying to get him done for manslaughter..." She sat up straight and turned towards me. "Matt dying like he did was just horrible, unbelievable. And when I think about all of us hanging out here, it's like it was yesterday – and now he's gone and for no good reason. Just stupid, going too far... But you can't blame Will. Will's as gutted as the rest of us. We were all friends."

"But, Meg," Mimi said gently. "I can understand all that, but why get involved now? You split up with Will before you came to London, yeah?" Megan nodded. "And he's a big boy – a very big boy, I hear. He can look after himself, can't he?"

Megan was sobbing now, her body shaking, her face in her hands. She pulled a tissue from her sleeve and dabbed her eyes. "He asked me to help," she said. "And anyway, the police want to speak to me too."

"We know," I said.

"How come?" Megan asked, her voice jumpy.

"Well, apart from it being in the Argus," I said, sounding more sarcastic than I intended, "we had a visit from the police this morning – an Inspector Richards."

Megan looked surprised. "So you've spoken to him. What did you tell him?"

"Nothing," I said. "I've got nothing to tell, Meg. But I did say I'd encourage you to contact him. You can't avoid him forever you know."

"Okay. Consider me encouraged, but I'll see him when I'm ready."

Mimi looked at me across Megan's back with a grim shrug. "But can't you see how this looks?" she said. "You're shacked-up with Will and avoiding the police. It looks like you have something to hide… especially with Will's history."

Megan sat bolt upright, knocking Mimi's arm away in the process. "Look, I'm telling you, I'm going to stand by Will like he's stood by me. And what's it got to do with you anyway?"

"It's got everything to do with me. You're about to go to Rio and you're running around with a – well, let's not beat about the bush – a drugs cheat. For fuck's sake, it's not exactly what we had in mind when we agreed your PR plan!" I gave Mimi a wave to calm it down but she wasn't having any of it. "Where are you staying anyway?" she continued. "Will's place?"

Megan ignored that and turned to me. "Liam, I want you to come with me to see Matt's father."

I think my mouth dropped open. If it didn't, my brain simulated the sensation. "To see Matt's father? Why?"

"Because I haven't seen him since, you know, it all happened. I went to London… without speaking to him."

"But his wife's gunning for Will."

"They've split up. Graeme lives on his own now."

"Can't Will go with you?"

Meg shook her head. "You're kidding, right? Graeme isn't after Will's blood like Matt's mother, but he wouldn't let him across the doorstep."

"What do you think, Mimi?" I said.

"I can't see any reason why not. 'Meg and her coach visit the bereaved father' sounds better than the other headlines we've been getting…"

"Fuck the headlines. I'm doing this because I want to."

Mimi cringed at that. "I know, Meg," she said, "but that's what you pay me for – you know, to think about the headlines; about how things look."

Megan stood up and turned to face both of us, her face

flushed and angry. "I know," she said. "But I'm sick to death of worrying about how things look. I'd just like to do something because it's right for a change. Liam?"

I nodded.

"Tomorrow morning," she said. "I'll meet you on the footbridge. You know, in town – the new one across the river. Graeme lives near there, and I've told him I'll be there about ten."

She turned and started to walk away.

"Meg," I shouted. "What about your training?"

She stopped and looked back, smiling. "Relax Liam. It's okay. I went for a run this morning. I'm in good shape."

"And the Diamond League?" I said.

"We'll see." She paused for a moment. "Friday seems a long way off."

And then she went, bounding across the grass, up on her toes. You rarely see an athlete striding so effortlessly, seemingly defying gravity. It always makes me think of the old song, Poetry in Motion.

* * *

Mimi and I walked back along the path towards the hotel. In the field to our right, a cricket match was drawing to a close with two batsmen walking off to applause from the fielding team and a gaggle of spectators. It seemed so simple and civilised.

Mimi was silent. I think we both felt reassured by seeing Megan and hearing her talk about Matt, but I had stopped myself from quizzing her more about Will, and his hold on her bothered me.

"So what do you think?" Mimi said finally.

We'd stopped where the footpath crossed a road before carrying on past the amphitheatre. The hotel entrance was only a short walk to the left.

"It was good to see her," I said, "but I still don't know what to make of it all, especially Will."

"Yep, me too. Her wanting to see Matt's father, that's good. Clears the air. But Will? The way she leaps to his defence..."

"Hmm. Like Marion Jones with C J Hunter," I mumbled, and regretted it immediately.

"C J who?"

"Nothing – it's okay."

Mimi looked bemused but didn't push it.

"I need a good walk, to clear my head," I said abruptly, making it obvious I meant on my own. "You don't mind, do you? I need to think things through."

I thought Mimi looked slightly hurt, but maybe I was flattering myself. I touched her arm and, to my surprise, she stepped forward and kissed me on my left cheek, more softly and slowly than the usual parting peck.

"No worries," she said. "Do some thinking, and if you have any brainwaves..."

"I'll let you know."

She threw me one of her sparkling smiles and laughed. "I sure haven't had any," she said.

* * *

I didn't realise how dark it was becoming until I was on an unlit path near the amphitheatre. The sun was starting to disappear and the lights of The Priory, across a field to my left, were glowing brightly in the gloom. The path curved around the Roman wall enclosing this side of the village and ran through two small meadows until it reached a busy road.

Ahead was the old stone bridge carrying traffic in and out of Caerleon. I stopped on the footbridge alongside it and looked down at the water below. The tide was coming in again, already so high it lapped into the bushes on the banks. Eddies and ripples reflected the lights from the pubs facing each other across the river, their gardens buzzing with boisterous drinkers. I leaned on the railing watching the river, the water rising just as it did when Roman boats were moored here, so certain and predictable.

But history depends on the angle you look at it from. All day I'd been picking over the events of the last two years or so, wondering if things were as I'd thought they were, if Megan was who I thought she was; remembering how she turned up at Copthall on a cold February evening, only 19 years old and not yet in the British team, but eager to take those final, hard steps into the small band of elite athletes.

I had seen so many athletes flounder at that point, lacking the will or the ability and having to face the brutal truth they might end up an also-ran. But I could tell Meg wasn't one of them, and we soon pinpointed what she needed to do. We made plans for perfecting her hurdling, improving her start and increasing her leg speed. But most of all, she needed more strength. Only if she was much stronger would she hold her form all the way to the line.

And that was the toughest part. She may have mixed – as I now knew – with bodybuilders, but it was obvious she hadn't done any really heavy lifting herself. She was very strong by any normal standards, but not world-beater strong. And so the really serious work began: hills, circuits, weights – pushing ever harder, talking her through the doubts and despair. I told her it would take 18 months, and to think of the World Championships in Beijing as her goal.

The chemists and conspirators behind Tim Montgomery called him 'Project World Record'. They turned him from being good but not exceptional into a world record breaker in three years. A controlled experiment, like a rat in a lab. Meg had made a similar dramatic improvement, and I wondered how people were talking about me now – if they were saying she was my 'project'. My enemies – rival coaches, athletes I'd offended – were bound to be gossiping about Meg, and I could imagine the raised eyebrows and 'no-smoke-without-fire' innuendos. But I also knew I hadn't pumped her with steroids and I couldn't see how it could be done without me knowing. I don't remember any 'roid rages or mysterious absences. She always told the anti-doping agency where she was and had been tested randomly many times. She'd never tested positive.

But then Marion Jones never failed a drugs test either.

I shook my head, trying to cast off the doubts that had plagued me all day.

It was dark now and the air suddenly had a chilly edge. The crowds were thinning in the pub gardens. People were passing me on the bridge, giving sideways glances as if they thought I was going to jump.

I walked back off the bridge and crossed the road to find the path to the amphitheatre. As the light from the road lamps and cars faded, I had to rely on the sound of my feet grinding the gravel to ensure I didn't wander off course.

I heard soft voices and footsteps coming towards me. Eventually a young couple emerged from the darkness about ten metres away. They passed, the guy nodding and murmuring, "Alright". I reached an open gate. The path began to climb towards where I sensed the amphitheatre was. I could see the distant lights of Newport beyond the meadow to my left. To my right loomed the Roman wall, the stones black now, the top outlined by a feint glow from the village.

The path got steeper and turned to a point where it crossed the top of the fortifications, opening up a view of the floodlit hotel and the village. There was a tall hedge to my left. From memory, I knew the amphitheatre was behind it. I would soon reach the road that crossed the path and be able to turn right to The Priory.

Another figure appeared from the gloom. No crunching gravel had preceded it. My mind computed that.

"Alright," said a male voice from the tall silhouette passing me slowly. I sensed the strides were wrong. They were too short and too slow.

But it was too late. I tried to stretch my stride, ready to run, but the man had grabbed me from behind, his arms locking mine. I wrestled to free myself, but my resistance was pathetic. He tightened his grip, jerking me upright, suddenly and painfully.

"Don't fucking bother, you snooping cunt," he said.

Someone else's hand was pulling my hair now, lifting my head. A face was in my face, his nose pressing into mine, a sickly smell of tobacco and alcohol on his breath.

"Evening, Jim, or Liam, or whatever the fuck your name is. Out for a nice stroll are we?"

Before I could tell him to fuck off, the first blow landed – a fist or was it a knee, driven into my stomach. I gasped and gulped for air. I tried to double up, to protect myself, but the man behind still had me locked upright. I flexed my abdomen. More blows came in. I lost count of how many, of where they landed, or any sense of time.

But I do remember falling face first onto the gravel and a voice saying, "Get the message: keep your fucking nose out!"

And then: "D'you get it? Get it? Geeeet it?", as boots thudded into my ribs. And then the sound of heavy feet running away; and the vomiting – I remember the vomiting – and its acrid taste in my mouth, my rib-cage on fire with pain.

I'm not sure how long I lay there or how I managed to get back to the hotel. I have no memory of it. But I do have a dream-like recollection of standing outside Mimi's door and of not having any strength to knock on it.

11

MIXED SIGNALS

GOING FOR BREAKFAST SEEMED LIKE a good idea compared to twisting and turning in bed like a contortionist. I'd spent the night constantly changing the arrangement of my limbs, hoping to find a position that wasn't painful. Success was never more than temporary. Periodically, I'd give up and walk around, killing time examining my wounds in the mirror, plucking gravel from my skin, and checking my wee for blood.

"Have you seen this?" Mimi said, announcing her arrival by sending a glossy magazine flying like a Frisbee and landing it on my poached eggs.

"Nice shot," I said, grumpily, peeling it away from the runny yoke. The cover was of a man with an unnaturally contoured six pack. "What about it?"

Mimi snatched the magazine back, shaking a blob of yoke into my tea. She flicked through the pages and thrust a double-page spread at me with a photograph of Megan draped across a bed in a minimalist nightie and some text headed 'Pillow Talk – with Megan Tomos'.

I still wasn't quite sure what Mimi was so angry about. Meg had done several photo shoots she might in later years regret, and Mimi was the architect of most of them.

Mimi sensed my confusion. "Read it."

I took the magazine from her, wincing as a pain shot from my ribcage to my neck. I felt like someone in jackboots had been using me as a trampoline. Most of the damage was concealed under the loosest fitting T-shirt I could find, but I was still acclimatising to a very limited range of pain-free movement. Even moving food from plate to mouth was a challenge.

"What the hell happened to you?" Mimi said.

I sighed and winced again. She touched the one visible mark – an emerging bruise in the centre of my forehead that was beginning to make me look like a brainy creature from outer space.

"God, Liam, where did you get that?"

Bad as the pain was, and much as I enjoy female sympathy, I was finding it difficult to admit I'd been so easily outgunned by two punks. I wanted to say, "You should see the other guy," but I knew they had probably walked away without a mark – and the usual pleasure of my lame jokes was far outweighed by the effort and discomfort each word would cause.

"Two punks jumped me," I said, finding four syllables about as much as I could bear.

"What?" she said. "Where? When?"

"Walking back. To the hotel. Last night."

"Oh my God, darling. Why on earth…?"

"No idea, really. Except one of them said, something about, keeping my nose out."

Mimi had sat down. Her mouth was hanging open like it knew it was its turn, but was waiting for her brain to give it instructions.

"Fuck. What are we getting into here?" she said finally.

I had spent most of the night asking myself the same thing and only managed to come up with more questions.

"I don't know," I said. "But I'm going to avoid dark foot-paths from now on."

"Let me look," Mimi said, not waiting for permission, reaching to pull my T-shirt up.

"Not here," I said, patting her away, conscious the other people having breakfast were glancing in our direction between every mouthful. "Let's have some breakfast and talk later."

Mimi nodded slowly with a lingering worried look. She took a piece of toast from the basket on the table and started to butter it absently, her eyes still on my forehead.

I picked up the magazine. It was one of those lads-mags that had long sunk from tasteless to semi-pornographic, but the photograph wasn't as bad as it could have been. It was the headline that gave me a foretaste of what was coming: 'Meg begs for quieter life'.

The preamble was a teaser for the boys: pin-up girl, hot favourite for gold in Rio, sends male pulses racing every time she peels off her track suit. But then it went into question and answer mode. The first few were predictable. How does it feel to be the poster girl? What do you do to relax? Who is your role model? What's been the best moment in your career, and what's been the worst?

But when they asked how she copes with success, the answers started to have an edge. Meg moaned about people, 'thinking they know you just because they've read something in a magazine' and 'jumping to conclusions about stuff they know nothing about.' She said she's 'coping' by 'trying to see more of old friends'.

I looked up at Mimi who was watching me read. "You weren't in the loop on this?" I said.

"Are you kidding?" she said, sounding exasperated I'd even asked. "I normally write the frigging answers myself, but this one was sent straight to Meg by one of my staff. And it gets worse." Mimi was pointing at the questions on the second page.

DID YOU ALWAYS WANT TO BE AN ATHLETE?

> *I sort of fell into it. It's just what I was good at. But I think I've been too obsessed with it. I've put winning before everything else.*

WINNING AT ANY PRICE?

> *Almost any, yes. You get so caught up in the whole thing, you think nothing else matters, and you don't let anything get in the way of success.*

IS THAT THE TRAIT YOU MOST DEPLORE IN YOURSELF?
> *Yes*

BUT IF YOU WEREN'T AN ATHLETE, WHAT WOULD YOU WANT TO BE DOING?

> *Something worthwhile. I want to give something back. You know, help kids in trouble, who've lost their way. I don't know yet.*

I laid the magazine down in front of me and read some of the answers over again. I put phrases together – too obsessed, putting winning before everything else, not letting anything get in the way of success. And the 'giving something back'? It would have sounded so worthy, if I hadn't read about Marion Jones reinventing herself as a crusader for young people facing 'tough choices'.

I couldn't reconcile this interview with the Megan I thought I knew. But what did I know? I'd just taken a beating from thugs who must have some connection with all this – who were obviously linked to a gym that Megan also had some connection with, if only via Will. That was a fact – and a very painful one. I looked across at Mimi. "What do you make of it?"

"Fuck knows," Mimi said. "I'm frigging livid she did it behind my back – and it's panicked Jackie. She rang me at seven, furious. She read it to me and said she'd had a call from a sponsor asking if it had something to do with the police inquiry. What could she say?" Mimi shook her head. "I thought I'd better shoot out to get a copy. And the more I read it, the more it sounds like she's admitting something. Sooner or later, other journalists are going to spot it and start speculating, and that's all we need."

I tried nodding, but my throbbing forehead reacted badly. I touched the bruise, and Mimi put her hand over mine, like she was blessing me.

"Let's get out of here," I said, not really wanting the moment to end but feeling so nauseous I thought my breakfast might reappear.

We made our way to Mimi's room, her arm around me, my steps tentative. The day was cooler but I was glad it was still T-shirt weather. I didn't fancy trying to manoeuvre myself into more than one layer.

"Take your top off," Mimi said once the door was closed.

I wanted to say, "Are you serious?" but she got the general idea from my expression.

"Really, take it off."

She helped pull it over my head, saying, "Oh my God," at least three times as the bruises and cuts across my torso came into view. I looked at myself in the mirror, and it wasn't pretty. Some of the bruises to my stomach and chest were starting to turn black. The skin across my ribs was raw and swollen. I had taken such a pounding that hardly any part of my upper body was unscathed.

"Oh Liam, this is awful," she said, running her fingers tips lightly across my chest. "We really didn't sign up for this."

It was indeed awful. I had never been in a proper fight, never mind taken such a beating. But Mimi's touch was helping, making my skin tingle with each gentle circling movement of her fingers. She was studying every lesion, her face only inches from my skin. I was looking down at the top of her head. Without thinking, I started stroking her hair with my left hand, and after a few moments, she began kissing my chest with moist open lips, moving slightly higher with each one until she reached my neck and then the dimple in my chin. Our lips met, and we kissed in silence for a very long time, tongues reaching deep into each other's mouths, hungry and feral. I sensed she could feel how aroused I was. I was embarrassed and surprised by my lust. It had been a long time.

I think we would have made love then and there if I hadn't been so bruised and battered, but it was hopeless. Each time I tried to hold her more closely, stabs of pain would ricochet through me like electric shocks. Kissing and caressing were one thing, but I needed a body in much better working order to go any further.

Mimi sensed my grimaces and pulled back. We looked at each other, neither of us knowing quite what to say. I didn't want to be presumptuous and say we'd have to come back to this another time. Mimi looked awkward and flushed.

"Thank you," I said, stupidly. "I mean that was…"

"Yes, it was," she said with – much to my relief – a broad smile forming and her dark brown eyes starting to moisten. We kissed again as if to confirm that, even after a pause for reflection, this was how we wanted to be with each other.

When we stopped, she looked back at my chest. "Liam, you've got to get this checked-out. Who knows what's going on under there – you could be bleeding internally, anything."

"I'm not pissing blood," I said, but Mimi frowned and I was touched by her insistence.

"I *will* go… I will, later… if I'm still struggling."

We stood there in silence again for what seemed a very long time, beaming at each other like a pair of school kids with a crush. This was bizarre. Since splitting with Kelli when Danny was little, I'd hardly spent any time intimately with anyone. Okay, there'd been a few one night stands. Athletics is one of the few sports where men and women compete at the same events and socialise together. Musical beds is fairly common. But these moments with Mimi were pathetically schmaltzy, and yet I was enjoying every lingering second.

* * *

I could hardly see Megan on the footbridge when I arrived. She was near the middle, only the top of her head visible in a crowd waving pens and notebooks at her. The most noticeable figure, towering above all of them, was male and standing over Meg like a security guard. I assumed it was Will and felt irritation welling up as I shuffled gingerly towards them, trying to avoid my arms brushing the bruises on my torso.

The bridge arched across the river Usk, dangling from a crane-like structure that was taller than any building in the city. Underneath, the river basin was filling fast again with the rising tide, the water now only a few feet below the paths on each bank.

Will nodded to me warily as I approached and broke away from the group to walk in my direction. Terry's description of him as a beast was an understatement. He looked about six foot six, and his red track suit was swollen with enough horsepower to pull a lorry.

"She won't be long, pal. Fans, eh?" he said, with a lilting Welsh accent that was far more pronounced than Megan's. He ran a hand through his long blond hair, pushing it away from his angular face to show more clearly his sky-blue eyes. He was looking earnestly at me like a boy meeting his girl-friend's father for the first time.

I was practically speechless at the sight of him, all the anger surfacing in such a surge it took me by surprise.

"Good," I said, looking at my watch.

"I'm Will by the way."

"No kidding," I replied.

"You guessed then."

"I didn't think you were coming with us."

"I'm not," he said. "What happened to your forehead?"

"It met a hard object. I bumped into two of your mates from the gym – or they bumped into me."

"I don't know what you're on about."

"Doesn't matter."

We stood in silence for a minute or more. Will was standing sideways on to me, looking back at Megan, trying to catch her eye to hurry her up. Finally, she peeled herself away. So much for hating celebrity, I thought.

"Hi Li. You've met Will then," she said, sliding her hand

into his and looking up at him with eyes that seemed alarmingly besotted.

"Yes. Shall we go?" I said.

Megan managed to take her eyes off Will for long enough to notice my face. "Who gave you that?"

"I'll tell you about it later. Let's go."

Megan seemed reluctant to let go of Will's hand and gave him a nod as if wanting him to say something.

"I used to play rugby over there," he said, gesturing with his free hand towards a sports stadium just visible between the flats on one side of the river. "Rodney Parade. Some big matches, big crowds, but I blew it. Made a stupid mistake…"

"Yes, I know all about it," I said. "I read the papers."

"I wasn't using 'roids to cheat, Liam. I was injured."

"Yes, okay. I've heard the story."

"And I've taken my punishment."

"Yes," I said, looking down at their hands, still clasped together. "But now you're dragging Meg down with you."

"That's not fair, Liam," Megan jumped in.

"It's not?" I said. "What kind of friend would embroil you in this mess just before Rio?"

"It's not his fault."

I looked at her expecting more, but she simply tugged Will's arm to get him to lower his head for a parting kiss and turned to lead me in the direction of some flats near the rugby ground.

12

THE SHRINE

MEGAN TOOK A DEEP BREATH and blew it out forcefully, like she was on a start line, adrenalin pumping. We were standing at the outer door of a small block of flats overlooking the river. The buzzer went to release the door, and Megan pushed it open.

As we climbed the stairs to the first floor, she whispered, "I told you didn't I, I haven't seen him since Matt… you know. I've really no idea how…" But she stopped when she noticed the door of the flat was already open a few inches. The ruddy face of a man of around fifty was peering through the gap. On seeing Megan, he threw the door wide open and stepped forward with arms outstretched.

The two embraced as if I wasn't there. Nothing was said.

Megan was slightly taller. The man – I assumed he was Matt's father – buried his face in her shoulder. Then he stood back and inspected her like a proud parent.

"It's fantastic to see you, Meg," he said. "Really fantastic. Mind you, I see your face everywhere. But it's not the same as the real thing."

Megan was smiling radiantly. I don't think I'd ever seen such a broad grin on her face. I was beginning to wonder if I'd ever be introduced.

"Oh, this is Liam by the way – my coach."

I stepped forward and shook Mr Davies' hand.

"Graeme," he said. "Come in, we can't stand here all day."

We followed a dark, narrow hallway into a small living room with French doors opening onto a balcony overlooking the river. A breeze was catching the net curtains hanging either side of the opening, sending them swirling against a metallic garden table and chair on the balcony.

Graeme pointed towards an armchair – I think he'd seen I was struggling – and I eased myself into it. It was so comfortable I felt light-headed with relief.

On a day like this, with the sun flooding through the French doors, the flat was bright and seemed more spacious than it really was. The lavender walls were freshly decorated. The beech flooring was polished and pristine. But it was small – two armchairs, a small chest of drawers and a coffee table filled the space. In winter, I imagined it would be cramped and dark, a desolate place for Graeme to be cooped-up with his memories. But maybe I was making false assumptions? Maybe he liked being alone and welcomed the separation from his wife? Maybe he was a party animal, only using this place as a bolt-hole, and he was actually out and about every night? But, looking around the room, somehow I didn't think so.

There were photographs everywhere: on one wall, an

overly-posed professional portrait of Matt; on another, school photos; on the drawers, multiple holiday snaps in a single big frame.

Without any apparent qualms, Megan was browsing yet more photographs packed onto the mantelpiece. She seemed completely at home, not hesitating to pick out frames from the back to see the pictures properly. It was like someone had flicked a switch, and she was in a different mode, from another time."

"Grae!" she exclaimed more than once, holding pictures up and waving them towards the doorway to the kitchen where he was making tea – a noisy kettle coming to the boil very slowly – and Graeme would peer into the living room, smiling and sometimes saying when and where a photograph was taken.

"Grae, look at this… Oh my God – when *was* this?" she said, holding one of several small children showing-off for the camera at a birthday party.

Graeme squinted at the image from the doorway. "That was when we first moved to Caerleon. Matt was eight… Yes, eight I think. Must have been. And that's you, with the fireman's hat on. You always wanted to be one of the boys."

Megan turned the picture round to look at it again herself. "Oh my God," she said quietly, shaking her head. "Oh my God."

Graeme came in with a tray crammed with a white bone china cups and saucers, a matching tea pot and a plate of cakes that looked like flattened scones. He slid the tray carefully onto the coffee table, placing it right in the middle with each side parallel to the corresponding edge of the table. Graeme was a man of precision - checked shirt immacu- lately ironed, the crease of his brown canvas trousers looking hazardously sharp.

Tray in place, he moved closer to Megan to look over her shoulder, their faces only inches apart. "You must remember that," he said.

"Of course I do. We stuffed our faces with chocolate cake, and all felt sick. Actually, I think Will *was* sick."

"Julie could make a great cake – fair play to her." Graeme was nodding slowly like he was shaking a memory of her out from the back of his mind.

"I'm so sorry about, you know…" Megan started.

Graeme touched her arm. "Meg, it's just one of those things; we probably would have split up anyway." He spoke softly but firmly as if signalling he didn't want to talk about it.

Megan slotted the photograph back into its place on the mantelpiece and picked up another one.

"These cakes are nice," I said to break the awkward silence, and still not sure what they were.

"Lovely Welsh cakes," Megan said, turning away from the mantelpiece and taking one from the plate.

Graeme sat down in the other armchair, facing me across the coffee table and pouring milk and tea into each cup without a drop going astray.

It struck me there were no sports pictures on display. I may not be the world's greatest father but my own flat has a photograph of almost every team Danny's been in. There must be a dozen or more for football, cross country and cricket. But here, there were none – unless you counted Matt as a small boy standing alongside his father proudly holding a fish he'd caught. It looked like Terry was right: Matt's steroid use wasn't about winning medals. You definitely didn't need them to catch fish.

Graeme handed cups of tea to Megan and me and sat back down in the armchair stirring his tea, staring through the French doors, lost in thought. "Do you remember that time you and Matt bunked off school?" he said, still looking beyond the balcony.

"Yeah, just me and Matt."

"And no one knew where you were."

"And the Head went mad. We were only about nine!"

"What was his name…? He phoned me."

"Adams. Mr Adams."

"That's it. He was in meltdown. You'd disappeared, last seen in the playground at lunchtime."

"Gone into town, like we were grown ups. We thought we were dead daring, going in and out of the shops!"

"That was it. You went down town. But at the time we thought you'd been abducted or something. And I had to tell Julie. My God she was tamping. Worried sick, of course, but furious too, really furious. Blaming Adams for being incompetent. Blaming you…"

"And no mobiles in those days. Well, kids didn't have them anyway."

"No. You phoned our house from a call-box. You didn't have enough money for the bus. Lucky I was there, because I was going to go to the school with Julie. But she told me to wait at the house."

"You came to pick us up. Thank God. We were dead relieved it was you, not Julie.

"And I dropped you off at yours. I don't think your parents knew about the panic."

"Not until later. Mr Adams phoned them. And then Julie as well. She told them it was all my idea."

"Ha. She did. That's right. Of course she did."

Megan went out onto the balcony and looked across the river towards the centre of Newport. I stirred my tea and wriggled a little just for something to do. I was in the line of vision between Graeme in his armchair and Megan with her back to us on the balcony. I had so many questions. I wanted them to fast-forward ten years or so. I wanted to ask how Matt got into steroids and what part Will played in it. I wanted to know how the boy in these photographs had ended up dead after a party. But I couldn't think of anything to say that would edge the conversation in that direction without sounding crass. I am often accused of insensitivity – putting my foot in it is rarely a problem – but the rawness of this man's loss was palpable even to me. I kept my mouth shut and sipped my tea.

Megan eventually swivelled round, looking at us almost as if she was surprised we were there.

"So how are you doing, Grae?" she asked.

I turned my head to Graeme like I was watching a very slow tennis match. He looked slightly bemused. I think we all knew Megan wasn't making polite conversation. But for some reason Graeme chose to take it that way.

He wasn't doing badly, he said. He'd given up his job as a deputy Head Teacher. It was all too stressful, too much management, too many targets and tables. A looming inspection was the final straw. He took redundancy and now he was doing some supply teaching. He was back in the classroom, doing what he loved: teaching English – even finding that some of the kids were actually interested. I joined in on that point, and we had some teacher talk, swapping stories and empathising with each other, even though we were in different parts of the system.

Graeme wanted to know all about Rio. Was Megan excited? When would she be going out there? Who was the biggest threat? How did she rate her chances?

Her replies were robotic. She reeled off the answers she'd given so many times to similar questions over the last few months.

"I am *so* proud of you, Meg," he said.

I looked at her. She seemed shocked, incredulous he might say something like that. She gave a half-nod to acknowledge the remark.

If I wasn't an atheist, I'd say there was someone else in the room. This was as close as I've ever come to believing in ghosts. Whatever it was, whatever Matt meant to her, whatever was swirling round in her head, Megan wasn't going to let it go. It was obvious – even to someone as thick-skinned as me – that she had come here for more than small talk and reminiscing.

"Grae, I'm *so* sorry about Matt. I can't tell you…" The sentence disappeared into an intake of air. She held her breath for a few seconds, composing herself. Graeme sat motionless; his face braced for whatever was coming next. "I know how much he meant to you. But if I'd have seen you, on our own – you know – not at the funeral, but face to face, I just wouldn't have known what to say."

"It's alright, Meg." Graeme's lips hardly moved. It was as if he was talking to himself.

"But it's not. I should have contacted you. I should have written… Done *something*." Megan sat down on the chair on the balcony and looked at her hands as if they held some great fascination. "But I was just so shocked. I couldn't believe it – I can't believe it – that he's gone, just like that. I'm so sorry."

"Don't be, Meg. There's no point. We have to move on. There was nothing you could have done."

"But I ran away. I couldn't face it."

"You had to, Meg. You couldn't let yourself be dragged down by Matt's troubles. You had to get away. It was for the best."

Megan was staring at her feet. I expected her to cry but she seemed controlled like she had more to say and was composing herself for the next part. Graeme got up and shuffled past me to stand over Megan.

"Let it go now," he said.

Megan looked up at him, her lips parted like she was about to say something. But no words came out. For some reason the will seemed to have left her.

* * *

After leaving Graeme's flat, we stopped on the footbridge. The tide was on its way out now sucking all manner of debris out to sea. Nature's waste, human waste, the river made no distinction. It did its job with relentless power and efficiency. We leaned on the handrail and watched a raft of branches and leaves make its way towards us until it disappeared under the bridge. Megan was so subdued I was beginning to feel uncomfortable.

"Nice man, Graeme," I said, truthfully but mostly to make conversation, in a breaking-the-silence sort of way.

"The best," she said, throwing her head back as if the heavens were where he belonged.

I decided it was time to be practical. It was Wednesday; there was a degree ceremony in the morning, and the small matter of a race against the top Americans on Friday evening at Crystal Palace. The week had not exactly been textbook preparation for her last appearance before Rio, but I was hoping the distractions in Newport might at least take her mind off the Olympics and help calm her nerves. Clutching at straws is one of the less scientific aspects of coaching.

"So, what about Friday?" I said with my firmest enough-of-all-this tone.

"What about it?"

"We need a plan. When are you going to go back to London? I'd prefer you to go back tomorrow after the degree ceremony, so you aren't travelling on the day."

Megan was looking at me as if my mind had been washed down river with the tide.

"Are you serious?" she said. "I haven't seen the police yet. I don't know what's going to happen with them."

That threw me. "What d'you mean? What could happen? They want to speak to you. You speak to them. That should be the end of it – shouldn't it?"

Megan turned away. My words seemed to have hit a nerve. I pushed up from the handrail into a more upright position. A pain shot through my chest, one of my ribs protesting. I had been beaten up – I had no idea why – and Megan wasn't giving me any clues. I had been tiptoeing around her, not wanting to provoke another explosion or disappearing act. I wanted to be on her side, to believe in her, but she was giving me nothing to go on.

"So who's Gary?" I said, struggling not to sound irritable.

Megan looked at my forehead as if she'd forgotten about it and was noticing it for the first time – or maybe it was a convenient diversion.

"So what did happen to you?"

I touched the sore spot. "It was probably a warning," I said. "Two thugs jumped me last night, said it was for snooping. I think it was to do with me going to the gym."

"Going to the gym?" she repeated, her voice rising. "You went to the fucking gym?"

I hesitated, not sure if I wanted to turn the screw, but wondering if I had much choice. "Yes," I said. "And Gary was there, and he knew you."

"Everyone round here knows me, Liam."

"I don't mean knows you because you're famous." I said, hearing my own voice and surprised how agitated I sounded. "I mean he *actually* knows you. In fact, he said to say 'hello', like you were friends."

Megan shrugged, her face morphing into the truculent expression she'd had at the hotel on Sunday.

I pressed on. "He had ginger hair, and he's a cop, and he also stopped us on Monday evening – me and Mimi. We had to pull over. Mimi was breathalysed."

I couldn't tell if Megan was surprised.

"What are you trying to say Liam?"

"I'm saying it's odd. All these coincidences. So many coincidences."

"And *I'm* saying: Liam, mind your own fucking business. I've already told you not to meddle, and then you go off to the gym. Who do you think you are?"

"Look," I said, doing my best to sound calmer. "I'm just trying to help."

"No you're not. You're meddling. If I say I'm going to see the police, that's all you need to know. I'll see them, and I'll answer their questions. And I don't need an inquisition from you."

"But you're putting everything at risk…"

"My God! Don't you think I know that? I'm not stupid. But I'm telling you, I've got no choice – simple as. There's stuff to deal with here, and it's got to be done."

"But, Meg, we've worked so hard – *you've* worked so hard – all those years of training to get into this position. You're on the verge of what could be the biggest moment of your career, maybe of your life. Don't you think you owe it to yourself, and to me, not to…"

"I owe you nothing Liam. You're my coach. That's it. If you go poking your nose into stuff that's none of your business, don't blame me if things go wrong. You get what you deserve."

"And I deserve this…?" I started to lift my T-shirt. But it was pointless. Megan had flounced off. She was already several metres away and moving fast, and I wasn't going to shout after her with other people passing who'd obviously clocked who she was.

I turned back to look at the river, resting my arms on the handrail again. The tide was nearly out now, leaving the river basin as grey and empty as I felt.

I texted Mimi:

```
Bad row with Meg. Mentioned gym. But she
didn't ask which one. Back soon. Xxx
```

13

PARTNERS IN CRIME?

BACK AT THE HOTEL, I knocked on Mimi's door. I was tempted to go right in and grab hold of her – the one pillar of sanity in this circus. But we weren't on barging-in terms yet.

Mimi opened the door, flicking her hair back with one hand and looking up at me with an amused smile.

"Liam, every time you turn up, you look worse!" she said, taking my hand and tugging me towards her.

We stood there silently locked in a hug for a few seconds until Mimi pulled back and placed her hands softly on either side of my face, touching my cheeks so lightly they tingled.

"You look really wiped out."

I felt really wiped out. I think my body was using so much energy fixing my wounds, it didn't leave anything in the tank for all the other dramas going on. I slumped onto the bed, stretching out on my back, my eyes closed.

"Hey, no sleep until you tell me what that text was all about."

"Right, yes – ginger and the gym," I mumbled.

I looked up at Mimi standing over me, her eyebrows raised expectantly. I noticed for the first time that she was wearing shorts, revealing more of her slim, copper-skinned legs than I'd seen before. My eyes drifted down them in a bleary sort of way.

"Concentrate," she said with a smile.

"The thing was…" I said, trying to muster my thoughts. "The thing was, when I mentioned the gym, she didn't ask which one."

"You mean…"

"Well, it could have been any gym, right? There's loads. So she makes out she doesn't know this Gary guy. She blanks me on that, but then she gets annoyed about me going to the gym. But she didn't ask which one."

"You're not making sense. You told her you'd seen Gary at the gym?"

"Yep."

"And she pretended she had no idea who Gary was?"

"Yeah, she said everyone knows her."

"But she took it for granted which gym you meant, and why would she if she didn't who he was?"

"Exactly, Sherlock."

"So what does that mean?"

I laughed out loud. Mimi looked annoyed, her hands on her hips now. But I wasn't laughing at her. I was venting a manic sense of helplessness, a get-me-out-of-here frustration.

"What does that mean?" I said slowly. "I've no fucking idea, not a clue." I closed my eyes again. "It all revolves around one gym. Whatever 'it' is. But I don't get how this Gary fits in."

Mimi sat down on the edge of the bed. "Don't go to sleep. You haven't told me about Matt's father yet."

"Okay, but I can't do that on an empty stomach." I looked at my watch. It was nearly three. If I wasn't going to be allowed to sleep, I needed food and strong coffee.

* * *

"Let's explore," Mimi said, and my heart sank because I knew it meant dragging my bruised body further and could delay satisfying my hunger. But it wasn't up for debate, and I followed her through the hotel to the exit that led directly onto the village high street.

The centre of Caerleon was a triangular space at a T junction called The Square where a Dickensian-looking post office faced an Indian takeaway and a half-timbered pub advertising all day sport. It all looked unpromising, and I contemplated suggesting we turn back, but Mimi was already heading down the street towards a place called the Fwrrwm, which I guessed – fairly quickly for a Londoner – was the way Welsh does Forum.

It was, we were told by a sign at the entrance, the site of Porta Praetoria, the main gate of the Roman city. But what really caught my eye was a sandwich board advertising an eatery called The Snug. My hunger was borderline desperate now.

The Fwrrwm turned out to be an eccentric enclave of craft shops facing a garden randomly littered with wood and stone carvings of mythical beasts, Roman legionnaires and Arthurian knights. We found The Snug in a stone building alongside the shops and chose a table near doors opening on to the garden.

"Odd place," Mimi said, nodding in the general direction of a large, surprisingly erotic carving of a naked woman with an animal of some sort on her lap.

"Yes, not exactly Frankie & Bennie's," I said.

We ordered extravagantly. Correction, I ordered excessively: steak pie and chips, ice cream, chocolate fudge cake, several coffees and a slice of what the menu called Bara Brith to go. Mimi was uncharacteristically restrained, choosing only a salad and mineral water.

In between shovelling food down myself, I told her about Graeme: what a pleasant guy he was; how little bitterness he'd shown; how his flat was something of a shrine; photographs of Matt everywhere; and, above all, how fond he obviously was of Megan and how she'd apologised for running off to London and not staying in touch after Matt died.

"And I met Will," I said.

"You met Will? He went with you to see Matt's father?"

"No, he was there, on the bridge, with Megan."

"Well?"

* * *

"He *is* a beast. Terry wasn't exaggerating, and a bit thick with it. It felt like he was trying to suck up to me. He made some feeble excuse about the steroids. Like Terry said, something about being injured."

"Hmm," Mimi said, twisting to pull a tablet out of a shoulder bag that was dangling from the back of her chair. "I did some research while you were out." She started tapping the tablet. "I looked up C J Hunter. I was curious because you'd mentioned his name."

"That was a bit random," I said, worried where this was leading.

"Maybe, but there are some strange parallels - like how he was doing drugs when he was dating Marion Jones and how she defended him when he first failed a drugs test. You know, at the Sydney Olympics."

"Of course I know. I was there."

Mimi threw me a quizzical look, as if to say 'what's your problem?' My problem was hearing her say out loud some of the things I'd been thinking. I wanted to keep them boxed up at the back of my mind. But, as ever, there was no stopping her.

"And he was a beast too. Just look at him."

"I know, but what's your point?" I said. "Megan's another Marion Jones just because they both like big men? It's history repeating itself? You can't condemn someone…"

"Yes, yes, of course, but look at this…" Mimi held the tablet up so I could read an article she'd found about Jones.

I scanned it knowing the story already: after leaving prison, Jones set up a charity called 'Take A Break', supposedly to help kids avoid making the mistakes she'd made. The piece was full of platitudes about how this project was enabling Jones to 'give back' and coach people 'to live a better life'. She'd even been used as a 'celebrity' speaker by the US government in Eastern Europe and was quoted saying 'the idea of making good decisions is a message that is needed all over the world'. I could feel the chocolate fudge cake churning in my stomach.

"So?" I asked, though it was obvious now where Mimi was going with this.

"Don't you think some of those phrases are like Meg's 'Pillow Talk' interview? All that stuff about helping kids in trouble and giving something back."

"They're just clichés. Everyone uses them."

"I know, but we have to face facts, Liam."

"What facts? The trouble is there aren't any."

"Will's a drugs cheat?"

"Okay, but Meg's never failed a test."

"Nor had Marion Jones. In fact, she never did. She was only nailed in the end because she was caught trying to cash a dodgy cheque."

Mimi was animated, her volume one notch below shouting. The Snug had gone quiet. Maybe it was only a lull in the conversations on the tables around us, but it felt like people were listening. I dropped my voice.

"Look, Mimi, I know what you're saying, and don't you think the same things have been going through my mind? But I'm her coach, and I just can't believe I wouldn't know. There'd be signs. She'd have muscled-up quickly or had outbreaks of 'roid rage. I'd have noticed something, some change in her."

"Unless it started before she came to London…"

That hit me in the pit of my stomach.

Mimi paused, and we looked at each other in silence.

"Liam, you have to face that possibility," she continued. "It could be the Megan you know is the one already shaped by steroids."

She was right, of course. How *could* I be sure? Megan could have started using steroids at the same time as Will. Did I know the authentic Megan? Was her determination and her competitive aggression the personality of a champion or a chemical product?

Mimi reached across the table and squeezed my hand. "You know much more about all this than I do, but the C J Hunter thing got me thinking, that's all," she said softly.

I shrugged and used my free hand to drain the last of

coffee. "Yep, it does get you thinking," I said finally. "But, if nothing else, vanity makes me want to think it was the programme I put her through that made her what she is now."

Mimi squeezed my hand again. It was out there now, spoken about between us for the first time. And all we could do was wait and watch until the truth emerged.

I paid the bill and asked for a receipt, out of habit. You never know, I thought as I put it in my wallet, this could all turn out okay and I could still send Jackie an expenses claim.

As we walked back up the High Street, Mimi put her arm through mine and leaned her head into my shoulder. The village was busy now with school kids making their way home and tourists mooching around. We stopped outside the local post office, vaguely looking at its display of souvenirs and paintings of the scene around us by local artists.

"You can stay in my room if you want," Mimi said hesitantly, without looking at me, hurrying to add: "There's no point wasting money on two rooms."

I laughed. "I'm still keeping the receipts… hoping the sponsors don't walk."

"Yeah, but sponsors aside…"

I looked down and she turned her head, her eyes meeting mine.

"I'd love to," I said.

We kissed, oblivious to the congestion we were causing as people came in and out of the post office or tried to post letters in the nearby pillar box. After a collision or two, we sidled sideways to get out of the way and stood, again like a pair of 16-year-olds, not quite sure what to say.

"But you've no idea how out of practice I am," I said finally, for want of a better line. "You could be very disappointed."

"I'm a good coach," Mimi said with a smile, and gave me a peck on the lips.

I was going to pull her closer, but a muffled phone started playing one of those annoyingly repetitive call tunes. She rummaged in her bag and tapped to answer.

There was a lot of head shaking and nodding and "Yeps," and a couple of, "he-said-whats?" It wasn't sounding too good.

"I'll call you back," she said, pulling the phone away from her ear and tapping it off.

She didn't seem in any hurry to explain.

"Well?" I said.

"That was The Mail."

"And?"

"They're running a story saying Megan's avoiding the police. They've spoken to the police. They're saying she still hasn't been in touch and they want to hear from her as soon as possible – you know, 'to help them with their inquiries'."

"Shit. I told her to…."

Mimi put a hand on my shoulder. "And they've spoken to Terry – your mate," she said, with more than a hint of irony, and paused, waiting for me to take this in. "He's quoted. He's mentioned you and said 'even her coach is in the dark' and something about you being at your wits end because Megan's disappeared. Liam, they're making it sound like she's on the frigging run."

I looked across the high street at some people leaving one of the pubs, bantering about something I couldn't hear above the traffic and shielding their eyes from the sun that was drenching that side of the road.

I turned back to Mimi, our eyes meeting and our minds probably thinking much the same thing.

"That's fucking helpful," I said. "I thought I could rely on Terry. How did they nobble him?"

"They didn't. They said he phoned them."

14

SUSPECT OR WITNESS?

"RICHARDS IS ON HIS WAY over," Mimi said.

"Richards?"

"Inspector Richards. Remember him?"

I rubbed my eyes and looked at the shape of my body mummified by the bedclothes, my feet sticking up, and Mimi towering over them dressed in jeans and an emerald green blouse, no make-up but looking eager to go somewhere.

"I said we'd meet him by reception."

"What time is it?"

"Nearly seven."

"While I'm at it, what day is it?"

Mimi started to say Wednesday but decided instead to pick up a cushion from the armchair and throw it in my face. She wasn't a bad shot either.

"Right," I said, sitting up and swivelling round to drop my legs over the edge of the bed. I was completely naked, and I sensed Mimi looking closely at me. The cuts and bruises on my torso were less inflamed now, but it had been as comical as it was painful earlier when we tried to manoeuvre our way round them to make love for the first time.

Mimi had lived up to her claim to be a good coach – a great one, in fact. I'd felt inhibited and self-conscious by the time we reached the room, over-thinking what was about to happen and wondering if I'd live up to expectations, whatever they were.

But she seemed to have no such inhibitions, undressing almost before the door was closed and then helping me along. I had forgotten how exhilarating sex could be – or possibly I had never known. The anaesthetic and soporific effect was so intense it sent me into the heaviest sleep I'd had for days.

Now, as I sat contemplating where my clothes were and whether I needed a shower before seeing the inspector, my whole body still felt weighed down and sluggish. I stretched, which was probably a mistake because I felt a cracking sensation in my ribs and let out a pathetic shriek.

Mimi had gone into the bathroom. I could see her reflected in the dresser mirror running some lipstick across pouted lips.

"Come on, Liam," she said, half-turning to see my reflection.

But I didn't move. I was struggling to recapture the memory of a dream. It was like trying to grab a feather floating in a breeze, each attempt seeming to push it further away. It was something to do with Daniel, something about picking him up from school.

I stared at the wall, my eyes half-closed, hoping the dream

would come back, but the only image I had was of a locked glass door and Danny on the other side of it. I remembered an incident when Danny had only just started school and Kelli went to collect him, and the teacher thought she was his nanny and asked for some ID, and how incensed she was about it. She phoned me, so furious and upset she lurched from sobbing to ranting. "He's my goddam son and that racist bitch wouldn't let me have him," she kept saying, and I tried to rise to the occasion but she didn't think I got it, and I suppose I didn't entirely.

"Liam!" Mimi sounded irritable now, coming back into the room and staring at me. "What the hell's up?"

I looked at her, still sitting naked on the edge of the bed, my mind somewhere near a Sussex school.

"What is it?" she said.

"Only a dream," I replied, and I knew by her look I'd have to explain – not only the dream but about me and Kelli and how our relationship had fallen apart, conceding my neglectfulness but skirting round some of the worst examples.

"What's brought this on?" she asked, when I'd finished my potted history.

I looked around the room and then settled my eyes on her. "This, I suppose – us," I said, gesturing in her direction. "And yesterday at Graeme's, all those photos of Matt were so sad. It made me think of Danny and, you know…"

"I'm beginning to," Mimi said.

* * *

Inspector Richards was leaning against the reception desk when I arrived, looking like he had better things to do and wanted me to know it. Mimi had gone on ahead and was buying us all drinks at the bar.

"Good evening, Mr McCarthy – you look like you're struggling."

"It's nothing much," I said, trying to suppress a wince as I hobbled towards him. "A minor run-in with some local thugs."

The Inspector raised his eyebrows, and was about to say something, but Mimi arrived with the drinks, and we took them outside. The evening sun was casting long shadows from the trees and umbrellas across the hotel terrace. We sat in an arc around one side of a table to fit the shape of the shade.

The Inspector was wearing a light brown checked jacket with darker brown trousers and gleaming beige shoes. His only concession to the heat was to wear his white shirt without a tie. He put his glass of orange juice down on the table and, looking across at Mimi sipping her white wine, gave me an expectant nod.

"So tell me about these thugs, Mr McCarthy," he said.

So I told him pretty much the whole thing. Admittedly, I made it sound like I put up more of a fight than was actually the case – which nearly made Mimi laugh out loud – and I didn't mention that we had seen Megan the same evening. But I told him about my visit to the gym and said I thought the beating was linked to that in some way – that they had called me 'Jim' and I had only used that name there when signing-in at the gym.

Richards nodded and tut-tutted in all the right places, but I sensed as the story unfolded that he wasn't impressed with my amateur detective work.

"Well, to be honest Mr McCarthy, I've got to say it's a very sorry tale," he said. "What's a man like you doing going to a gym under a false name?" He paused as if contemplating his own question. "Mind you, I'm not condoning what happened

– of course I'm not – but you were asking for trouble."

This I found annoying. I may have been naïve. I may even have been stupid – but why was that asking for trouble?

"I see," I said. "If I give a different name because I want to keep a low profile, that warrants a beating, does it, inspector?"

"No, no, no, I wouldn't suggest that for a minute. What I'm telling you is it's best to leave the policing to the police."

"Funny you should say that," Mimi chipped in. "One of your men was at the gym."

"What? What do you mean?"

"Gary," I said. "Ginger hair, built like a tank. He turned up at the gym when I was there."

"And how do you know he's a police officer?"

Mimi sighed. "Liam recognised him from the night before. He was one of the officers who stopped us in the car."

"I recognised him and he recognised me," I added. "And when I was at the gym he came over, and said something about me signing in as Jim."

"And you're sure he was one of the officers who stopped you?"

"Yes, of course he's sure!" Mimi said firmly, her frustration at the inspector's sceptical questions obviously growing.

"And you say his name's Gary, ginger hair." We did some synchronised nodding. "I see, yes. Well, I know who you mean. But I am surprised…" Richards hesitated. "Well, let's just say he wouldn't normally be out in a patrol car."

Now it was synchronised quizzical frowning. The inspector looked uncomfortable.

"He's CID," he said. "That's all. But, to be fair, I'm sure DS Lewis had his reasons."

Richards pulled out a black notebook and jotted a few things in it, taking his time as if needing to digest the 'ginger' angle.

"Be that as it may, Mr McCarthy," he said finally, "my main concern is Miss Tomos. She still hasn't made contact with us, and we have no idea where she's staying – mind you, that's assuming she's still in Newport. Perhaps you can help us there?"

I had left Megan out of the story of the beating but I didn't want to tell any lies. "She was definitely in Newport earlier today," I said. The inspector raised his eyebrows. "I went with her to see Matt's father, Graeme Davies."

"Well, well, well," Richards said. "Haven't you been busy on your short visit here, Mr McCarthy? So where can I find Miss Tomos now?"

"I've no idea, I'm afraid," I said to more eyebrow-raising. "Really, I left her in town around lunchtime, and she didn't say where she was going or where she was staying."

"And you didn't ask?"

I shrugged. I wasn't going to mention her storming off.

"Was she with Driscoll?"

"Not when I left her. But I saw him earlier, before we went to see Graeme."

"He went with you?"

"No, it was just me and Megan."

The inspector was making notes of everything I said now, and it was beginning to feel more like an interrogation than a casual chat.

"You are telling me everything, aren't you Mr McCarthy? There's nothing you're holding back?"

Mimi wriggled and reached forward to put her wine glass down on the table. "Inspector," she said. "He's been beaten-up – look." She lifted my T-shirt. "And you're talking to him like he's done something wrong."

Richards put his hand up as if to say he'd never doubted me and didn't need to see the evidence. "I can arrange for you to make a complaint about that. I'll get an officer to take a statement. But my primary concern at the moment is the very serious question of Miss Tomos and her whereabouts, and it seems to me, if I may so, that the two of you are not... Well, how can I put it? You're not moving heaven and earth to ensure Miss Tomos makes herself available to me."

"That's not true, inspector," I said. "I told her she needs to get in touch with you, and she's promised she will."

"I'm glad to hear it because I wouldn't like to have to charge you with obstructing a police inquiry. Let me make it clear, Mr McCarthy, if you know anything that would help me; if you find out where she's staying, you should tell me immediately."

"Of course. You do know she'll be at the university degree ceremony tomorrow?" said Mimi.

"Yes, I do indeed, but I would prefer not to have to confront her there, in public – with the media present. I'm sure you wouldn't want photographs splashed all over the papers of Britain's golden girl being arrested."

"Arrested?" we both said at once.

"What do you mean arrested?" I added.

The inspector closed the notepad, slid it into the inside pocket of his jacket and looked across the hotel gardens towards the field and the amphitheatre beyond.

I was stunned. The thought of Megan being arrested had never occurred to me. Mimi and I exchanged looks, both of us waiting for Richards to answer. I wondered what Mimi was thinking. To me, this didn't sound like a policeman trying to flaunt his power and importance. Richards seemed old school and understated.

"Look," he said turning back to face us. "I've been treading carefully because of the status Miss Tomos has. I respect the young lady's achievements. And I've been prepared to, well, cut her some slack." He paused to take in our nods of acknowledgement. "But – and I'm not obliged to tell you this Mr McCarthy, Miss Jacobs, but I will as a courtesy and because you'll know soon enough anyway – we are going to exhume the body of Matt Davies. The coroner has given the go ahead, and I've spoken to both parents this afternoon. And yes, Mr McCarthy, I did know you'd been to see Graeme Davies. He told me, and he appreciated your visit, and was pleased to see Megan. But that isn't the point. I have an inquiry to conduct, and she is part of it."

"But why exhume the body?" I said, tentatively, thinking of Matt's father alone in that room surrounded by his pictures of Matt as a boy looking so happy and hopeful.

"I'm not at liberty to go into detail," Richards continued, "but you're intelligent people and I'm sure you realise we wouldn't be doing this unless something new had come to light – well, in this case, something that was overlooked the first time around. Which means we need to do some more tests. We don't dig bodies up for the fun of it."

Mimi was more subdued than I'd ever seen her. She looked dazed. All traces of irritation had vanished.

"Will the media be told?" she said.

"Of course," the inspector replied. "We'll be issuing a statement tomorrow. The body will be exhumed on Thursday night."

Mimi looked at me as if expecting me to say something, but I was struggling to know where to begin. I left her to rise to the occasion.

"We'll do whatever we can to help inspector," she said, sounding calm and professional. "When we see Megan tomorrow – assuming we see her – we *will*, not for the first time, emphasise the seriousness of this. We can't force her to listen of course, but we will tell her we think she should contact you without delay."

The inspector nodded and frowned slightly as if straining to summon the right words. "I don't want to make threats Miss Jacobs – it's not my style – but, to be fair, I think you need to know that if the tests on the body confirm our concerns, and if she doesn't volunteer herself, I may have no choice but to issue a warrant for her arrest. I need to establish whether she's a witness or a suspect in serious crime."

I gasped, loudly enough for Richards to stop and look from Mimi to me.

"I'll give you 48 hours," he said, standing and straightening his jacket and turning to walk briskly to the car park.

15

PEER PROBLEMS

"DAD, DAD. IS THAT YOU?"

Danny had caught me in the no-man's-land between sleeping and waking. At first I thought the phone ringing was part of a dream. Even after answering it I was disorientated and slightly surprised to see Mimi lying next to me.

I mustered a mumbled, "Danny, hi! What's up?"

"What's happening with Megan, Dad?"

I could hear him breathing, softly and rhythmically, on the other end of the phone. Mimi stirred and rolled over, her naked back to me, her dark hair fanning across the pillow.

"I don't know yet Danny. It's complicated."

"They're saying she's disappeared."

"Who's saying?"

"Everyone. It's on Twitter… There are photos of you."

"Are there?"

"They're saying you don't know where she is."

"You shouldn't believe everything you read, Danny."

"But *do* you know where she is?"

"I saw her yesterday."

"So what's going to happen? What about the Olympics? Is she going?"

"Sorry Danny. I don't know yet."

Mimi bolted into an upright position, frowning and clutching the duvet to keep herself covered. I knew what she was thinking. We had agreed not to admit to any doubts about Rio. But that was for adults. I couldn't lie to Danny.

"So Dad, when are you going to come back to London? Am I going to see you on Sunday, like you said?" His voice, beginning to break, seemed to go up half an octave as he emphasised those last three words. It took me a few seconds to get my bearings. I looked at my watch, which was pointless as it didn't show the date. It said 8.20. I realised it was Thursday morning. Who knows what could happen between now and Sunday?

"Shouldn't you be on your way to school?" I asked.

"I am. I'm outside school now. So Dad, what about Sunday?"

"Yes. Sunday. I'll see you then."

"Promise?"

Mimi was following my amateurish parenting closely. She nodded vigorously and gestured with a hand like she was pushing me along, urging me to sound more reassuring.

"Of course! Definitely. Tell Mum, okay?"

The breathing again. I could sense him thinking.

"Dad."

"Yeah?"

"Are you okay?"

"Of course. Of course I am. Yep. Don't worry about me… but I've got to go now, okay? Sorry son – we have to be somewhere soon."

"We?"

"See you Sunday, Danny."

"Yes. Don't forget."

* * *

Mimi and I decided to skip the hotel breakfast. We had to be at the university for ten thirty, and I couldn't rock-up in a lived-in tracksuit and a crumpled T-shirt. I needed to buy some clothes, and there was no time to worry about style – as if I ever did. The solution was the nearest retail park, and grey trousers, white shirt and navy jacket from the first store we found. I tried them on and kept them on, dumping my sorry-looking coaching clothes in a carrier bag.

While I was changing, Mimi had bought a full set of newspapers. The coverage wasn't good. The Mail front page led with the Terry story, under a headline: 'Meg mystery deepens – coach at wit's end'. As expected, they made it sound like Megan was on the run and I was 'in the dark'.

"For fuck sake! He really screwed us," I said.

"Not here, Liam. Let's go somewhere quieter," she said, looking over her shoulder. Paranoia was setting in.

We left the clothes shop and found a small family-run Italian coffee place housed, incongruously, in a Tesco the size of an aircraft hangar. We ordered coffees, succumbed to the tempting sticky pastries and sat as far away from the other customers as we could with the pile of papers in front of us. Finding the Meg story wasn't hard. It was either on the front page or jumping out at us from one of the early news pages. This definitely wasn't a sports story any more.

I was still smarting over Terry. "The next time he fancies a pint I'll pour it over his effing head," I said.

Mimi looked up from the paper she was reading. "Ha! I've got some better ideas, but let's save that for another time."

The Mail piece was the most damaging, lent credibility by the quote from Terry, someone who had spoken to me. The others were more speculative: 'Drug cloud over Olympic star'; 'What's Meg got to hide?'; 'Meg avoiding steroid death probe'. None of them made specific allegations. The editors knew Jackie – with libel lawyers on tap – would be trigger-happy if they published anything they couldn't back-up. But that didn't stop them recycling the story of the police inquiry ladled with innuendos.

"There's nothing new here," I said, "except Terry's treachery."

"Hmm, well, it's kind of new," Mimi replied, picking up her steaming cappuccino and looking at me like she was about to explain something to a child.

"What do you mean?"

"What I mean is that the news is there's no news. There's no news of Megan. Four days go by, and she hasn't shown up. She still hasn't made contact with the police. That's the story. And it looks bad."

I put the paper I was reading down. It was depressing me. The previous night had been bad enough. After the inspector's not-so-veiled threat, we had retreated to Mimi's room only to be inundated with calls. Mimi had to fend off journalists, insisting to me she couldn't go to ground when they were people she dealt with day-in, day-out. And I spent a few hours placating athletics officials and trying to track Megan and Jackie down.

Megan didn't respond to my calls, and I agonised over

texting her. I even started tapping in a few words, but how do you tell someone their dead friend's corpse is being dug up?

As for poor Jackie, I thought she was going to pass out when I told her. She groaned and went silent and then mumbled something about calling me back. When she phoned again an hour later, she said her day had been spent acting as a punch bag for angry sponsors, placating them with the offer of a clear-the-air meeting at Crystal Palace on Friday and promising – optimistically – that Megan would be there to answer their questions.

I knew how fickle sponsors and their army of 'brand guardians' could be. One minute they are gushing with false jollity about everything being 'exciting' and 'brilliant'. The next, the athlete loses form, and they are ever-so sorry darling but this isn't working for them. There are honourable exceptions – especially the sponsors who love track and field for its own sake and who gain a vicarious pleasure from supporting an athlete through thick and thin. But at the higher levels of the sport, the big corporates take over, and it's clinical: the only thing that matters is Return On Investment. When an athlete is yesterday's success story, it can be as brutal as the treatment of anyone who's surplus to requirements. Jackie had said, "If they're half-way out the door now, imagine what will happen when they hear about the body being exhumed."

Of course Jackie was no saint when it came to driving a commercial bargain, but I could empathise with her. The only thing I couldn't make my mind up about was who to feel angrier with: the sponsors or Megan for dragging us into all this.

Mimi's phone was vibrating on the table now, sending a ripple across my half-drunk coffee. She answered with a curt, "Yep". I gathered it was someone from the university in a panic. Mimi tapped the phone off, scooped the papers up and said, "We need to go. The uni's crawling with paparazzi."

* * *

The university campus was on a hill above Caerleon. There was only one way in, and it was jammed with photographers and fans being kept at bay by security guards in florescent yellow jackets and uniformed police. They had managed to keep a channel clear for cars to approach the barrier, but the photographers pressed forward when they recognised us, and some of them were leaning across the bonnet as we inched towards the man checking passes. Mimi showed him our invitations through the windscreen, not wanting to lower the window, and he lifted the barrier and waved us through.

We followed signs for the Sports Hall tucked away behind the main building where the flustered university PR man was waiting at the entrance, clutching a clipboard in one hand and a phone in the other. This was obviously not a normal day at the office for him. He was young and looking around anxiously like he was desperate for the cavalry to arrive.

"You must be Mimi," he said as we approached.

"Any sign of Megan?" Mimi replied with a nod.

Yes, she's with the Vice Chancellor," he said. "She knew the back way in." He chuckled nervously.

Mimi threw him a sisterly smile and turned to me. "This is Liam McCarthy, Meg's coach."

The university man shook my hand and gestured us towards the door. "We're running late," he said. "The parents and students have been in their seats for quite a while."

He directed us along a balcony overlooking the hall to the

rows of seats on a retractable stand that filled the back third of the gym. Our seats were among the parents. Students filled the rows on the floor area, all of us facing a stage furnished with two lecterns and a row of upholstered throne-like chairs.

Within seconds of sitting down, we were on our feet again as digital horns heralded the arrival of the academic hierarchy in a colourful array of gowns, hoods and hats. They trooped in from the balcony, down a central aisle and onto the stage, looking suitably ceremonial and generally very pleased with themselves.

One of the academics remained standing to tell us she was using the powers vested in her to declare the congregation open for the conferment of degrees, diplomas and other awards. She invited the Vice Chancellor to speak. I still couldn't see Megan.

The Vice Chancellor's speech was mercifully short, and soon the woman running the show was on her feet again announcing that she was presenting Megan Cerys Tomos to everyone – and there was Meg, popping up from among the students wearing a golden gown and a soft black hat. As she stepped onto the stage, my frustrations with her melted away, warmed by a sudden unfathomable sense of pride. As she stood there, looking composed and dignified, alongside the woman speaking of her accomplishments, I felt proxy for her poorly father.

Megan, we were told, was – at twenty-one – already one of the most successful Welsh women athletes of all time. In her chosen event, the 100m hurdles, she had set European and Commonwealth records and won a gold medal at last year's World Athletics Championship in Beijing. She was a Welsh speaker, born and bred in Newport, and had attended Caerleon Comprehensive School, where she was head girl and gained straight As at A-Level. Megan was destined for university, the woman explained, but winning gold medals at European and World Junior Championships had whetted her appetite for sporting success and, two years ago, she decided to put her university place on hold and move to London to work with a top hurdles coach. Her performance in Beijing had made her an international star, and in a few weeks she will go to Rio, aiming for an Olympic gold medal.

"Megan," the speaker continued, "Rydym ni'n falch ohonoch chi, mae Cymru yn falch ohonoch chi ac rydym yn dymuno pob llwyddiant i chi yn Rio mis nesaf. Megan, we are proud of you, Wales is proud of you, and we wish you every success in Rio next month. Is-Ganghellor, yr wyf yn cyflwyno Megan Cerys Tomos ar gyfer gwobr Cymrodoriaeth y Brifysgol. Vice-Chancellor, I present Megan Cerys Tomos for the award of Fellowship of the University."

Applause rippled around the hall. I had nothing to compare it with, but it sounded polite rather than enthusiastic. It had stopped by the time Megan had taken her certificate and stepped behind the lectern, leaving an uncomfortable pause as she unfolded her notes and smoothed them flat. I had never heard Megan make a speech and my stomach was churning even faster than it does when she's on the start line. I squeezed Mimi's hand, and she smiled anxiously back.

"Diolch yn fawr Is-Ganghellor am yr anrhydded hwn," Megan said tentatively. "Yr wyf yn falch iawn i'w dderbyn. Mae wir yn arbennig iawn i mi. Thank you so much Vice Chancellor for this honour, which I'm very proud to accept. This is really special for me. When the letter informing me of the university's decision arrived a few weeks ago, it came as a complete surprise. It means a lot to me to be recognised in this way in my home town, by a university attended by so many of my friends."

Megan looked up from her notes and scanned the room

as if she was searching for some of those friends. The hall was so quiet the slightest cough sounded like a firecracker.

"That's why," Megan continued softly, "I want to dedicate this award to an absent friend. Someone who should have been with us today."

Mimi gasped like she had just been winded by a blow to the stomach. This obviously wasn't in any script she'd written. I was gripping Mimi's hand more tightly than could have been comfortable. Ahead of us, among the students, there was a ripple of movement and some shushing.

Megan seemed undeterred. "Some of you will know Matt Davies, who went to Caerleon Comp and who I first became friends with when we were at Infants' School. Matt died two years ago; a terrible loss to his parents Graeme and Julie and to his many friends. He should have been here today. He could have gone on to do great things, but he was taken away from us far, far too soon."

The student part of the audience seemed divided. Most of them were listening intently, but some were visibly uncom-fortable, fidgeting and whispering to each other. The Vice Chancellor was looking sternly at that group, but someone – a female voice – said something; it sounded like she intended it to be a whisper, not mean for everyone to hear, but the word carried around the silent hall.

"Hypocrite."

Megan paused and looked across the audience in the direction of the voice. There was more shushing. Heads were bowed in embarrassment. Everyone was fidgeting now. My eyes were locked on Megan's face. I held my breath, wondering if she'd explode or manage to regain her balance; stay composed, like she would if she hit a hurdle painfully.

Megan looked down at her notes, her hands gripping the podium. She continued. "Those of you who knew him will know how kind and generous he was, and how much pleasure he took in the success of others." She faltered and then looked up, saying, but beginning to choke on the words: "especially in mine."

For a second, it wasn't clear if Megan had finished. The Vice Chancellor stood up and stepped forward to stand at her shoulder.

Megan picked up the certificate and waved it defiantly, saying: "Felly, yr wyf yn neilltuo'r wobr hon i Matt Davies, ffrind arbennig, a gymerwyd oddi wrthym cyn iddo gael cyfle i wireddu ei freuddwydion ei hun. So I am dedicating this award to Matt Davies, a special friend, who was taken from us before he had a chance to fulfil his own dreams. Fy annwyl Matt. I ti mae hwn, ble bynnag yr wyt ti. My dear Matt. This is for you wherever you are. Diolch yn fawr."

The hall was silent. I was thrown by Megan's use of Welsh. Speaking her first language, she sounded so different. I looked at Mimi, who seemed as stunned as me and was staring at the platform speechless.

Some of the students started to clap. The Vice Chancellor joined in enthusiastically. Soon a few of the students were standing and waving at Megan. Most people were applauding, but it was noticeable that the students around the source of the voice were not joining in, and some were shaking their heads, vigorously, making a point.

A man in the parents' section stood up and walked out. It may have been paranoia, but I sensed him staring at the back of my head as he passed behind me on the balcony.

Megan was still behind the lectern as if paralysed by the moment. The Vice Chancellor turned to her and, in a kindly way – like she was helping an old lady across the road – steered her towards a steward standing by the steps down from the stage. Megan sat down where she had been before, and I could only see the back of her head.

The woman running proceedings announced that the Vice Chancellor would now present degrees in business studies and a queue formed near the steps.

Mimi leaned towards me. "We need to get her the fuck out of here," she whispered.

A woman in front of us half-turned, an eyebrow raised. I held her look and she turned back. I was trying to think of a way out, but I couldn't see how it could be done inconspicuously.

"It would only make matters worse," I said.

The ceremony became a succession of roll calls. Most of the students walked briskly across the stage; others milked their few seconds in the limelight by bowing or waving to friends. I kept an eye on Megan as best I could in the movement of students to and from the stage. She was sitting bolt upright and not obviously showing any emotion.

The roll calls seemed interminable. My thoughts drifted to the students whose exam papers still lay on my desk. They were second years, so the delay didn't matter much, but I imagined it gave them something to talk about in the union bar.

It must have been more than an hour into the ceremony when Mimi nudged me. She was nodding vigorously towards the front of the hall and starting to get out of her seat. I look across the rows of students. No Megan. There was a gap where she'd been sitting. No question about it.

Mimi was already on the balcony now. I followed her. There was no way of doing this inconspicuously. Parents and students were looking up at us. Even the Vice Chancellor caught my eye with a concerned look.

We found ourselves in the Sports Hall reception area. It was deserted apart from two stewards waiting for the ceremony to finish.

Mimi was checking her phone. "Shit! They've announced the body is being exhumed." She was tapping her way through story after story. "It's frigging everywhere. She must have seen it."

"We've got to find her," I said, heading briskly in the direction of some double doors that seemed to lead into the main university building. We followed dark and deserted corridors past student shops and coffee bars until we reached an exit taking us out onto gardens at the front of the building. We could see most of the campus and the village of Caerleon beyond, but the only people around were stewards killing time.

We stood there in silence, going through the motions of looking in different directions as if there was a possibility Meg would amble into view.

"She could be anywhere," I said.

"I've texted her."

I nodded. "What are the police saying?"

"Not much. The only new thing is they mention something about a blood sample taken at the scene." Mimi was reading from her phone. "They say it wasn't considered significant in the first investigation, but now they want to do some tests."

"Try Meg again."

Mimi tapped her phone and went through to voicemail. "It's Mimi and Liam – call us," she said.

"There's no point in hanging around here," I said. "We'll only get caught by the media. Let's go back to the hotel. Leave your car – we'll find a way out on foot."

Mimi was still fussing with her phone, pulling faces as she trawled through Twitter and Google. You didn't need to be a genius to guess what was out there.

I walked down some steps to the intersection of two driveways. The gate we'd used earlier was to the right, but ahead was what looked like the original approach to the main building. It was rammed with parked cars. The gates at the far end were closed, but there seemed to be a gap for pedestrians to one side.

I called back to Mimi. "Let's try down there."

She looked up and started walking towards me still focused on her phone, even as she negotiated the steps.

"There are some evil bastards on Twitter," she said. "Listen to this…"

"Not now," I said. "Let's get out of here first."

Mimi took the point. We set off down the drive, trying hard not to break into a jog to avoid giving a photographer with a zoom lens a great shot to sell.

The hotel was only a short walk from the campus, past the Infants' School where Megan had first met Matt. We walked in silence, holding hands, like a couple of lost children. When we arrived at the hotel room, it felt like a refuge, a place where we could close the door on this madness. Except for the phone. The calls were relentless. They were all from the media, following up the police announcement. Mimi ignored them.

I slumped into the armchair and Mimi went into the bathroom. I heard her sit down on the loo and pee. I thought about how embarrassing that would have been only a few days ago, and wondered if maybe we should just pack our bags and go back to London; leave Meg to it. Why were we bothering? She didn't seem to want our help. We didn't really know what she needed help with. Mimi emerged from the bathroom, straightening her skirt with one hand and waving the phone at me with the other.

"It's Meg – a text," she said, "but I haven't a clue what she means."

I took the phone. The message said:

'See you at the hotel. Need to talk. I was there.'

Mimi and I looked at each other, bemused. The phone vibrated again: another message from Meg. It said: 'When he died.'

Mimi tossed the phone on the bed and joined me in the armchair, her head buried in my shoulder.

16

AFTER THE PARTY

MEGAN BARGED THROUGH THE UNLOCKED door and scanned the room desperately like there might be enemies in every corner. She had a manic look: spiky hair wilder than usual, smart clothes dishevelled, beads of sweat draining mascara from her eyes. She wiped her cheek with the back of a hand, smearing mascara even further across her face. Her eyes settled on us. Mimi was disentangling herself from me and standing up.

"What's going on?" Megan said.

"Nothing much," Mimi replied, throwing me a guilty, childlike smile. She went into the bathroom and returned with a handful of tissues for Megan.

"Didn't look like nothing much to me," Megan said, taking

the tissue and slumping into the other armchair.

I shrugged. I didn't have much idea what was going on between Mimi and me, let alone want to explain it to Megan.

Mimi settled herself on the bed, upending two pillows to cushion her back against the wall. We formed a triangle and sat there in silence avoiding eye contact. Megan was dabbing her cheeks with a tissue. She seemed to be calming herself and preparing to say something, to explain her text. But Mimi spoke first, treading carefully with, "You okay?"

Megan nodded but didn't look up.

"They had no right..." Mimi started.

But Megan looked at her sharply, frowning. "Yes they did. Of course they did. Well, *she* did anyway."

"She?" Mimi said.

"That girl who heckled. She's a cow, but face facts, I was asking for it."

Mimi looked across the bed at me as if expecting some help, but I didn't want a repeat of my row with Megan on the bridge. I was trying to keep my usual lack of tact in check and wait as long as it took for Megan to open up. But she seemed frozen in some angry, dark place and sat there motionless, tanned legs outstretched, staring sullenly at her scuffed and dusty black leather shoes.

We fell silent again. Mimi fidgeted and looked like she was about to try again, but I gave her a short sharp shake of my head.

"Have I ever told you I used to go out with Matt?" Megan said, nodding to herself, like she was visualising it. "It was in Year Ten, the summer term. He asked me out, and I was so surprised I said 'yes'." Megan lifted her head and looked at me, swallowing a truncated laugh as if the thought of her and Matt was funny and grotesque at the same time.

"You know we'd been friends from primary school, right?"

she continued. "You saw the pictures at Graeme's. And that carried on at the comp. Like I said, we used to hang-out around Caerleon. We were in the same circle, and Matt was a lovely boy. He was kind and popular, a bit of a joker. Some people said he was a show-off, but that wasn't fair – it was only his way of, you know, trying to get people to like him. We all do that I suppose."

"And you liked him?" Mimi said.

Megan looked back at her as if the question needed careful thought.

"Of course I did, yes," she said slowly, "but I was only 15, and to be honest, I'd never thought about him as someone to go out with. He was this kid I'd known forever. He was just Matt. And then suddenly, out of the blue, he goes all serious and wants us to be a couple; wants me to be his 'missus'. And I'm telling you, he actually called me that, for God's sake!"

Megan shook her head, locked in eye contact with Mimi. "We stopped socialising with everyone else," she said. "It always had to be only us. He'd become really intense. D'you know what I mean? Needy." She looked at Mimi, who smiled like she knew exactly what she meant, and I thought I must remember to ask her about that.

"Anyway," Megan said. "It was annoying, and really claustrophobic. Especially the texts all day long. I'd wake up to them. I'd go to bed and 'ping' there was another one. And then the selfies started. And, well, it all got a bit strange…" She flushed and held the tissue up to her face, like a child wanting to hide. "I mean really explicit, a bit weird. I felt more and more uncomfortable about the whole thing, and I thought, 'I've got to end this' but I didn't know how to do it. There isn't a good way, is there? So I told him one day after school and he just disappeared – went off somewhere and then rolled up later drunk and started calling me a bitch in front of everyone when we were hanging-out at the barracks. After that, he ignored me for weeks, and later I heard he'd been talking about me." She shook her head, choking on a sob. "Telling the boys I was a stuck up bitch and a frigid cow, stuff like that."

She paused for a moment, took in a deep breath and then turned back towards me like she'd suddenly remembered I was in the room.

"I couldn't believe it," she said. "Matt and I had been so close – or that's what I thought – and things were never really the same again."

"Did Graeme know about all this?" I said.

Megan laughed. "What – you mean, all of it? The dirty photos?"

"Any of it," I said. "About you going out and things turning sour."

"He must have known about us going out, but I never spoke to him about anything like that and Matt probably didn't either. What's he going to say? He knew his dad liked me. I don't know. Julie's attitude changed. I stopped going to their house for a while, but whenever I saw Julie she was always snooty – like I was trash, not good enough for her Matt."

"So what happened after that?" Mimi said.

Megan took in a long breath and fell silent for a moment.

"Things gradually settled down," she said, looking at Mimi, "and I began spending more and more time training and competing. I was away a lot, and we had our GCSEs so I didn't go out as much as I used to, but Matt and I still had the same friends, hung out with the same people at school."

"And Will, was he part of that, in your circle?" I said.

"Yeah, sort of. Will was mainly Matt's friend at first. I didn't really know him that well, but Matt started going to the gym with him not long after we split up. Talk about out of character: he was really skinny and he'd never done any sport. He'd always have an excuse for missing games, like he forgot his kit or something – but then suddenly he was into working out. And then this one time, the first time I'd seen him with his top off for ages, I just laughed out loud: he'd shaved his chest and he had these huge pecs and a six pack. I couldn't help laughing. Which he didn't like, not at all."

Megan paused, gulping like she was struggling to suppress tears. "But how was I to know how things would turn out?" she said, talking mainly to herself, staring at her feet again. "I had no idea he'd become a 'roider. Not at first, but then Will told me, and I was shocked – really shocked – especially when Will said most of the boys were at it."

I wriggled in my seat, and Megan shot me a look as if to say, 'I know what you're thinking'. But she was wrong. At that point, I was only thinking about finding a position that didn't make my ribs ache. The pain from the beating had eased, but sitting seemed to compress my chest and push the ribs into each other. I straightened my back.

"So when did you start dating Will?" I asked to move things along, a wince in my voice.

"About that time," Megan replied. "The end of Year Twelve. We went out right through my last year at school." She laughed and shook her head. "We were the 'celebrity couple'. Will was rugby captain; I was head girl and – you know, the athletics glory girl and all that. I suppose I loved it to be honest, and by then Matt had latched himself onto us again. It was weird. It was like he was our biggest fan, and he seemed okay too, doing his body building and being the centre of attention at parties."

She broke off for another long look at her scruffy shoes. "But then he began turning up at the parties less and less.

He had new friends outside school. They'd go to Bristol or Cardiff and Matt was always telling everyone how wrecked he'd been and how they should try this or that." She gave me a sideways glance, checking to see how I was reacting. "Most people had tried weed. I didn't do it, I didn't like the smoke. I didn't even drink. It was odd watching people getting high, but you never knew if they were putting it on; like they'd have one draw and make out they were off their heads. It was pathetic really. Everything was 'good stuff'. No one ever said, 'this is crap'. D'you know what I mean?"

She directed that at Mimi, perhaps thinking I was too out of touch to know what she meant. Mimi nodded.

"Anyway, Matt was into other things by now," Meg continued. "Weed was child's play for him. He was like a walking pharmacy, a bag of pills in one pocket and a bottle of vodka to wash them down in the other." She stopped as if wondering what to say next.

Mimi started to get up. "Do you want some water?" she said.

"And he began to make money from it," Megan said.

Mimi sat back down.

"Will thought Matt was making a lot of money; said he was dealing in everything. Steroids. Weed. Meow meow."

I gave her a puzzled frown.

"Love him," Megan said to Mimi, laughing at me and sounding very Welsh.

She was right. I had no idea what meow meow was. I'm not sure Mimi did either, but she kept quiet.

"It's an amphetamine, Li," Megan said. "I couldn't believe how low he'd sunk. He started acting like he was some kind of drug baron, like something out of Breaking Bad. He had his own little fan club of girls too. But give me a break, I mean this was Caerleon for God's sake." She paused as if trying to remember something. "Yes, I'll have some water please."

Mimi went into the bathroom and came back with two glasses of tap water. She handed one to Megan and took a gulp from the other, then gave the remainder to me. The room had become unbearably hot. With no windows open, the afternoon sun streaming in and the heat from three warm bodies, it was like a sauna. I didn't want to risk anyone overhearing our conversation, but Mimi was one step ahead of me. She opened the door, letting a refreshing breeze in, and leaned outside, looking both ways to see if anyone was around. "Let's leave it open for a few minutes," she said, standing by the door.

Megan was fidgeting, trying to pull something out of a small pocket in her skirt. "I keep this," she said, handing me a tatty photograph. It had been cut down so only Matt was in it. He was standing outside a pub, wearing a waistcoat and collarless shirt and drawing on a cigarette. I hardly recognised him. His face was grey and emaciated, his eyes sunken in dark cavities. There was a smile on his face, as if he was pleased with himself, but in a grim way – not like the innocent boy with the fish I'd seen at Graeme's flat.

I passed the photo to Mimi who was still guarding the door. She stared at it for a while. She hadn't seen Matt's image, other than a much younger school photograph of him that was being recycled in the papers.

"He looks shocking," she said, handing the photo back to Megan, closing the door and going back to her place on the bed.

"That was taken after our A-Levels," Megan said. "We were still friends then, just about. I think we were going out to celebrate the end of the exams. Not that Matt was very bothered about the exams. He was expecting to fail, and he didn't seem to care."

Megan was gripping the arms of the chair now and I sensed she was bracing herself, like she was through the foothills and the climb was about to get steeper.

"It's the last photo I have of him," she said. "I hardly saw him that summer. Everything was coming together for me. I reached the finals at the AAAs in Birmingham and then I went to the European Juniors in Italy, which was fantastic. I loved it. This fabulous old city called Rieti; athletes from all over Europe…"

I smiled and nodded. Rieti was special. I'd gone out to those championships with one of my juniors and helped out coaching the relay squad. I didn't speak to Meg but I saw her compete. She was only 18 – younger than most of the other competitors – but she held her own. On her time in the qualifiers, she could have been among the medals, but nerves and the heat got the better of her in the final.

"You did well," I said.

"Ha, but I bombed in the final," she said, reading my mind. "Still, I was pleased. It whetted my appetite. But then when I came back, I found Will was really miserable. He'd injured himself – pulled a hamstring in pre-season training. It was supposed to be his breakthrough year, and he was gutted. He couldn't do anything for weeks, and by the time he could train again, the season had started and he was struggling to make the squad. I think he only had two full games before Christmas…" Megan paused. "Well, I mean, before he failed the test." She looked hard at me, a fixed unblinking stare. "I know it looks bad, Liam, but I had no idea. Not until he got done."

I was still struggling with this. I wasn't sure I was ready to say I believed her beyond any doubt. Mimi sensed my difficulty.

"So what happened between you and Will," she asked, "when you found out he'd failed a drugs test?"

I was watching Megan closely now to see if her body language gave anything away, but she didn't blink or flinch or wriggle or give me any sense of feeling awkward.

"I dumped him of course," she said, with a welcome hint of indignation that it might be in doubt. "We had a massive row at his flat. By this time, he'd got a job and had left home – we were practically living together – but I walked out on him. My parents were thinking of moving back to west Wales, so I had most of my stuff at Will's, but I couldn't stay there."

"But you were together the night Matt died?" Mimi said.

"Yes, that was a few weeks later, after Christmas. I'd moved everything back out of his flat by then, and I was living back home, but I didn't know what to do, what with my parents planning to leave Newport. I'd been thinking about going to London, but…" Megan's face turned as red as it does after a hard training session.

Mimi looked across the bed at me and raised her eyebrows.

"But… you know," Megan said, "I couldn't let him go completely."

"So you were still seeing each other?" Mimi said.

Megan looked at me sheepishly and then turned towards Mimi. "He was a shag," she said, with an embarrassed chuckle. "We ended up in bed a few times, and I think Will hoped we'd get back together. He kept apologising – over and over again – for being such a twat, for ruining his own career and risking mine. And I suppose I was still fond of him. But there was no way back, not for me."

"So that night…?" Mimi asked, tentatively.

"That night…" Megan closed her eyes and sat completely still for a long moment. She still hadn't opened them when she started speaking again, sounding like she was reeling off lines from a script. "It was just a normal Saturday. None of us had any money to go out. It was a few weeks after Christmas and we were all skint. So Will had a house party, at his flat. There weren't many of us there. It was boring to be honest. We sat around playing drinking games, same old things."

"And Matt was in a bad way?" I said.

Megan laughed. "Oh no. Matt wasn't there. God knows where he was. We never found out where he'd been. He could have been anywhere. Matt did his own thing – you never knew when he'd turn up. He was really out of control by then. He had been for months: always looking for the next high, wanting it to be better than the last. Our parties weren't exciting enough for him."

"So… I don't understand?" I said. "What happened? I thought Matt died after the party."

Megan was staring at the wall, looking like she was ready to break down, her face drained and tense. Mimi sat up and dropped her legs over the edge of the bed so that she was close enough to Meg to take her hand.

"Everyone had left," Megan said, closing her eyes. "They'd gone home or gone clubbing. Including that girl who heckled me today, Hannah. She was there but left early. I suppose it was about two o'clock in the morning by the time everyone had gone. I don't know, I lost track of time. I was going to stay over with Will, and we were in his kitchen, clearing-up and talking. Then Matt turned up, banging on the front door. Will went down to let him in, and he had to practically carry him up the stairs."

Megan let out a long breath and drew another one in. Mimi squeezed her hand.

"Will sort of dropped Matt onto this chair in the kitchen, and he slumped over the table. I just looked at him. If I'm honest…" Megan stopped and bit her lower lip, staring at the wall again. "If I'm honest, I was pissed-off with him. I was angry. I know it sounds terrible but I had no patience left for him. I'd had enough of seeing him like that. But Will gave him some water, and it was odd... Matt started getting agitated and stood up and was pacing around the kitchen. I can't remember exactly what he was saying. Most of it didn't make any sense anyway. He was slurring his words, just ranting about stuff, randomly slagging people off."

"Was it directed at you?" I asked.

"A bit. I was always a bitch when he was drunk and drugged-up. But there was also something about Gary..." Megan looked at me.

"That would be the Gary you don't know?" I said.

She waved a hand irritably in my direction, and Mimi looked equally annoyed. I knew it was bad timing, but Megan's pretence she didn't know Gary had dented my trust in her.

"Yes, Gary the cop," Megan said. "I don't really know him, but Will says Gary runs the whole steroid thing from that gym you went to; the gym Matt and Will used. And Matt was ranting about him."

"Ranting about what?" Mimi said softly.

"I don't really know, it's all a blur. They'd fallen out about something. I never found out because I lost it with him myself. To be honest, I didn't give a fuck about his problem with Gary. I was angry with him for so many things – for supplying Will, for dragging me into the whole steroids thing, for the state he was in. So I told him what I thought. For months, I'd been bottling it up, and I just let rip. I told him..." Megan bit her lower lip, so hard she drew blood, "... he was a waste of space. That's what I said. I can't believe it now, I said he was *a waste of space*."

Mimi was still holding Megan's hand. She squeezed it again. "You weren't to know," she said.

Megan looked at her like she wasn't there, as if seeing something else. Their faces were inches apart.

"So what happened then?" Mimi said.

Megan recoiled, still staring at Mimi but not right through her, seeing her now and frowning as if she was surprised by the question.

"He died," she said. "He died right there, in front of me, practically at my feet. I'm telling you, it was the worst…"

Megan looked down at the floor like she was imagining Matt stretched out, and we followed her eyes, absurdly staring at the same spot as if we could all see him.

"I'd never seen anyone die before," Megan said, like she was gathering herself, becoming almost matter-of-fact. "It was so, I don't know, absolute. One minute I was saying 'You're a waste of space' and he was looking at me all shocked, and the next, he was clutching his chest and falling, like his knees had given way. The next thing we knew, he was on the floor, on his side with vomit spewing out of his mouth, everywhere. And he rolled onto his back and Will tried to pick him up but he was still writhing around, and then he stopped, just stopped moving completely, and Will let him go and his head dropped onto the floor. And that was it. He died. Will checked his pulse, and he said 'He's dead'."

Megan slumped back in the chair like a valve had released the pressure from bottling this story up for so long. I couldn't be sure but it seemed like this was the first time she'd told anyone about that night, or told anyone the truth about it.

"And Will phoned for help, did he?" I said.

"He must have done," Megan said, "but, to be honest, his first thought was to push me out of the door, literally. All I remember is he stood up and grabbed me by the shoulders and said, 'You've got to get out of here'. We didn't talk about it. I was so stunned I didn't argue, and the next thing I remember is running down the street. I got a taxi home from town and luckily my parents were down in Pembrokeshire for the weekend, house-hunting. The following week I moved to London." She shook her head, teeth gritted, seeming to want to suppress any tears. "I ran. I ran away… like a coward, a selfish fucking coward."

Mimi turned to me and raised her eyebrows, as if to say, 'So now we know'. My mind was on the night she turned up at Copthall asking me to coach her. I calculated the dates. The newspaper reports said Matt died in the early hours of the January 11th, a Sunday morning. Megan was in London nine days later, talking to me about her ambitions. I tried to picture her that evening; what she was wearing and how she looked, but it wouldn't come back to me. All the different impressions of Megan seemed to blend into one – and besides, how would I know if there was anything unusual about her behaviour that evening? I didn't know what her 'normal' was. I had never spoken to Megan before.

"Are you ready to tell the police all this?" Mimi asked.

"Of course…" she said, "and Graeme. I want to tell Graeme first."

Mimi ran a hand through Meg's spiky hair, but she seemed distracted.

"Oh my God… I can't believe they're digging Matt up," Megan said, shaking her head. "What's that all about? It's gross."

Megan looked searchingly into Mimi's eyes and then turned to me. For want of anything to say, I shrugged. I had no idea what that was all about.

17

THE BLOOD SAMPLE

"SHE NEEDS A LAWYER," MIMI said.

"Why?" I said.

"Liam, get real!" She threw her hands up in despair. "The police are exhuming Matt's body. They're treating his death as suspicious. And you *don't* think she needs a lawyer?"

We were still sitting in Mimi's room, an armchair each, shadows lengthening across the bed. Megan had gone to my room to phone her parents to tell them the full story about the night of Matt's death, before they heard it anywhere else. She'd looked terrified as she left to make the call, but I think she realised she couldn't delay it any longer.

I hardly knew her parents. They'd turned up to watch a couple of races, but they couldn't travel far because of her father's health. I had no idea how they'd react or whether they might suddenly arrive in Newport to take charge – but I was ready to carry on as proxy parent, at least for now.

"But she hasn't done anything wrong," I said.

Mimi looked even less impressed. "Well, for a start, she lied to the police," she said.

I needed to think about that. "Is that actually a crime?" I replied eventually.

"It depends why she lied. What if she lied to protect Will?"

"How would saying she wasn't there help Will?"

"Okay, but lying never looks good when there's a corpse involved."

I cringed at that, conscious Megan was only a thin wall away. "And bringing lawyers in will only make things look worse," I said. "It'll make her look guilty. Why not let the police do their job, and see what happens?"

From the incredulous look on Mimi's face, I could see this was an argument I was never going to win.

"Your confidence in the police is sweet, Liam," she said.

I smiled. She had a point. We couldn't risk leaving it to the police. Mimi knew she'd won and started flicking through the messages on her phone.

An image of Danny in a school play came to me – I've no idea why – and I couldn't think when it was. All I could remember was his eyes darting across the audience until they settled on me, like no one else was present. Then he said his lines and when he'd finished, he turned in my direction to check I'd been watching.

"But what I'm not clear about…" Mimi started, putting her phone down on the arm of the chair.

There were so many things I wasn't clear about it wasn't a sentence I could finish for her.

"I'll call Jackie," I said, "about a lawyer."

Mimi smiled. "And to tell her to pull Megan out of the Grand Prix," I added.

The Grand Prix hadn't even been worth a discussion. We both knew it was literally a non-starter.

"Yep. Okay," Mimi said, "but what I'm not clear about is this blood sample found at the scene. Presumably, it's what Richards meant when he said there was something over-looked the first time around. I was going to ask Megan if she knew, but…"

"No, it wasn't the best time to ask," I said.

Mimi shook her head in agreement. We had both been treading carefully when Megan finally opened up. Too much cross-examination could have sent her back into her shell – or sparked another storming rage.

I called Jackie. She wasn't in the best of moods – and that was before I'd even told her Megan's latest revelations. The story about Matt's body being exhumed was everywhere. The sponsors were now calling the 'clear the air' meeting at Crystal Palace a 'summit'. The top executives had decided to come along, and these were people who could pull the plug on Megan on the spot. They didn't like the sound of the police statement. They wanted to know exactly how Megan was involved. They wanted 'assurances'.

I listened to all this patiently. When she'd finished, I launched a guided missile into her evening.

"Megan was there when the boy died," I said.

Jackie made an eerie hissing sound like she was asphyx-iating on the other end of the phone. It took her several moments to digest this news. "So she was actually there?" she said finally. "You mean, that night – she saw him die?"

"Yes, she witnessed the whole thing."

"And she's been keeping this small detail to herself?"

"Yes."

Jackie sighed so loudly my hand reflexively pulled the phone away from my ear.

"So much for my fucking heart-to-heart with her after the trials," she said. "So what's the… what's she saying now?"

I think she was going to say 'bitch'. I took in a deep breath and gave Jackie a potted version of Megan's confession. When you broke it down to the bare essentials, it sounded pretty grim: Megan had dated both Matt and Will; there was bad feeling between her and Matt; Matt was heavily into the drugs scene; he'd been using steroids for some time and probably supplied them to Will; Megan gave him a mouthful of abuse the night he died; and then she watched him die and ran away.

I stuck to the essentials, leaving the part about Megan calling Matt a waste of space out. There was no point raising the temperature. Even so, Jackie punctuated every other sentence with, "You're winding me up," or "Please tell me this is a joke".

When I'd finished, we both fell silent. I sensed Jackie was computing all the angles. It normally took her a nanosecond, but this algorithm had more variables than most.

"And you believe her, right?" she said finally.

"Why wouldn't I?"

"Well, she hasn't exactly been very open until now – and there might be more. Are you sure she's told us *everything*?"

The last word was loaded with innuendo and, of course, I knew what she meant. What Mimi had said about the possibility of Megan using steroids before she came to London had been playing on my mind. I didn't feel certain of anything anymore, but I still couldn't bring myself to think of Megan as a liar and a fake. I still couldn't square the idea she might be a cheat, with the Megan I'd picked up off the track when she'd run so hard the lactic acid had reduced her legs to jelly.

"Yes," I said. "I think she has told us everything… if you mean what I think you mean."

"You know exactly what I mean, Liam. Is she fucking clean?"

"I think so," I said.

Jackie fell silent again. Mimi and I sat looking at each other, and I remembered Megan in the next room and felt strangely disloyal having this conversation.

"Well," Jackie said eventually. "I guess Megan being a drugs cheat might turn out to be the least of our worries – the police could try to nail a manslaughter charge on her."

"We were talking about lawyers…" I said.

"How could she deceive us like that?" Jackie said, though now sounding resigned rather than angry.

I took the question to be rhetorical and waited. It was time to get practical, and I was confident Jackie was inching towards her customary calm efficiency.

She didn't let me down and was soon issuing instructions. I switched the phone to speaker so Mimi could hear.

Jackie knew a law firm she trusted and would get someone down to Newport the next day. She wanted Mimi to speak to UK Athletics about a press statement on Megan pulling out of the Grand Prix. Above all, she thought we should be economical with our answers when quizzed by sponsors, the press or anyone else on why the police were so interested in Megan – no hint whatsoever of her being present when Matt died.

"They don't need to know the sordid details at this stage," she said. "All we need to say is that it's in the hands of the police, and there's no suggestion Megan's done anything wrong, and we can't discuss it for obvious reasons."

The only disagreement among us was over whether or not Mimi should go back to London. Jackie wanted her at the Grand Prix where the sponsors and athletics media would be.

For her, it was all about the sponsors, and she needed Mimi's help in "managing the fall-out" at Crystal Palace. But Mimi thought she should stay in Newport. This was now a crime story with a celebrity in it, and the news reporters would be camped out here.

"The place is swarming with them already," she said. "This is where the body is. Not to mention Megan. Body plus Megan equals story. Newport is where the story is – and the risk to Megan's reputation."

Mimi was right, I thought, but Jackie was adamant.

"Okay, okay, but *I* want you at Crystal Palace," she said, without adding 'and I sign your invoices'.

And then she turned her attention to me. "And Liam, are you across this steroid situation?"

"What *situation* would that be?" I said.

"Well, whatever's going on down there with everyone wanting to look like Arnold Schwarzenegger."

"Not really," I said. Unlike Mimi, I wasn't accountable to Jackie.

"Well, Liam darling, don't you think you ought to be? We need to understand all the angles."

"I'm an athletics coach, not a social worker," I said, feeling irritation welling-up, "but I did go to one of the gyms – and I took a beating for my trouble."

I hadn't mentioned this part of the saga to Jackie until now.

"A beating?" she said. "What is it about that place? You went to the gym and got beaten-up?"

"Not exactly," I said. "The beating was later in the evening, on a dark footpath, but they said something about me going to the gym."

Jackie took a moment to digest this. "Good God, what are we getting into?"

I didn't answer that.

Mimi gave me a look. I'm not sure what it meant, but she said: "And Jackie, we haven't talked about this blood sample."

"Blood sample?" Jackie said.

"You know, the police mentioned a blood sample as a reason for exhuming the body."

"What about it?"

"I wish I knew," Mimi said.

* * *

By the time Megan came back to Mimi's room, we had ordered supper from the restaurant. The receptionist had protested the hotel didn't do room service, but the owner – once I'd tracked him down – made an exception. His knowing look when I told him we still needed two rooms after all and one would be taken by a new female guest, whose name I couldn't give him, suggested either he had a pretty good idea what was going on – or he thought I was a pimp. I was past caring what anyone thought as long as they didn't tell the press where we were.

I'd chosen bream and salad for Megan – diet is still the coach's prerogative, even in a crisis – and steaks for me and Mimi, who'd rediscovered her appetite.

Megan looked anaemic. I'd seen her in a bad way after gruelling training sessions with all the blood drained from her face, spent on the track – but this was worse, a deathly greyness. She settled on the bed, rearranging the pillows Mimi had used earlier. Mimi and I were still slumped in the armchairs.

"What?" Megan said, conscious I'd been watching her.

"How were your parents?" I said.

She looked confused. "I've been asleep," she said.

"But you rang them, didn't you?"

"Yeah, yeah," she said, waving the issue away. "They'll get over it."

"And what about Tom?" Mimi said.

Megan wriggled, irritated. "What about him?"

"It's finished, is it, definitely?" Mimi persisted.

"Yep, he's useless," Megan said, laughing now. "Pretty, but completely self-absorbed. It wasn't going anywhere. I think I was kidding myself it might do."

"I've ordered you fish for supper," I said, thinking that it was time lighten things up. "Bream – your favourite."

That earned a smile. Meg could smile in a charming and heart-warming way, glowing like she was really pleased you had shown her a kindness or paid her a compliment.

The room fell silent. Mimi was back on her phone, flicking through messages and emails and occasionally typing a reply. Megan was resting her head against the wall with her eyes closed. I was staring at a pile of newspapers on the bed, unsettled by a feeling I'd forgotten something.

The food arrived, and we ate in an atmosphere of morbid calm. None of us wanted to speak about 'it'. None of us had the energy to speak about anything much else.

Then what I'd forgotten came to me.

"The car!" I said.

Mimi leapt to her feet. "Shit, yes – I'll go now," she said, starting to fumble for her keys in the pocket of a jacket draped over the armchair.

"Leave it," Megan said. "I'll take you in the morning."

Mimi didn't need any persuading. She slumped back into the chair and looked across at me.

"My father was a lawyer," she said.

I wasn't sure what to say. Was she making small talk, or

suggesting he could help? Megan looked equally bewildered.

"Just thinking about him," Mimi continued. "He'd be good in a situation like this, but he's retired now – and he's in South Africa, so that's not much use!" She turned to Megan and then back to me. "And where the hell did you get a name like McCarthy anyway?" she said.

Megan laughed.

"That's a bit random, isn't it?" I said.

"Come on," Mimi said. "You must be Irish or something, are you?"

I had to think about that one. I was a Kilburn boy with an Irish father, but I'd never felt much of a connection. He'd gone back to Cork when I was about seven, leaving me with my Londoner mother and Essex stepfather.

"My father was Irish," I said, "but I don't even know if he's still alive. He went back to Ireland when I was a kid. I only saw him a couple of times after that."

"Still, that makes you half-Irish," Mimi said. "What about you?"

Megan looked blank. "I'm not Irish at all!" We all laughed and it eased any remaining tension in the room, but she knew what Mimi meant. "Mine are West Walians to the bone," she added.

"And Welsh-speaking?" Mimi said.

"Oh, yes. Welsh-teaching in fact."

"I knew they'd been teachers in Newport but I didn't realise they taught Welsh. No wonder you sounded so authentic today."

Megan laughed. "Not really. I'm very rusty. Don't forget, I was brought up in Newport, and hardly anyone speaks Welsh here. I'm a big disappointment to my Mum. She's passionate about it – Cymdeithas through and through."

Mimi gave her a quizzical look.

"The Welsh Language Society," Megan said, sounding more Welsh than ever. "That was her big thing. She was a bit of a troublemaker in her day."

"So what about Jacobs then?" I asked Mimi. "Where does that come from?"

Mimi laughed. "The Bible you idiot," she said.

"Okay, okay, but in your case?"

She took a moment to think about that. "I'm not sure how far back it goes. It's one of those names Jewish people adopt when they're ditching something that sounds too German or east European. It goes back a few generations, as long as my family's been in South Africa."

"South Africa?" Megan said.

"Yes, it looks like you're the only pure Brit in the room," Mimi said with an exaggerated South African lilt. "But actually I was born in London. My parents were exiles."

Megan looked puzzled.

"From Apartheid," Mimi added, and turned to me, laughing. "Maybe that's why I find it hard to trust the police."

"So tell us about your parents, then?" Megan said.

Mimi looked at me as if to check I didn't have a problem with the way this was going – but why would I? It seemed to be distracting Megan from her own worries, and, besides, I was interested – Mimi and I hadn't had the time or energy to talk much about personal stuff. I shrugged with a 'why-not' look.

She turned back to Megan. "They came here in the sixties, after Rivonia... You know, when Mandela, Sisulu and the others were sent to prison? My father was a young defence lawyer and had to get out in a hurry. My mother joined him later, and they settled in Golders Green." She seemed to find that funny. "There were loads of other exiles around that part of London. My father worked as a solicitor, but I think he spent most of his time on politics – or 'the struggle', as he liked to call it. When I was kid, people from 'down South' would come and go all the time. We always seemed to have someone staying with us, mainly Africans who'd been in prison or who'd left the country to join the… well, you know, to work 'underground'."

Mimi stopped, possibly wondering if this was getting too heavy, and I think she was going to leave it at that. But Megan seemed fascinated. "Go on," she said.

"That's it, really. I haven't got any brothers or sisters, and it was exciting for me as a child having all this going on: the coming and going…" She dwelt on that, watching herself run an index finger along the arm of the chair, creating a dark trail in the green upholstery. "But sometimes I also resented it," she continued. "Sometimes it felt like my father knew more about what was happening in Soweto than in his own frigging daughter's school – but, you know, I understand it now. Someone had to do what they did."

I was struck by how calmly she said that, leaving no room for doubt that she meant it.

"So they went back to South Africa?" Megan asked.

"Yep, after Mandela was released. My dad went first again, to Jo'burg to work on the release of other prisoners, and my mother stayed with me for a few years, until I went to university. And then she went out to join him, and they settled in Cape Town."

"Didn't you ever think about going there yourself?" I said.

"Not to live, not really," she said. "I went there after uni for a few months, but I couldn't settle. I'm a Londoner really, and this is where my career is."

Her career. The word made her pause, and, as if on cue, Megan's phone started vibrating. She picked it up off the bed with a frown, read whatever the message was and tossed it back down.

"It's only Will," she said, "ranting about what's on the news. It's on now."

Mimi reached for the remote lying on the bed, but Megan was quicker, lurching forward to grab it.

"No," she said. "I don't want to watch it." She sat back down on the bed, leaning against the wall, one hand holding the remote, the other tapping her thigh. Her phone started ringing. She answered it with a brusque, "Hello," and Will's voice could be heard across the room. Some of the words were clear: "The body, the blood sample, the bastard," – but it was hard to make much sense of it.

Megan told him to calm down, but Will continued, still sounding agitated.

"I know he's a bastard," Megan said, "but don't do anything stupid."

Will went silent.

"Listen," Meg said firmly. "Turn the telly off and go to bed. I'll call you tomorrow." She tapped the phone off without waiting for an answer.

I was on my feet now, feeling agitated myself. Mimi didn't seem to know whether to sit or stand, but there wasn't enough room for both of us to pace around.

"Calm down about what?" I asked.

Megan shook her head. "Oh, just the whole thing. What's on the news – it's wound him up. That's all."

"And which 'bastard' is he talking about?"

"Forget it, Liam," Megan said. "It's nothing."

But it didn't sound like nothing to me.

"Who was he talking about?" I repeated, and Megan knew I wasn't going to let it go.

"It's just Gary, that's all. He thinks Gary's been stirring trouble for us."

I nodded. I could imagine Gary sidling up to Richards,

whispering in his ear, deflecting attention from his own activities.

Megan stretched and moved to the edge of the bed, dropping her feet on the floor. She was facing towards Mimi, who was still sitting in the armchair. They were as close to each other as they had been a few hours ago, except they'd reversed places. Megan touched Mimi's hand and kissed her on the cheek.

"Thanks for tonight," she said. Mimi kissed her back on the opposite cheek.

"So about your training schedule tomorrow?" I asked awkwardly, not wanting to let her go without finding out where we were on the small matter of her athletics career.

"Ha!" she said. "Not much chance of that."

"But seriously, what about Rio?" I said.

"Not now, Li. I can't think straight. Let's talk about it again." And she smiled that charming, disarming smile, leaned forward, gave me a peck on the cheek and left us with a mischievous, "Sleep well".

18

TRUTH IS TRUTH

THE NEWS WASN'T GETTING ANY better. BBC Breakfast led with the story of Matt's body being exhumed.

'Police investigating a suspicious death in Newport say they expect to be interviewing Olympic medal prospect Megan Tomos later today', the male newsreader told us.

Mimi groaned. "Isn't there a war or something they should be reporting?"

She was already up and about, not wearing a thing, checking and replying to messages and emails on her phone. I was still in bed, my paunch discreetly covered by the duvet.

A few days into our relationship, and she was much less inhibited than me, but then the paradox was she could easily pass for an athlete, whereas these days my pecs were in danger of becoming man-boobs. I didn't have much to flaunt, and made a mental note: Liam, sort it out.

The news reader had finished the bulletin and handed back to a presenter perched on a couch in the studio, who said: "*Now we're going live to Newport for an update on the Megan Tomos situation.*"

"Oh my God, we're a frigging 'situation' now," Mimi said, glaring at the screen, hands on naked hips.

I felt numb, beyond anger, as if my immune system had hardened me against further shocks.

The screen switched to a male reporter standing on the lawn in front of the university with a dark haired, over-generously made-up young woman by his side: "*Thanks Sian. Now, I'm here,*" he said, gesturing towards the red-brick building behind him, "*at the University of South Wales, where yesterday Megan Tomos was heckled as she received an honorary fellowship in front of hundreds of students and parents. There were no cameras allowed at the event, but we understand the heckler called the Olympic medal prospect a 'hypocrite' after she dedicated her fellowship to a friend – Matt Davies – whose death is being investigated by the police.*"

The reporter turned to the woman, holding a microphone that looked like a dead kitten between them. "*Now, Hannah, you were there yesterday, receiving your degree. Tell us what happened.*"

"Oh fuck, here we go," Mimi said.

The girl hesitated, then looked straight at the camera like she was about to jump through the screen. "*It was disgusting,*" she said. "*Really bad. She had the cheek to talk about Matt like they were bosom buddies, when everyone knows...* everyone knows she hated him.*"

"*Now Hannah, we have to be careful, of course,*" the reporter said, "*but you knew Matt and you felt it was inappropriate?*"

"*Yes, I was at school with Matt and Megan – and she was dead out of order.*" She looked back at the reporter, checking herself. "*Sorry, I mean she had no right to bring up his name. It was wrong, and I'm glad someone… someone said so. She deserved it.*"

The reporter seemed to be trying to interrupt, but the interviewee was in full flow now.

"*Everyone knows there's been a cover-up,*" she said. "*Just because of who she…*"

"*Thanks, thank you, Hannah,*" the reporter said abruptly, pulling the microphone back and turning towards the camera. "*I'm afraid we're going to have to leave it there, and just to be clear, before we go back to the studio – there is no suggestion of any wrongdoing by Tomos. Her spokesperson has issued a statement saying she has pulled out of tonight's athletics Grand Prix at Crystal Palace so that she can help the police with their inquiries. Sian, back to you.*"

The thud on our bedroom door was so violent it nearly burst from its hinges. Mimi darted for the bathroom, leaving me scrabbling for some clothes as Megan burst in wearing a crumpled T shirt and track suit bottoms, her hair dishevelled like she'd just jumped out of bed. She probably had.

"That fucking cow," she said, loudly enough to wake the whole hotel. "That bitch has always hated me. I'm going to…"

"Calm the fuck down," Mimi said, having reappeared with a towel around her.

Megan was pacing and shaking with rage. "She's the cow who heckled."

Mimi grabbed her, a hand holding each forearm. "Calm down," she said again, firmly but more softly.

I had managed to put some shorts on and went over to the pair of them and took over from Mimi in holding on to Megan, who was shaking now in a slower, shuddering way, her head bowed, looking at the floor. I couldn't see her eyes, but rivulets of tears had reached her chin and were forming into watery pearls ready to drop onto her T-shirt. She was sobbing so hard I thought she might collapse if I let go of her.

Mimi started to stroke her hair with one hand, holding her towel in place with the other. She looked at me as if to say 'talk to her'.

"Meg," I said hesitantly. "Listen to me. I'm not just your coach, I'm a friend – and you need to listen to me on this. You listen to me on other things. Listen on this."

I paused, struggling to find the right words but feeling Megan had now finally accepted we could help her.

"Meg, you can handle this like you handle everything else – stay strong, stay focused," I said, resorting to the language of coaching. "Concentrate on what *you* have to do. Execute *your* plan. You know what you have to do today. We'll go to see Matt's father and you can tell him what you need to tell him. And then we'll go to the police. Who cares what that girl thinks? Who cares what anyone thinks? All that matters is what you know in your own heart to be the right thing to do."

Megan looked up at me now, and I let go of her arms. Mimi handed her a tissue, and she wiped her cheeks and chin.

"I know," she whispered, nodding, as if convincing herself. "I know... but I'm telling you, it's just so hard, hearing that bitch like that."

"But who is she anyway?" Mimi said.

Megan looked past her like she was struggling to remember. "Just someone who used to hang-out with Matt sometimes. Not a girlfriend though. She was at the party, but she wasn't really one of us, if you know what I mean. And she never liked me – she told everyone I was, you know, a big-head."

"And now she's jumping on the bandwagon, seizing her chance to give you a kicking," Mimi said, and reached out to pull Megan towards her.

It was odd watching them hug: the mismatch of Megan's height and broad shoulders and Mimi's delicate frame, the reverse of their strength in other ways.

I left them to it and sidled quietly into the bathroom to shave.

* * *

By the time I came out, Megan had gone back to her room, and Mimi was dressed and busy packing. I'd forgotten she was going back to London today, and now I felt a sudden pang of disappointment.

We had been in this together all week, like we were under siege and our lives depended on each other. I couldn't imagine her not being there.

She was standing with her back to me, folding clothes into a small suitcase, wearing a wine coloured top, an off-one-shoulder thing that fell on one side to show a delicate shoulder blade moving in tempo with her packing. I ran a hand across her smooth copper skin until it reached the back of her head. She turned into me, pressing her head sideways against my chest, her arms around my waist. She didn't say anything.

"All being well," I said softly "I'll see you tomorrow."

Mimi leaned back and kissed my neck and my chin and then settled her parted lips on mine. Our tongues circled and touched, our bodies rocking gently. We stayed like that for a long moment. Then we stopped and looked at each other in silence. I wondered now if what had happened between us was merely comfort in a crisis, and I had no idea what Mimi thought. There were no clues as she stoically went back to her packing.

* * *

Megan was waiting for us in the hotel car park, the doors of her Audi 4 open already. She looked composed now in smart jeans and a sky-blue silk blouse, her hair organised in its normal spiky arrangement.

The sun was already high in the sky, and a haze shimmered over the field next to the hotel, making it look as if the two horses trying to find some edible tufts of grass were ankle deep in water. There was no sign of the hot weather breaking.

Megan laughed as we approached holding hands. "When's the wedding?" she said.

"Ha ha," I said, knowing the teasing was mainly directed at me.

I threw Mimi's case onto the back seat and climbed in after it. Mimi sat in the front with Megan. It took barely five minutes to reach the university where we found the car park nearly empty and only a few people coming and going from the university buildings. There was no sign of the BBC camera crew or Hannah, but we didn't want to hang around any longer than necessary.

Megan pulled-up next to Mimi's car, and in seconds Mimi was setting off for London with a little wave through the windscreen. I felt a quiver of sadness in my chest, but I was trying hard to follow my own advice to Megan and stay focused on the job in hand.

Megan swung her car round, and we drove off towards Newport through Caerleon's one-way system, over the old stone bridge and along a road following the river into the city centre.

Megan seemed pensive and said nothing until we reached the small parking area near Graeme's flat.

"I'll park by there," she said, nodding towards a tight space.

I realised she meant I needed to get out straight away, as the space wouldn't be wide enough for the doors to open on both sides. I jumped out and watched her park with absolute precision. As she switched the ignition off, I could see her shoulders rise and fall with a long sigh.

We walked over to the flats and repeated the ritual of pressing the bell and waiting for Graeme to release the door.

"Okay?" I said as we stood there.

She nodded without looking at me.

The buzzer went and she pushed in and practically ran up the stairs, taking them two at a time. Graeme was at the door but this time there were no beaming smiles or warm embraces. It was hard to imagine what Graeme was thinking after all the nastiness in the media over the last two days, but he hadn't hesitated when I'd phoned to say Megan wanted to see him again. He'd been subdued but not hostile.

Graeme let us go into the flat first, patting my back as he ushered us through. I felt a kinship with him, though I can't put my finger on why.

"Well, Meg," he said. "I don't see you for years and now it's twice in a week. What's that they say about London buses?"

He meant it in fun, but I sensed Megan tightening at the implication of a criticism.

"Now then," he continued. "Can I get you a cup of tea?"

Megan shook her head and I held a hand up to pass. I didn't want to rush him – this couldn't be rushed – but we had no time to waste on refreshments and small talk with the police clock ticking.

Megan sat in one of the armchairs and I pulled-up the chair from the balcony. Graeme took the other armchair.

"So Meg," Graeme said in a kindly way, like he was counselling one of his pupils. "What have you come to say that you didn't say the first time around?"

Megan was looking at her hands, exactly as she'd done on Wednesday.

"Grae," she said, still not able to look him in the eye. "When I said I was sorry, you know, about running away, I meant… I was trying to say…"

Graeme didn't wait long to see how Megan would finish the sentence. "I know exactly what you meant, Meg," he said, leaning forward as if to emphasise their closeness.

Megan lifted her head slowly.

"You ran away *that night*," Graeme continued. "Of course I know – well, I suppose, strictly speaking, I guessed. It seemed likely. I thought that all along."

"But why didn't you say?"

Graeme shrugged. "What's to say?"

The room fell silent. My discomfort had evaporated. I knew now that Graeme was in control here, and felt confident whatever he had in mind to tell Megan would probably contain more wisdom than the rest of us had mustered in the last few days.

"I suppose," he said, sounding like he was reflecting and correcting himself, "I suppose I wanted to hear you say it first. I wanted *you* to tell me." He nodded as if agreeing with himself. "And you have. And I knew you would – but I suppose, if I'm honest, I hoped you'd do it sooner."

Megan flushed and fidgeted at this gentle reprimand.

"Look, Meg," he said. "I interpreted what you said on

Wednesday as an apology for running away. I know that was what was on your mind, and why you came to me before you went to the police. I know you well enough to believe that of you."

I could only see part of Megan's face, but it was obvious the tears were welling-up. She had her hands clasped together now as if trying to keep her composure. Graeme didn't make any move to comfort her, but he looked across at me, and I sensed he thought that was my job. I reached out and put an arm around her shoulder.

"Look, my lovely," he continued, "I've had a long time to think about all this; about what might have happened that night, and I have a pretty good idea how things were with Matt. How, well, how lost he was... But he wasn't a child anymore, and I was helpless. I could see him sinking, sliding deeper into a kind of quagmire. I had nightmares about it, about trying to grab him and pull him out, and not being able to reach him." Graeme fastened his gaze on the posed professional photograph of Matt, as if remembering something. "Julie wanted me to do more, of course," he said. "We argued about it, but what *could* I do? You can't lock a 19 year-old boy up. And I couldn't talk to him. Every time I tried it went wrong, and anyway, he needed professional help. It's like anorexia, you know? Anorexia for boys – that's what they say."

Megan looked baffled, and I wasn't sure what he meant either, but it was obvious he hadn't finished.

"I think I can guess what that night must have been like – how he was when he turned-up. I'd seen him in a bad way so many times myself. I know you'd tried to help him and stay his friend, Meg. I guessed he was as bad with you as he was with me – pushing us away."

Megan was shaking her head now, and Graeme stopped.

"But you're wrong," she said. "It *was* me that pushed him away. I had no patience with him. If I'm honest…" she seemed to be choking on the words, "if I'm honest," she tried again, "I think I'd, well, written him off. And I'm ashamed of myself for it. It's not so much that I ran away that night, I'm ashamed about how I'd treated him for a long time before that."

Graeme thought about this. It obviously wasn't in his script for the meeting, but he didn't seem surprised either.

"But Meg," he said finally, "we're all in the same boat here. We all have regrets; thinking we should have done this or that, but it won't make any difference, will it? We can't help him now."

Megan looked back at him, seeming to realise how generous he was being and the fondness he was displaying towards her - and I wondered if somehow she was, for him, the link to the better memories of Matt. He would forgive almost anything to keep that connection.

Megan broke the silence abruptly. "I think the police are gunning for Will," she said.

Graeme straightened his back, as if reeling at the mention of Will's name.

"I don't know why you care what happens to him," he said.

Megan looked confused. "But why not? You don't agree with Julie, do you?"

Graeme was shaking his head.

"Matt collapsed," Megan said. "Will didn't touch him… I was there, Graeme. I saw it happen."

"I know, Meg, and I believe you. I'm not saying Will killed him – not in that way – but he may as well have done. Matt was impressionable, weak. Will knew that, and made the most of it."

Megan bristled at that. "What do you mean?" she said.

"Oh, come on, Meg," Graeme replied. "You don't believe

all this rubbish Will's been peddling about using steroids as a one-off? He'd been at it for years."

Megan looked at me as if wanting me to say it wasn't true – but what did I know? I was going on what Megan herself had told me, and the only back up for it was Terry – who'd betrayed me. Will had peddled the story that he'd used steroids only to recover from injury, and people assumed Matt was his supplier. But I had no reason to believe Will. Why couldn't it have been the other way round?

"I didn't see any change in him," Megan said, echoing my thoughts about her. "I would have noticed something if he'd started earlier."

"It depends how early, Meg," Graeme said. "Will's been at it since he was 15 or 16, well before you started dating. Why would he go to that gym for all those years? Apparently everyone knew what went on there. All the boys were doing it. A whole gang of them from school. For Matt and boys like him, it was a social thing. It was a fashion or a fad, call it what you will. Everyone wanting to man-up and have big shoulders and a six-pack. Only a few of them were doing it for sport – a few of the rugby boys, maybe the boxers. And don't kid me that Will wasn't part of it. He was going there every day. If anything he was the ring leader, the one everyone looked-up to – Matt included."

Megan was subdued, staring at Graeme in a daze. She stood up and walked past me out onto the balcony, grabbing the rail with both hands and looking across the river towards the city centre.

"But why didn't he get caught earlier?" I asked. "Wasn't he tested before?"

Graeme smiled. "He was good at it, that's why," he said. "Look, what people say – and I believe them – is he only did it for short periods of the year, when he was training intensively.

A lot of them do that: an 'on cycle' and an 'off cycle' they call it. So Will got away with it because they don't test very often at the lower levels, but then he was injured, and he took a risk, just as he was rising through the ranks and likely to be tested more often. He used them too close to the start of the season, and he got caught and blew everything."

Megan turned around to look back into the room. "So you blame Will?" she said.

Graeme thought about it. "Like I say, not directly," he said. "Not in the way Julie does, thinking there was a fight or Will pushed Matt, wanting him charged with manslaughter. But I do blame him in the sense that… in that he led Matt on. Why didn't he look out for Matt instead of making him think he could be something…? Matt could never compete with Will, or any of the rugby boys. He was out of his depth. The only way he could make himself stand out was by being more extreme, more daring with the drugs, taking more risks to show off, be the big guy."

I looked across at Graeme and realised suddenly how much this was taking out of him. He looked exhausted. His ruddy face was ashen and lifeless now. He had been talking about Will in a matter of fact way, sounding resigned rather than malicious. It was inconceivable that he didn't believe every word he was saying. Why would he lie? But it was possible this version of events had the power of truth for him not because it *was* true necessarily, but because it made Matt's death less painful.

I didn't care about Will, one way or the other, but I did worry about the effect this was having on Megan when she was about to face the police. She was also looking drained and anxious. I realised now that she hadn't come back to Newport to see Will – or not only to see him. She did seem to have an affection for Will and enough faith in him – at least until the last few minutes – to want to help him prove he didn't directly cause Matt's death. But she had come back mainly to make her peace with Graeme and, through him, with herself.

I looked at my watch. The solicitor Jackie had arranged was waiting for us at Celtic Manor. We were supposed to be there by midday.

"Graeme, I'm sorry, but we have to go," I said. "We're due to see a lawyer in ten minutes."

Megan looked at me as if I'd said something outrageous. She seemed to be lost in thought, probably somewhere deep in the past, trying to see Will through this new prism; trying to reconcile Graeme's interpretation of events with her own.

Graeme stood up and went over to her. "You know what Shakespeare says?" he said. "Truth is truth until the end of reckoning."

Megan smiled as if she'd heard him say that before.

"You will have to find the truth for yourself, Meg," he said, "and hang on to it when you do."

19

BY THE BOOK

MEGAN PULLED THE CAR OUT of the space with the same precision as she'd parked it, but I doubted her look of grim determination had anything to do with driving. She unlocked the passenger door to let me jump in.

I was eager to usher Megan into the right frame of mind for meeting the police. She had to be calm and clear-headed – her chances of going to Rio hinged on this interview, on the police believing her story. But from my sideways glances at her as she drove, it was hard to tell her state of mind or which episode in these bewildering events she might be dwelling on.

"Li, you can stop looking at me like that," she said. "I know what you're thinking."

"You do?" I laughed. "That's good, because I've no idea what I think about anything right now."

That brought a flicker of a smile to her face.

"I know what you mean," she said.

"So what do you think I'm thinking?"

"You think I'm naïve, and that Will has lied all along about the steroids, and that I'm dumb for still having anything to do with him."

"And what do you think?"

Megan was negotiating a junction that took us onto a dual carriageway that seemed vaguely familiar from an earlier visit to Newport.

"The track's on the right by there," she said, pointing ahead of us.

The main stand came into view across a car park, and Megan kept glancing over to it.

"Will used to pick me up from training, every Tuesday and Thursday, without fail," she said. "He was never late, and we'd go to get something to eat together and talk about stuff; how training had gone, our ups and downs. You know what it's like. One minute you're on top of the world thinking you can win anything, and the next you feel you're going nowhere: training's hard, you can't see any progress, and it feels like there's no point..."

Megan gave me a sideways glance now. "That was us," she continued. "We shared that. We helped each other through it. If I believe Graeme, I'd have to believe that was nothing – that it was all meaningless: that Will was conning me and playing me along."

"And you don't?" I asked.

Megan's eyes had returned to the road ahead, and Celtic Manor was looming on the horizon.

"Li, we went out for nearly two years," she said. "We

practically lived together for God's sake. And we talked for hours. No. I don't know. I don't think I'm that gullible..." She threw me another look and sighed. "But maybe I am."

I smiled, and we fell silent. I didn't want to press her any harder.

The dual carriageway had reached a roundabout where we turned onto a road that led to the entrance to Celtic Manor, just as Mimi and I had done in what seemed like another life.

"But I am beginning to think about things in a different light," Megan said as we reached the hotel's over-sized portico. "I always wondered why Will gave Gary the time of day. I never could stand him, even before I knew he was bent. But Gary seemed to have a hold..."

The men in red and gold plus-fours were rushing towards us, but this time there seemed to be an air of panic about them. I heard someone shout, "There she is". People seemed to appear from all directions, running towards us. Megan reacted quickly – a little too quickly. She crunched the car into gear and accelerated with such force we were thrown back in our seats. Photographers were leaping out of the way, snapping pictures as they went. We were clear.

I looked back. There were about twenty of them, some dusting themselves off, others still trying to snap 'Britain's Olympic golden girl' fleeing like a runaway bride.

"Wankers!" Megan said, looking in the mirror.

I felt sick – my hotel 'breakfast' consisting of two biscuits was rattling around inside me – and the sudden acceleration jolted my still-sore ribs. We were soon down the hill, joining the road into Newport. Megan stopped in a lay-by, pulled on the hand brake and banged her head theatrically against the steering wheel.

"What now?" she said.

"I'll call Richards. We may as well go to the police station."

I pulled his card out of my wallet and dialled the mobile number.

"Richards," he barked.

"It's Liam McCarthy, inspector. We were due to see our lawyer at Celtic Manor but the place is crawling with media. We're thinking of coming straight to you. The solicitor can join us there."

"No," Richards said firmly. "There's the same problem here too. It's like a circus on the green across the road: vans, satellite dishes, TV cameras everywhere."

"So what do you suggest?" I asked, thinking they should have thought of this.

"We'll do it at one of our local stations," he said. "Go to Maindee. It's on the way into town. I'll text you the postcode."

Megan was already pulling out. "No need – I know it for God's sake," she said.

"I'll call them," I heard Richards shouting as I tapped the phone off.

It took us only ten minutes to reach Maindee. It was an area with more empty shops than open ones, and Meg's top-of-range Audi stood out badly.

We found the police station, housed in a rambling red-brick building that looked like an old Victorian school. Outside were two uniformed officers. One signalled to us to pull into a bus stop across the road. He ran over. I lowered the window.

"Hop inside with my colleague please, and I'll park the car," he said.

The female colleague ushered us into the building, fussing over Megan like she was royalty. I followed, playing courtier.

Our mini-procession passed through a small reception to an even smaller interview room with red bucket seats and a dark wooden table. The yellow walls were bare and shining under the glare of fluorescent lighting. It was about as far from the glamour of the Olympics as you could get.

I had phoned the lawyer en route, and he was on his way in a taxi. The policewoman told us Inspector Richards would be here any minute. She asked if we wanted tea, and we both said yes, like it was the best offer we'd had all day.

"So this is it," I said when she'd gone.

We were standing facing each other across the table. Megan looked nervous. We each pulled-up a chair and sat down. Our opportunity to talk properly about the interview had gone, but I thought I should say something if only to break the tension.

"Meg," I said, "you're not here to protect Will. Stick to what you can actually remember, and don't …"

Megan nodded, but in a 'yeah, yeah, shut up Liam' way.

She had a point. I don't give last-minute advice to athletes on race days, so why do it now about something I know as little about as she does?

"The lawyer will be here soon," I said.

But she shrugged like she didn't care.

We both stared in silence at different walls until the policewoman reappeared with a tray carrying a teapot and several mugs, looking sideways at Megan like she really wanted to ask for her autograph. She seemed disappointed when I thanked her and said I'd do the pouring. I didn't want any distractions

My mind wandered to the conversation in the car as we were arriving at Celtic Manor.

"So what were you going to say about Gary before? About him having a hold over Will, I presume?"

Megan shook her head. "I'll tell you again," she said and smiled. "I mean, another time."

I didn't push it, but I was worried about Will and about

what Graeme had said about him and how this Gary character fitted in. It felt like I was in a race where I didn't know anything about any of the other competitors, on a track I'd never used before.

The waiting dragged on, and it was all the more frustrating because wait was all we could do. I wondered if that was the point – if it was a device to unsettle Megan. "Let her stew for a while," I imagined Richards saying.

Eventually, Richards and a younger man in plain clothes burst in, Richards saying, "Good, you're here," and dropping a file on the table. I stood up out of habit. Richards and I shook hands, and he nodded towards Megan.

The other man was introduced as DC Simmons. He was about the same age as Megan and – wearing a slick grey suit – looked as if he'd dressed in his best clothes for the occasion.

"Your brief's on his way, is he?" Richards said, more to Megan than me.

"No need to wait," she replied. "I haven't even met the guy."

The inspector and I sat down. He was facing Megan and I was next to her.

"Look, we're going to do everything by the book here," he said, lining a pen and pencil up next to a large notepad. "I have to tell you this is a very serious matter. It's not every day we exhume a body." He paused, as if wanting to let that sink in. I sensed Megan tightening next to me; not liking the implication that he doubted this was anything other than the most important thing in the world for her too.

"And I know you must have other things on your mind," he continued.

I knew I had to stop this before Megan did far less tactfully.

"Inspector, we've just come from seeing Matt's father again," I said. "Megan fully appreciates how serious this is."

Richards didn't flinch. "Mr McCarthy, let's be clear here.

I'll conduct this inquiry as I think best. I'm not a mind reader, and I need to be sure Miss Tomos understands that we are treating this as a suspicious death. I will be cautioning her just as soon as the lawyer arrives."

Megan touched my clasped hands resting on the table. "Yes, I do understand that, inspector," she said.

Richards turned to his colleague, who was still hovering by the door. "Simmons, pop next door to get another chair," he ordered.

Our lawyer, a trim man, probably in his forties, arrived just as Simmons was struggling back with another red bucket seat. After dancing round each other in the doorway, Simmons put the fifth chair next to Megan and resumed his seat next to Richards, leaving the lawyer standing and surveying the cramped room with what looked like a sneer.

"I'm in the right place then?" he asked Richards, handing him a card. "Perhaps I could have a word with my client?"

Richards stood up immediately and gestured to Simmons to leave the room with him.

The lawyer, still on his feet, waited until the door was closed. He was blond, tanned and wearing a sandy-coloured flannel suit and a casual blue shirt open at the neck. Apart from the computer bag hanging from his shoulder, he could have been going on holiday. Maybe he was when Jackie phoned him.

"Right, Miss Tomos" he said in a precise well-spoken way. "Jackie asked me to get myself down here to represent you. I'm Nigel Winters." And, turning to me, he added: "You're presumably Mr McCarthy."

"Yes – Liam," I said. "I think we just need to get on with this."

"Yes, yes, I appreciate that, but we don't want to be in such a rush we trip over ourselves, do we?" he said with a smirk and the weary look of someone who had heard all this before. "Megan, my job here is to stop them overstepping the mark. If I'm not happy, I will stop the interview. If you're not happy, just say so or give me a kick. You don't have to answer their questions, and you should definitely take your time. Do you understand?"

Megan nodded. "Yep, okay – that's fine."

"Before we start," he continued, "is there anything you want to disclose to me? Anything I need to know over and above what Jackie's told me?"

"No, let's just get on with it," Megan said.

Nigel nodded, untroubled by Megan's abruptness. "Right, I'll get them back in and we'll see how we go," he said.

* * *

Once everyone had settled in their places, Richards took the lead again.

"As I said earlier, Miss Tomos, Mr Winters – I will be doing everything by the book here. Mr McCarthy, I'll allow you to stay as long as you don't interfere. If, as we go along, I think you could be a witness in the case, I'll have to ask you to leave."

I looked across at Winters, who was now sitting on the other side of Megan, and he nodded, so I did too and Richards continued. "Miss Tomos, I need to interview you under caution."

"Is that *really* necessary?" Nigel asked.

The inspector looked irritated. "Indeed it is, Mr Winters," he said. "I think it's in everyone's best interests, given the seriousness of the matter we're talking about."

"I'm okay with that, Nigel," Megan said quietly.

Richards moved on, not giving Nigel a chance to argue. Simmons pressed a button on the recording machine. Richards stated his name and the date and time – 13.43 – and then asked everyone to identify themselves for the record.

Richards picked up a sheet of paper from the table and read from it slowly: "You do not have to say anything, but it may harm your defence if you do not mention when questioned something which you later rely on in court. Anything you do say may be given in evidence."

I knew he must have done this a thousand times, but I suspected he didn't always take this much trouble. From the formality in his voice, I sensed he was carrying not only his own expectations but also those of everyone in the chain above him – and who knows how high it went.

"Now Miss Tomos," he said. "Let's start with your relationship with the deceased. Tell me how long you've known him and how you would describe your relationship."

Megan drew in a deep breath. "Inspector," she said, "before I answer that, there's something I want to say."

Nigel fidgeted but didn't intervene. Jackie had said she would brief him, and we all knew Megan had to get this over with.

"I was there when Matt died, inspector."

The words seemed to float across the table. Simmons, who was opposite me, wrote them down neatly on his notepad. The inspector's eyes fastened on Megan with, I thought, a benign expression.

"Thank you, Miss Tomos," he said. "It has been alleged by others that you must have been there, and, fair play, I'm pleased to have established that at the outset."

"There is of course a technical point inspector," Nigel said. "My client isn't medically qualified and she can't be absolutely certain her friend was dead when she left the flat."

Megan was visibly taken aback and looked at Nigel as if to say, 'how would you know?'

But Richards nodded. "Yes, I take your point, and we'll come back to that. For now, we'll take it that you saw Matthew Davies in a state where you thought he was dead, and you left before Will Driscoll called for help. Is that correct?"

Megan nodded.

"Miss Tomos, you will have to say your answers out loud for the record."

"Yes, I thought he was dead," Megan confirmed, saying each word precisely but without surliness, and we all watched as Simmons meticulously transcribed them. When he'd finished, Richards looked across at Megan.

"And then I ran away," she said, sitting rigidly upright, only a slight quiver in her voice giving away the pain of her admission. "For the record inspector, I'm ashamed of my actions."

Nigel was looking anxious, but Megan seemed far more composed than I'd seen her all week, and I felt greater pride in her than I had for anything she'd achieved on the track.

The inspector acknowledged her words with the shortest of nods.

"Now then," he said. "To return to my original question, tell me about you and Matt."

And Megan did just that. For more than half an hour, she talked about how they were friends from primary school and how close they'd been and what he was like. She explained how, when they were older, he'd unexpectedly asked her out and how things were never the same after that.

"Would it be true to say then that there was bad feeling between you?" Richards asked.

Nigel fidgeted and looked ready to intervene, but Megan seemed untroubled by the question, even though she must have known any truthful answer could be incriminating.

"Yes, that's true," she said. "There was bad feeling."

"It's alleged you despised him," the inspector said, "and you blamed him for Will failing a drugs test."

Megan thought about that. "Despised is too strong, inspector," she said. "I can't explain it. He was like a brother, when we were younger, but to be honest, I was disgusted by how he'd let himself go – how he was ruled by drugs and alcohol. He was like two different people. One minute the old Matt, and then the next this monster. And it's true, I did blame him for Will's rugby ban because I thought he'd supplied steroids to Will."

"Thought?" Richards said, in a reaction time that would compare favourably with a sprinter. "Are you implying you don't anymore?"

Megan wriggled slightly in her seat, enough to nudge me. "That's what Will told me, and I believed him – why wouldn't I?"

"But you don't have any evidence it was true either, do you Miss Tomos?"

Megan shook her head, and the inspector pointed towards the recording machine.

"No, none," she said.

Nigel's concern now seemed to be approaching panic. "Is there much more, inspector?" he asked. "I think my client needs a break."

The inspector looked at his watch. "It's 15.08. We'll resume at three-thirty with some questions about the night of the death."

* * *

Nigel used the break to spell out to Megan the scenario Richards was building: a picture of circumstances that would make manslaughter or worse seem plausible – but Megan was adamant that she had nothing to hide.

"I'm trying to answer his questions as best I can," she said. "I've been running away from all this for two years, thinking it would go away, and it didn't. I need to face it now, for everyone's sake."

Nigel looked unimpressed. "You won't be saying that if you end up being charged," he said.

"Charged with what exactly?" I enquired.

"Anything from perverting the course of justice to murder – what do you think?" he said.

"So what do you want me to do? Lie to him?" Megan said, her composure giving way to irritation.

"But Meg," I said. "After what Graeme said this morning, you must have your doubts?"

"What do you mean?" Nigel said.

Megan shook her head but I pressed on. "Graeme Davies – Matt's dad – thinks Will was more involved in the steroid scene than he's letting on. He blames Will for Matt's steroid problem."

"He would though, wouldn't he?" Megan said. "It makes it easier to accept if he can blame someone else."

"Look Megan, let's get this straight," Nigel said. "I may not be up to speed on all this yet but one thing needs to be clear – I'm not here to help you protect Will, or whatever it is you think you're doing. You're my client, and my job is to keep you out of prison. Don't speculate or give opinions. Just stick to the facts. You don't need to get drawn in to his agenda. And remember, you're under caution, so ask for a break to discuss things with me if you have the slightest doubt what you should say. Understood?"

It was 15.30. Richards and Simmons swept back into the room, giving Megan no time to respond.

"Right you are," the inspector said. "Let's get back to business."

He sat down, looked at his watch and said: "Interview resuming at 15.31."

Chairs scraped as Simmons took his place next to the recorder and the three of us pulled our chairs into a line facing Richards across the table.

"Now, I want to talk about the night in question," he said, "and may I remind you you're still under caution. Miss Tomos, from your statement at the time, and I'm assuming you aren't disowning most of that?"

"No. No, only that I left before Matt turned up," she said.

"Okay, so take me through the evening." And when Richard's said that, he meant every detail. We spent the best part of the next hour going through the names of everyone who came to the party, what time they arrived, what sort of relationship they had with Matt, how long they stayed, and who left with who. Megan wasn't allowed to skate over any aspect of it or dismiss anything as boring. She was pressed to be specific. As she answered their questions, both Richards and Simmons were checking them against lists and notes they pulled from the file.

Nigel seemed relaxed about all this, but for me, as a newcomer, it all seemed irrelevant to the main issue. I thought how tedious TV dramas would be if they were anything like this.

Richards stopped proceedings again at 16.30 and left with Simmons, saying he would be back in ten minutes.

We spent the break pacing around the tiny room, making small talk and checking messages. I sent a text to Mimi saying we were still with the police and I'd call later.

It was nearly half an hour before the two of them returned. Richards was clutching some notes, which he tucked into the file on the table. Simmons pressed the record button again.

"Right," Richards said. "Thank you for your patience. Interview resumed at 16.57. I'd like to talk now about Matt's arrival. What time that was, and what sort of state he was in? We know from the autopsy that he'd had a lot to drink and there were traces of steroids and amphetamines in his blood, but was he in a bad way when he arrived? Do you remember what time it was?"

Megan was beginning to look jaded now, grey shadows forming under her eyes. She was shaking her head.

"I really don't know for sure," she said, sounding brittle. "Maybe two or two-thirty."

"Okay, let's do it this way," the inspector said. "Matt was declared dead at the scene at just after four-thirty." I felt Megan wince. The inspector saw it too and softened his tone. "Working backwards," he continued, "allowing for the time it took the paramedics to arrive, and the condition of the body, we estimate he died sometime between three and three-thirty. So how long had he been there when it happened?"

"Not long… not long at all," Megan said, haltingly, choking on the words and breaking into gasping sobs for the first time. I put an arm around her, and she lifted her head to face Richards. "I don't think he was there for… for much more than half an hour before it happened. He was in a terrible state. Will had to practically carry him up to the flat."

"You weren't with them at that point?" Simmons said. "You didn't go down with Will to let him in?"

The inspector looked taken aback and raised his eyebrows in Megan's direction to reinforce the question.

"No, I waited in the kitchen," she said, sounding composed again.

"And what happened when they got to the kitchen?" Richards asked.

"At first Matt was fairly calm. He sat down and slumped over the table. Will gave him some water, or something. I remember Will giving him a drink, but I'm not sure if he drank it."

Simmons pulled a piece of paper from under his notepad and placed it in front of Megan on the table. It was a floor plan of the kitchen, showing the fittings and furniture and a silhouette of Matt's body on the floor.

"So where was Matt sitting?" Richards said.

Megan pointed at one of the chairs, and the inspector said, "Miss Tomos is pointing at chair number three". They went through the same process to establish that, at this point, Megan thought Will was standing by the sink and she was just to Matt's left near the corner of the table and on the spot where he died.

"I fail to see how this helps, inspector," Nigel said. "My client has acknowledged she was in the kitchen and witnessed Matt Davies collapsing. It was more than two years ago and her recollection of the details is bound to be affected by the passage of time."

Richards ignored him. "Miss Tomos," he said. "What happened next?"

"Matt got angry," Megan said. Nigel slumped back in his seat, with a despairing sigh. "He was very agitated," she continued. "He started ranting about stuff and pacing around."

"Did he approach you?"

"Yes."

"Was there any contact?"

"No. Well, nearly – he came close to me, right in my face, shouting."

"And did you push him away?"

Megan paused. "No, not at all," she said. "I stepped back."

"There wasn't much room in that kitchen," Richards countered.

"I stepped back," Megan repeated, looking past Richards now like she was visualising it, "and he turned to face Will who was still by the sink. I remember that. And I remember clearly seeing Matt's face changing: his profile was different, like something had surprised him, and then I remember him grabbing his chest, and suddenly crumpling." Megan put her elbows on the table and buried her head in her hands. "I tried to stop him falling. I reached out, but I missed him… I wasn't quick enough."

"My client's exhausted," Nigel said. "Do you have much more to ask?"

Richards reached for the file and pulled out the papers he had tucked away earlier.

"We've had a forensic report on the exhumed body this afternoon," he said, looking at the papers but speaking to Nigel. "It's established a DNA match between a blood sample taken from the corner of the table and Matt Davies. You're aware of the blood sample?"

"Yes, but why has it suddenly come to light now?" Nigel replied.

"Because I'm being thorough, Mr Winters," Richards answered. "It was overlooked, regrettably, in the first investigation. The sample was taken but never tested against the boy's DNA. My colleagues were a little hasty in their conclusions, it seems. Which, I don't deny, is very unfortunate. We don't like having to exhume a body."

Megan was rigid.

Nigel was taking his time computing this revelation. "So what you're saying is, it looks like he bumped his head as he fell?" he said.

The inspector nodded and then realised he needed to say the words. "Yes, that is my point, Mr Winters."

"But does it have any bearing on the cause of death?" Nigel said.

Richards looked levelly at Nigel. "You mean, did he bang his head badly enough for that to be the cause of death, with obvious implications for anyone who pushed him?"

"*If* anyone pushed him," Nigel retorted.

"Yes, if anyone did," Richards agreed. "But, first things first, let's wait for the pathology report. That will show if his skull was fractured."

Megan flinched and looked down at the papers on the table – the floor plan and the report – a brutally stark record of what had happened that night.

Richards pursed his lips, as if mulling over what to do next.

"Miss Tomos," he said. "Just one more question, and then I think we'll adjourn until the morning. Say ten o'clock here?"

Megan nodded absently.

"You were saying Matt was angry and ranting. What exactly was he angry about?"

Megan was motionless for a long moment.

Then she turned to Nigel. "I'd like to speak to you about this," she said.

The inspector raised his eyebrows in surprise. "Okay Miss Tomos," he said absently, apparently perplexed by Megan's need to delay her answer. "Interview adjourned at 17.33. We'll be next door."

Megan waited for them to leave. She was looking down at her hands which were clasped together, resting on the table. Nigel stood up and did a lap of the room, finishing in the chair the inspector had been using.

"What's on your mind?" he said.

Megan looked at him as if sizing him up, deciding how much she trusted him.

"It was stuff about Gary," she said. "Matt was ranting about Gary."

"Who the hell's Gary?" Nigel asked.

"He's a police officer," I explained. "He was involved with Matt in some way in the steroid scene. It all revolved around one particular gym and Gary was in the thick of it. I saw him there myself the other day, and he stopped us – me and Mimi – the day before."

Nigel seemed sceptical. "Stopped you?"

"Breathalysed Mimi."

Nigel looked dismayed. He checked his watch as if he was wondering if he could still catch a train back to London.

"Okay," he said. "So you're saying – alleging – that Gary was a dealer, but what *evidence* do you have for this?"

"*Everyone* knows it," Megan said. "He's been hanging-out at that gym for years. Will says he runs the whole thing."

"Evidence?" Nigel repeated.

"None as such, I suppose," Megan admitted.

"Meg, you can't go around accusing police officers of being drug dealers without any hard facts. My advice is that you only tell Richards that there was some kind of problem between Matt and Gary. You don't speculate that it was to do with drugs. It's up to Richards to follow it up. Understood?"

Megan nodded, and Nigel stood up and opened the door.

"We're okay to continue," he told Richards, who was hovering outside.

We all resumed our places, Richards checking his watch and looking eager to move things along.

"Interview resumed at 17.41," he said.

Nigel took the lead. "My client has informed me that Matt was angry that night because of an argument he'd had with a police officer. She doesn't know the details of that argument or the exact nature of the relationship between Matt and this officer. But she has a clear and specific memory of Matt mentioning his name and being angry about something."

Richards looked at Megan. "And we're talking about?"

"Gary Evans," Megan said.

Richards laughed and looked across at me. "Your friend," he said. "He does seem to pop up a lot. Okay, Miss Tomos, and you're confirming what Mr Winters has said on your behalf, that Matt was agitated because of an argument he'd had with Gary Evans?"

Megan nodded. "Yes I do."

"And do you recall anything at all Matt said about Mr Evans?"

"No, not really" Megan said. "To be honest, the whole thing's a blur. I just remember him, Matt, being very agitated, and it was to do with Gary."

"Thank you," Richards said, giving nothing away. "I think we'll leave it there for today, Miss Tomos."

Richards gathered up his notepad, pens and file and ran his eyes across the three of us, settling finally on Nigel.

"Mr Winters, we'll resume at 10am tomorrow," he said. "I have a few more questions about the night in question and about Miss Tomos's relationship with Will Driscoll." He waited for Nigel to nod. "Thank you. Interview adjourned at 18.05."

20

WHERE'S WILL?

WE HAD OUR DE-BRIEF IN Megan's car, parked at the back of the police station. Nigel wanted to go over everything and tried pressing Megan about Gary, but she looked exhausted and exasperated, and ready to risk a manslaughter charge on him.

After twenty minutes, he gave up, told us to be at the police station half an hour early the next morning and left to find a taxi to take him back to Celtic Manor.

Megan grabbed a baseball cap and some dark glasses from the pocket of the driver's door and put them on, tugging the cap down as far as it would go. She checked herself in the mirror and seemed pleased with the effect.

"I know a back way into Caerleon," she said, her

eyes darting in all directions as we pulled away from the police station.

"Let's stop to pick up a takeaway," I said, suddenly desperate for food. As the tension eased, the adrenalin was replaced by a realisation I hadn't eaten since having those two hotel biscuits for breakfast. Megan drove into the city centre, crossing a bridge over the river and passing the blackened remains of a castle, before heading out again on a road lined with shops. A sign for Fish & Chips seemed to jump out from the rest, both of us noticing it at the same time, Meg giving me a hopeful sideways look like a child wanting a treat. Chips were normally banned.

"What the hell," I said.

Meg waited in the car while I went in. I don't know if it was the smell of the sizzling chips or the anxieties of the day evaporating but I felt strangely euphoric. It reminded me of exams ending, of that sense of a weight lifting.

I ordered extra-large portions of chips and picked the two largest fish from the golden pieces piled up on the display shelf. The woman serving was glancing at me as she shovelled the chips onto their trays and started wrapping everything. She was doing her best not to make it obvious, but she wouldn't have made much of a spy.

"Aren't you that man…?" she said eventually. "You know, the coach of that girl?"

'The coach of that girl' – maybe that's how I would be remembered, the title of my memoirs. There seemed no point in denying it. I looked over my shoulder. No one in the queue looked remotely like a journalist.

"Megan Tomos, you mean," I said, immediately regretting using her name and sensing a stirring of curiosity among the people behind me.

"That's the one," she said. "My word, she's in a bit of

bother, isn't she? Poor dab. Local girl. Everyone's talking about it."

"I bet they are," I said, putting enough cash on the counter to cover the order and picking up the two bulging parcels of food.

"Need a carrier bag?" she said.

But my back was already turned, and I waved to say 'no'.

Megan's alternative route to the hotel took us along a lane clinging to a hill above the river with Caerleon visible ahead, spreading out across the valley floor. The road was so narrow we had to stop half a dozen times at wider points to allow oncoming drivers to pass, giving everyone in each car plenty of time to check us out.

"Shit, this wasn't such a good idea," Megan said.

By the time we'd arrived at the hotel, my phone was buzzing with texts from Mimi.

```
Nice chips are they?
Tell Meg cap looks good too.
#MegMugShots is trending on Twitter
```

The last one made me bristle. I wasn't expecting Meg to become an online sport. So much for the end-of-exams feeling.

We went to my room, slumped into one of the armchairs and started devouring the fish and chips. Meg was staring at the floor, looking downcast and preoccupied. I juggled between stuffing food in my mouth and discreetly checking the photographs of us on Twitter. There were a couple of unflattering sideways shots of me leaving the chippie, and one taken on the lane of Meg through the windscreen with her cap and dark glasses looking like a fugitive. The picture of Meg had already been retweeted dozens of times.

It was nearly eight. Mimi and Jackie would be starting

their meeting with the sponsors any minute. I texted a 'good luck' message to Mimi, turned the TV on and switched channels to find the athletics.

The 100m hurdles was scheduled for eight-forty. The studio panel of athletes-turned-pundits was already talking about the race and Megan's absence and speculating about whether or not she would go to the Olympics. It was hard to tell how much they really knew. The news was out about Megan being with the police all afternoon, and they were talking sympathetically about how they hoped 'for the country's sake' she would be able to 'clear things up' – like it was a minor misunderstanding.

One said that, whatever happened, she couldn't see Megan making it to the Olympics now. "This disruption has come at *such* a crucial stage, she'll never be able to make up the lost time". But another thought her fellow panellist was underestimating Meg. "She's tough. Tough, tough, tough. A great competitor. I think she'll bounce back."

I sensed Megan tensing as they carried on along these lines.

"I can't fucking stand this," she said suddenly, leaping to her feet and tossing the remains of her supper in the bin. "Sorry, Liam, I need some space."

I felt bad for turning the TV on, but she was gone before I could say anything. I heard her slam the door of her room and thought I'd give her some time before checking if she was okay.

The TV was now showing one of the races. Judging from the tempo, it looked like a 5000m. I hadn't checked the programme and, at this point, didn't much care. I sat back and watched as the women jockeyed for position in the leading pack.

Megan came back in the room and paced around, switching between watching the race and playing with her phone.

I was distracted by Megan and missed who won the

5000m. The panellists were back, and Megan flounced out again. They started speculating about who would win the 100m hurdles. Megan's absence was a godsend for the Americans and the Russian, they thought, stating the obvious.

It was painful viewing in so many ways, and I was relieved when they finally went back to the track for the women lining up for the hurdles – 'Megan's race' as the commentator called it.

My coaching instincts kicked-in, and I was interested now, sitting on the edge of my chair and mentally ticking-off Megan's rivals as they appeared on camera. They were all there: three Americans, a Russian, a German - and three Brits for the home crowd to cheer. All of them looked in great shape, smiling to the camera, waving to the crowd and obviously relishing Megan's absence. It was just as well she'd gone back to her room.

The commentator was saying the conditions were perfect, a glorious summer's evening at Crystal Palace, with a slight following breeze for the athletes.

The starter brought them under orders, and they were away first time. The Russian led from start to finish, hurdling cleanly, crossing the line a clear metre ahead of the others. It was a comfortable winning margin for sprint hurdling. Her time was slightly faster than Meg's at the trials but not as fast as her season's best.

Mimi rang. "What did you make of that?" she said, sounding harassed and anxious.

"No worries for Meg," I said.

"Ha! Can't say the same for the sponsors," Mimi replied. "What a nightmare – they want assurances we can't give, and are bailing-out like they're on the frigging Titanic."

"Bailing-out? Already?" That was a shock, even by my low expectations.

"One's suspended its contract, another's given us until Monday. They don't give a shit about Megan. It's all, 'Darling, we have every sympathy but her brand is in tatters and she's not taking us down too'." Mimi fell silent. I could hear her breathing softly. "The cap and dark glasses didn't help either. They'd all seen it. She looked like someone on the run, like she had something to hide."

"Sorry," I said, feeling responsible. "How's Jackie?"

"How d'you think? Pissed off – to put it mildly. She's still haggling – as we speak – with one of the sponsors... So how did it go with Richards today?"

"I've no idea really," I said. "Megan admitted being there when Matt died, and he didn't seem too surprised. It helped to get that out of the way right at the beginning. Then there was the blood sample."

"And?"

"It's Matt's blood apparently, and the sample was taken from the corner of the table. So it looks like he hit his head as he fell and the question is, was that the cause of death? They don't know yet if he fractured his head. They're waiting for a pathology report."

"Holy fuck," Mimi said. "And if he did and he was pushed…"

"Exactly, and that little bombshell was dropped after we'd been there for five hours, and he wants us back tomorrow."

"Shit," Mimi said. "Does that mean we can kiss goodbye to the Olympics?"

I didn't know where to begin with that, and Mimi sensed it.

"You must be gutted," she said. "After all the work you've done…"

"I haven't given up yet," I said, trying to sound upbeat. "But, with them leaving for the holding camp on Thursday, it's touch and go. It looks like it's all down to Richards and his pathology report. I didn't get a chance to ask him when that would come through. If this drags on through next week, even if Megan's eventually cleared legally, it'll be too late for her to go to Belo Horizonte with everyone else. I suppose she could go later, direct to Rio, but it's not ideal, she won't have a chance to acclimatise."

Mimi fell silent, digesting the implications of that.

"Oh well," she said with an ironic tone. "The sponsors will walk, and I guess I'll have to find another client."

I didn't reply to that because 'the client' had walked back in. She was absorbed in reading something on her phone and didn't seem to have heard Mimi's last comment, which was just as well.

"I'd better go," I said to Mimi. "Meg's back, and she is still the world number one."

"Ha, right – that's okay then," Mimi said, disconnecting.

"What happened?" Megan was nodding towards the TV, which was still showing the athletics, but with the volume on mute.

"Well, you are still number one," I said, making an effort to smile and sound cheery. "Natasha Sholokhova won, but her time was nothing special, in the conditions."

Megan was still distracted by her phone.

"I've been getting some really strange texts off Will, and I've tried to phone him but he's not answering," she said.

"What sort of strange?" I asked.

"Like last night, except worse. The media's getting to him and he's saying stuff about Gary."

"What sort of stuff?"

She looked down at her phone. "About him being a back-stabbing bastard."

I shrugged. I felt like saying: 'So what do you want me to do about it, the two bastards deserve each other?' But I didn't.

Megan sat down and jumped up again almost in one movement. "I'm going over there," she said.

I groaned, feeling weighed down by a long day and too many chips, but I knew I had no choice.

"Not on your own you're not," I said.

* * *

By the time we reached Will's flat, the sun had gone, and it took me a while to get my bearings. We had passed the footbridge where I'd met Megan earlier in the week, and I realised we were on the same stretch of river as Graeme's flat but the opposite side.

Megan was becoming increasingly agitated. She had tried the bell and was pacing up and down looking at the black windows of a flat two floors above, seemingly trying to find an angle to see if there was some movement inside.

I stood by the car peering into the amber gloom at the dark shapes across the river, wondering which one was Graeme's building and imagining him sitting there, alone and brooding. It occurred to me suddenly, with a morbid jolt, that he may have consciously chosen a flat with a view of the place where his son died.

Megan had disappeared around the corner, but she was soon back, shaking her head, looking like she was ready to scream. We stood there for a few more minutes, Megan checking her phone and texting more messages until I suggested, tentatively, that this might be a lost cause.

"I'm sure he's fine," I said.

"But it's not like him," said Meg. "Not replying. Not replying to *me*."

"Maybe his battery's gone," I said, though I really thought it was more likely he was in a pub or a club somewhere and couldn't hear his phone or was too drunk to face a conversation with Meg.

Megan threw me a look as if to say I was a moron for not appreciating just how out of character it was for Will not to be responding instantly to her.

"Let's wait a bit longer," she said getting back into the car.

And so we sat there for a good thirty minutes, Megan in sullen silence and me trying to suppress my growing irritation.

"Look," I said, my last reserves of patience now nearly exhausted. "This is a complete waste of time."

She ignored me.

"And anyway, I don't get why you're so worried?"

Still no reply.

"For God sake, Meg, what is it?"

She looked across at me, her hands gripping the steering wheel like she was clinging to it for support.

"It's just that I think there's something going on between Will and Gary," she said.

"Meg, so the fuck what?" I said. "Why is it any worry of yours?"

Megan had let go of the steering wheel but she was now chewing her lower lip and looking at me like she had something to say and couldn't decide if she dared say it. I waited but with my eyebrows raised as if stay say 'get on with it'.

She drew in a long breath and let it out slowly. "The thing is, Liam," she said, "there's something I haven't told you."

"Something else?" I said, incredulous. "You mean something *else* you haven't told me?"

Megan was sitting upright, turned towards me but with her back pressed against the driver's door. It was as if she wanted to be out of reach in case my reaction was violent.

"Gary was blackmailing me," she said.

It took me more than a few seconds to process that one. I let the words hang in the clammy air and played them back to myself a couple of times.

"He was blackmailing you…" I repeated, almost in a whisper. "What the fuck do you mean, blackmailing you?"

"Gary found out about the blood sample. He knew it had been overlooked and said to Will that it was a 'smoking gun' and he could use it to make trouble for us – unless we paid him a lot of money."

"How much is 'a lot'?"

"Ten thousand."

"You're kidding! Ten thousand pounds. *And you paid it?*"

Megan nodded, cringing at the same time at the force of my reaction.

"When was this?"

"Last year, just after the World Championships. He must have seen all the stuff about me being the highest paid female athlete, so he went to Will, and told him he could be done for manslaughter and I could be done for perverting the course of justice… and I panicked. I was worried sick. I couldn't bear the thought, Li, the thought of people knowing I'd left Matt like that…"

"So you coughed-up ten grand?" I said. "For God's sake, what were you thinking? It only makes matters worse."

Megan fell silent, and we sat there for a few moments listening to our own breathing, Megan fiddling with her fingers.

"The money seemed like nothing – I suddenly had so much of it," she said, still looking down at her hands. "But then he came back for more, a few weeks ago. Another ten thousand."

"Shit!" I said, beyond exasperation, beyond words, even beyond anger.

I threw the door open, got out and paced around in a circle, unable to gather any coherent thoughts. I was tempted to walk away, to just get the next train to London. But before I could think anything through, Megan had pressed the ignition and was shouting, "Li, Li," through the open window and gesturing for me to get in.

I looked at her, and she held my look like she was clinging to her last hope.

I got in.

She drove back to the hotel recklessly as if she was past caring what happened to her – or me for that matter – taking speed bumps like we were riding rodeo. I gripped my seat and closed my eyes, trying to think straight, wrestling with the implications of Megan's latest bombshell.

Why hadn't she come to me for help? How could she have carried on as if everything was normal? Okay, I could appreciate the shame she felt about running away when Matt died: how hard that would be to admit, and the effect it could have on her career, and the bloody sponsors. But, once it had degenerated into blackmail… why hadn't she realised she was out of her depth?

The answer to all of it could only be Will. She seemed so blind in her loyalty him, naïve beyond belief. It was as if they were locked into a suicide pact by the events of that night.

When we reached the hotel, I was ready to give Megan a no-holds-barred grilling. I was determined to get to the bottom of everything before we had to face Richards again in the morning.

But Megan was too quick for me. She threw the door open and started to get out. I tried to pull her back, grabbing her nearest arm.

"We need to talk, Meg."

"Fuck it, Liam," she said, shaking me off. "I know I've

been stupid, but what the fuck was I supposed to do? Let Will go down for something he didn't do?"

I was about to say 'Yes!' but, before I could answer, she'd tossed the car keys at me and broken into a run, heading for her room.

My adrenalin was pumping so hard I could hardly breathe. I looked at my watch. It was nearly one in the morning. I wanted to phone Mimi and I fumbled for my phone, but I didn't even have it on me. It was too late anyway.

In the distance there were faint rumblings of thunder. The air seemed alive with electricity. A few drops of rain landed on the windscreen. I sat there watching them multiply.

21

IN HARM'S WAY

THE AIR FELT LIGHTER NOW, having been relieved of its humidity by the overnight rain, and there was a cool breeze on my face. I was sitting on a stone overlooking the amphitheatre, watching the sun emerging from behind a hill above Caerleon. The yellow grass around me was saturated from the overnight storm and the dusty earth had turned dark brown. Everything seemed in sharper focus: birds picking at the damp soil, a plane overhead, a church tower nestling in a cluster of houses on the hill. Everything except Megan.

I had hardly slept. I'd phoned Mimi at 5.30, waking her. She was grisly – not at all pleased about being woken up, and even less so when I told her why. Neither of us could make much sense of this new revelation nor understand why

Meg hadn't told us or why we'd failed to spot anything odd in Megan's behaviour.

Had we been blinded by our own ambition, treating her like a machine, only interested in our stake in her success? Or had all our endeavour been honest but betrayed by Meg's lack of openness?

"I can understand Meg being terrified of admitting she left Matt for dead," Mimi had said, echoing the thoughts I'd been wrestling with all night. "My God, poor thing – keeping that bottled up. But Will? What is it with Will?"

I had no answers to offer and after we'd picked at the wounds for twenty minutes or so, I suggested we save the post mortem for later, not least because I had a worry of my own.

"I'm supposed to be seeing Danny tomorrow," I'd said, "but I can see Richards spending all day grilling Megan. He likes to take his time and, well, it's hard to say how it's all going to go. I don't know whether I'll be able to get back this evening, but I don't want to let Danny down."

Mimi had anticipated this. "I'll sort it, even if it means driving him to Newport myself," she'd said, adding, "As long as you don't mind me talking to Kelli."

For a second, I'd felt uncomfortable at the thought of a conversation between Mimi and my ex-wife, but Mimi's eagerness to help me raise my parental game was touching.

"Thanks," I'd said, slightly choked.

It was gone seven now and some early Saturday joggers and bikers had appeared. I pushed myself up from the damp grass and walked slowly back to the hotel, past the path where I'd been beaten-up and along the gravel drive to the rear entrance. Breakfast was being served. I decided to make the most of it.

* * *

We arrived at the police station at the same time as Nigel. Megan was subdued driving there, but she did say, 'Sorry, Liam' in a hushed way, like a child nervously showing remorse for being in so much trouble. I touched her arm to show we were okay. I could see she'd probably had as little sleep as me.

"How are we today?" Nigel said with such jollity I almost laughed out loud. Little did he know what was coming.

We were ushered by the receptionist into the small interview room and sat down, Nigel facing us, where Richards had sat.

"I think we'd better start with what Megan told me last night," I said, not wanting to waste a second of the time we had before Richards arrived.

Nigel gave me an unflappable, 'go-on-then' look, like he thought nothing could surprise him or spoil his day.

"Gary has been blackmailing me," Megan said flatly.

Nigel looked at her sceptically. "I'm sorry – what?"

"Nearly a year ago, he told Will he'd found out about a blood sample that had been overlooked and said he'd make trouble for us unless I paid him ten thousand pounds."

"Ten thousand pounds – you paid him *ten grand*?" Nigel said, disbelievingly, sounding like someone was strangling him.

Megan nodded. Nigel lifted his leather bag from the floor wearily, rested it on his lap and pulled a notebook out. "Okay, you'd better tell me the whole thing," he said.

Megan went through what she had told me, adding a few details under Nigel's probing. She said it first happened the previous September, a few weeks after the Beijing World Championships. She was all over the media, and they were reporting she was being paid twenty thousand pounds a race, and that she had signed a sportswear deal worth nearly half a million pounds. Gary seized is chance.

"I suppose I thought I could buy my way out of trouble," Meg said, sheepishly. "Suddenly I had all this money, and ten thousand seemed like nothing to make it go away. I thought, even if I went to tthe police and confessed to what I'd done, where would that leave Will? It might have made things worse. I suppose I could have told them he didn't do anything – been a witness for him – but who would have believed me after I'd lied in the first place?"

Megan looked pleadingly from Nigel to me as if hoping one of us would agree with her and make it all seem better.

"Okay," Nigel said, putting his pen down, all jollity long gone.

"And there was a second time," I said, not letting Megan off the hook.

Nigel rolled his eyes and waited for Megan to explain.

"He demanded another ten grand, a few weeks ago," she said, "and I paid that too."

Nigel smiled as if tragedy had now descended into farce in his mind.

"Right. Well, I suppose we'd better tell the inspector," he said.

* * *

Richards arrived with Simmons promptly at ten o'clock. They were also in relaxed mode, breezing in wearing weekend clothes like they were ready for a walk in the park.

Simmons dropped the file and a notepad on the table.

Nigel moved to his place alongside Megan and gave Richards a mischievous smile.

Richards looked at his watch. "Interview resumed at 10.01," he said, before cautioning Megan again and insisting on everyone identifying themselves.

"Well, inspector," Nigel said when the ritual was over. "Miss Tomos is full of surprises. We need to bring another, separate matter to your attention relating to Gary Evans, the police officer my client mentioned yesterday."

"Okay, best get on with it, then," Richards said.

Nigel gave him a version of the blackmail story peppered with legal jargon and caveats – it is alleged, things 'apparently' happened. Simmons took notes. Richards kept glancing at Megan, checking her reaction to Nigel's account.

"Miss Tomos," Richards said, "can you confirm what your solicitor, what Mr Winters, has been telling us?"

Megan started to answer but her voice was drowned-out by the sound of a police car outside firing-up its siren. We sat in deafened silence while the car pulled away. And, as the noise of its siren faded, others could be heard in the distance, possibly half a dozen, not quite in rhythm or harmony.

A female uniformed officer half-opened the door and peered in looking flustered.

"Sir?" she said, and Simmons stood up and left the room with her.

Richards' eyes followed them and then he turned back to Megan and nodded towards the recording machine to remind her to confirm Nigel's statement.

"Yes, what my solicitor said is correct," she said.

"And how exactly did Evans communicate with you?" Richards asked.

Megan seemed surprised by the question. "Well, I didn't speak to him or anything, if that's what you mean?" she said.

"A letter, an email?" Richards suggested.

"Nothing like that. It was all done through Will."

"I see," the inspector said, letting the words hang in the air, sounding sceptical, acting-out an interview technique honed, no doubt, on tougher subjects than Megan. "So you don't have any physical evidence?"

"Physical? No – well apart from transferring the money," Megan said.

"And how did you do that?"

"Online," Megan replied, looking puzzled, like she thought Richards was asking the obvious.

"Online into what account?"

Simmons came in looking flustered. "There's an incident, sir," he said.

But Richards ignored him. He was still looking at Megan.

"Into Will's account, of course," she said. But Richards seemed to be waiting for something else. "I didn't want to have anything to do with Gary."

"Sir," Simmons persisted. "It seems the incident is at Grange Road, at the gym. They say Driscoll's involved."

Richards and Megan both stood up instantly and started for the door, but Simmons held a hand up in Megan's direction.

"It's a potential hostage situation, sir," he said. "Firearms are on their way. I've arranged transport."

Richards ran his eyes from Megan to me and then Nigel, looking at us like we were kids who would have to be babysat.

"I need to find out what this is all about," he said, "The three of you can follow with Simmons, but you're to stay in the vehicle until I say otherwise. Your presence could escalate things. Understood?"

He started to leave but stopped halfway through the door and turned back to emphasise his point: "You won't be doing yourselves any favours if this turns into a media circus."

As soon as Richards had gone, Simmons gathered up the file and notebook and told us to follow him. Our silent, stunned procession went through a door in the reception area into a drab and cluttered office and then along a dark corridor to the rear of the building. Simmons led and a female uniformed officer appeared from nowhere to take up the rear.

Outside, another officer, a man even younger-looking than Simmons, was holding open the front passenger door of a gleaming black Range Rover with tinted windows. Simmons reached past him to pull the rear door open, and threw his head sideways to indicate that we should get in.

"Inspector Richards?" the officer holding the door asked, as Megan climbed in followed by me and then Nigel.

"He's gone on ahead," Simmons replied. "We're to keep our distance for now."

It took us less than five minutes to reach Grange Road. The young driver had weaved his way through Newport like a boy racer, the siren sending cars scattering at random angles, creating an exhilarating but unsettling sense of power.

Megan grabbed my hand. I looked down at her fingers threaded through mine, struggling to remember if that had happened before. To my left, Nigel was keying combinations of words like 'gun', 'siege' and 'Newport' into his phone, searching for some reference to what was happening online.

"You can't do that, sir – no contact with anyone," Simmons said, assuming the tapping sound was Nigel sending a message. "We have to keep this locked down."

As we turned into Grange Road, the driver slowed down to walking pace. All I could see ahead, between the shoulders of Simmons and the driver, was a large unmarked white van with a satellite dish and aerials on its roof, parked in the centre of the road, its rear doors open. It was flanked by a police car on one side and a police minibus on the other. Beyond the white van, there was yellow tape across the road at waist height, fluttering and reflecting the sun, and then nothing until another clutch of police vehicles in the far distance.

Uniformed police in black flak jackets were patrolling the sealed-off stretch of the street. Some were marching up and down the short front paths, knocking doors and calling through windows. One was ushering an elderly Asian couple towards us.

"They'll be evacuating the houses facing the gym," Simmons said, sensing me leaning forward behind him to see what was going on. "We'll stay here for now."

Richards was climbing out of the white van ahead, and a uniformed officer followed. They started walking in our direction. The uniformed officer was much the taller and had a military look, a parade ground bearing, as if he was coming to inspect the troops.

Simmons lowered his window as they reached us. The tall officer leaned forward so that his head was framed by the window. He seemed a few years older than Richards; with white hair cut very short and grey eyebrows dense with thick curling hairs like an old toothbrush. His large nostrils had matching bristles. His eyes danced across the five of us and settled on Megan.

"Miss Tomos, I'm Chief Superintendent Anderson," he said, almost shouting because a helicopter had arrived over-head. "I'm in charge here, and I understand from Inspector Richards that you are connected to the suspect."

Megan's grip on my hand tightened. "I don't know what you mean? What's going on?" she said.

Anderson continued looking at her for a moment and then pulled his head back. "Simmons," he shouted. "Let's get you parked somewhere so that I can talk to Miss Tomos properly. Put it behind the command vehicle, at right angles, driver's side nearest. We'll circle the wagons, so to speak. I want to keep Miss Tomos out of view."

Anderson thumped the side of the car, signalling us to go. Simmons closed the window, and the driver edged forward and manoeuvred into position behind the white van.

By the time, the driver was satisfied the right angle was perfect, Richards and Anderson had caught up with us. Anderson walked round to Megan's door and opened it. We could see straight into the white van where a uniformed man wearing a headset and mic was sitting sideways-on facing a panel of screens and controls

"Now, Miss Tomos," said Anderson, noticing our curiosity and stepping into our line of vision,

"the situation we have here is that your friend, Driscoll… he seems to have gone berserk. Apparently, he arrived here about an hour ago with a crow bar and, we understand, a sawn-off shotgun…"

"You're kidding?" Megan interrupted, closing her eyes like she was going to start praying. It was about the only thing we hadn't tried, I felt like saying, but I kept my mouth shut.

"I don't joke about firearms, Miss Tomos," Anderson replied, acidly. "We're relying on information from one person – a woman – who managed to get out while Driscoll was herding everyone else into the office at gunpoint. I don't think she was making it up, and we have to assume the worst."

Megan nodded, looking chastened by Anderson's tone.

"We don't have any contact with the suspect, and that's very worrying," he continued. "He's not answering the landline in the gym or his mobile. Our negotiator can't even start trying to talk some sense into him – but you may be able to help. Perhaps he'll respond if he sees your number come up on his phone."

Megan let go of my hand and started patting her jeans to find her phone. She pulled it out of her left pocket and offered it to Anderson.

"In a moment," he said. "There are a few things we need to clarify first." He turned to a young, dark-haired man wearing a sky-blue polo shirt and jeans, who'd appeared at the shoulder of Richards. "This is Inspector Blake. He's our negotiator."

Blake stepped past Richards and held a hand out to Megan. "Ryan Blake," he said. Megan shook his hand limply.

"I'm a trained negotiator," Blake said, earnestly, like he was interviewing for a job. "Our objective here is to bring this to an end without anyone getting hurt."

Nigel was fidgeting next to me and leaned across. "I'm Nigel Winters, Megan's solicitor," he said.

"Yes, I know, thanks Mr Winters, but we don't need your help at the moment," Blake said, not taking his eyes off Megan. "Now, Miss Tomos, I've had a briefing on the case from Inspector Richards, but I need to get a better understanding of Will's frame of mind. When did you last speak to him?"

"Speak to him?" Megan repeated. "We haven't spoken since Thursday evening."

"But you've had contact? By text?"

Megan looked down at the phone on her lap and tapped it a couple of times. "A few texts yesterday, but he didn't answer when I tried to call him." Megan turned to me, her eyes watery. "See, I knew there was something…"

I sensed Blake was waiting for an explanation. "Megan was concerned about Will last night," I said. "He wasn't answering her calls and texts, so we went over to his flat – but the lights were off; there was no sign of him."

"Okay, Miss Tomos, Megan, so you spoke to him on Thursday evening – how was he then?" Blake asked.

"Very upset, agitated. He was ranting about Gary."

"About what specifically?"

Megan looked down again at her phone, avoiding Blake's

intense gaze. He was crowding her now, leaning into the car.

"Inspector Richards has told me about the blackmail allegation," Blake continued. "Was it that? Or had something else happened? Anything you can tell me might help."

"I don't know. He said something about Gary trying to bring him down. That he was a bastard and out to destroy us."

"Both of you or just him?" Richards said over Blake's shoulder.

Megan frowned, puzzled.

"You said 'him' and then 'us'," Richards explained. "Do you think something had happened between them, maybe something that didn't involve you?"

"I don't know," Megan said slowly. "Thursday was a bad day. I think it was the body being exhumed. It got to him. He completely flipped. But, now you say that, I think it was more about him than me. There was something like that about it."

"Have you...?" Richards started to say, but Blake held up his hand.

"We can come back to this later, inspector," he said. "Suffice it to say, for now, that our one witness, a woman who escaped, has identified the man with the gun as Driscoll and, from her descriptions of the others, it sounds like Evans is in there too. I think the sooner we can get some communication going with Driscoll the better." Blake picked up Megan's phone. "I want you to text him. Keep it light. We want him to stay calm. Just say: 'Will. What's happening? Are you alright? Is everyone alright?' That's all. Okay?"

Megan took the phone and started to key in the words, but Blake said, "Hang on a second. I have to get our technician to tap into your phone, in case he calls you back."

* * *

Will didn't call back, and it was a long half an hour or so before a text arrived, and then all it said was 'Sorry Meg'.

Megan looked deflated. We were still sitting in the back of the car. From so close, I could see a film of sweat above her upper lip and inflamed veins forming tiny red deltas in the whites of her eyes. She handed the phone to Blake to show him.

"Fucking great," she said, a quiver of anger in her voice. "What's he playing at?"

Blake showed no surprise. He was probably still in his twenties but he carried the impassive expression of someone who had seen all this before. I wondered if he had or if that was only part of the training.

He took the phone across to show Anderson and Richards, who were standing next to the van, looking out across the empty space in front of the gym. The three of them stayed huddled there for some time, deep in discussion, Richards doing most of the talking, Anderson occasionally pulling his lapel towards him to bark instructions into a small mic.

I was beginning to feel claustrophobic, not to mention anxious about the toilet arrangements. I tried to occupy myself by remembering sieges I'd seen in movies, but they all seemed a blur of rapid activity – nothing like this.

Next to me, Nigel was scrolling through emails on his phone, making the most of the absence of Simmons and the driver, who were propping themselves up against the front of the car. I didn't see any point in discussing the finer details of Megan's legal situation with him. I assumed Will's actions had changed everything.

To my right, Megan was beginning to fidget, knees twitching like she was in the athletes' holding area before a race.

"Those poor people," she mumbled a couple of times. She

seemed ready to explode, as if she might break cover, hurdle the tape and rush the building all on her own. No one would stand a chance of catching her.

It was a relief when some officers finally appeared with screens to shield the area between the two vehicles from view, and we were allowed to get out, but we were still a big crowd – the three of us and five police officers – for a space no bigger than my hotel room, with nothing much to say to each other as we shuffled around waiting for Anderson or Will to make a move.

On my toes, I was tall enough to be able to see over the screens. Behind us, there were now steel barriers keeping out a growing crowd gathering to watch the show. Ahead, I caught a glimpse of a posse of police wearing military-style metal helmets and clutching chunky black weapons, scurrying into position behind the low wall that separated the pavement from a small car park in front of the gym. Shifting my angle, I could see another heavily armed group moving tentatively down a path to the side of the building, keeping their heads below windowsill height, their backs almost horizontal. It all seemed so choreographed: the helicopter still high above us somehow acting like a puppeteer.

Richards had sidled up to me. "It's only a precaution, Liam," he whispered. "In case we need to react fast."

I nodded but still felt unnerved at the sight of the quiet residential street I'd walked down only a few days earlier looking like TV pictures of Belfast or Baghdad.

A few feet away, Ryan was in deep discussion with Anderson. He broke away to approach Megan.

"We want you to try calling him now," he said. "From the van. If he answers, we want you to appeal to him to let everyone go. That's the main thing. I'll sit next to you. If you get him talking, I'll tell you what to say. I might want you to mention me, by my first name, but we'll see how it goes."

Megan climbed into the van and sat on the bench alongside the technician, who connected her phone to his equipment and gave her a headset. Ryan sat beside her with Anderson and Simmons leaning into the van to listen. Nigel and I moved as near as we could without provoking them to banish us to the Range Rover.

Megan made the call. It rang through to voicemail.

She tried again.

This time he answered: "Meg?"

"Will, it's me, Meg. Will, are you okay?"

There was no reply. Someone shouted in the background. The only word I caught was 'maniac'.

"Will, listen to me," Meg said. "Let those people go."

The line was silent. Overhead, the helicopter roared relentlessly. The technician's screen was still showing the phone as 'connected'. Ryan handed Megan a note. She read it and sounded like she was reading from it. "Will, I've got someone who wants to talk to you. His name's Ryan."

"Will," Ryan said. "We're here to help you sort this out. There's nothing to gain by people getting hurt. Why don't you put your firearm down and come out?"

The helicopter seemed to have dropped lower.

"What's that noise?" Will screamed. "I can't think fucking straight with that fucking noise – on and on..."

Ryan looked at Anderson, who turned away and spoke softly into his lapel mic, telling the pilot to 'back off'.

"Will, it's only a helicopter," Ryan said. "It's going now. Everything's calm here. We just want to talk Will, to work something out. Let's talk about those people in there with you. How about letting them go? What harm have they done you?"

"Ha, that's a laugh," Will said bitterly, and fell silent.

Ryan took his time, waiting for the sound of the helicopter

to become a faint rumble, merging with the noise of traffic on nearby roads.

"How many people are with you, Will?" he asked.

There was no reply. Ryan waited again. Without the helicopter, we could hear Will's heavy but steady breathing on the line.

"Will, what do you think? Let them go," Ryan persisted, seeming to sense Will was torn, wondering what to do. "Then we can talk about everything else…"

Meg looked ready to burst.

She did. "Will, please!" she said, through heavy sobs, struggling to catch her breath. "Just let them go."

Will was still silent. It was hard to imagine what he was thinking; what he thought this would achieve and what calculations he could now be making. Whatever trouble he was in, whatever had happened between him and Gary, this had only made things worse. But these things seem to have a dynamic of their own, one action setting off a chain of events, spiralling out of control, like nations stumbling into war.

"Meg," he said finally. "Meg?"

"Yes, Will?" she said, sounding calmer.

"Don't be upset, Meg, I'll make it all up to you…" he said feebly, child-like.

Megan began sobbing again. "Will, if you want to make it up to me, for God's sake let them go."

On the line there was a kerfuffle of chairs scraping and a door banging. A male voice shouted 'yes'.

"They're coming out," Will said.

Ryan punched the air. Anderson spoke into his lapel, ordering the firearms team to be ready to receive them.

"But not Gary," Will shouted. "That bastard stays with me."

22

IN THE THICK OF IT

"LIAM, WHAT ARE YOU FRIGGING playing at?"

I held the phone a full arms-length away from my ear. I'd never heard Mimi so agitated. The words were tumbling out so furiously I couldn't make much sense of them, but the gist was that she'd seen an amateur video of the siege on Sky, was alarmed at seeing so many weapons on display and caught a glimpse of the top of my head apparently in the thick of it. TV can be deceptive, of course.

"Why the fuck didn't you call me?" she said, and finally took a breath.

"We weren't allowed to call anybody," I replied.

"Anybody? I'm frigging *anybody*?"

"You know what I mean. It was a lock down." I realised

I sounded ridiculous using their jargon. "That's what they called it," I added.

The line fell silent. I could hear a faint quivering sound at the other end.

"Have you been getting calls?" I said.

Now there was sharp intake of breath, and I knew immediately I'd missed the point, but I couldn't think of any way to recover.

"Liam, do you think that's it?" she said. "That I'm worried about pissing-off a few hacks?"

"Of course I don't," I said quietly. "I wanted to phone but I'm… well, not very experienced when it comes to sieges."

I hoped the silence meant she was smiling. I imagined her dark lips stretching a little wider, her cheekbones rising, and those warm brown eyes glowing. But there was no way she was she going to let me off the hook by laughing out loud.

"Okay," she said, sounding more like her composed, feisty self. "You better give the police press officer my number. We need to get our act together."

"Right, I'll tell Richards to tell his people to speak to my people," I said.

"Funny," she said.

"Right," I said.

"And text me every hour. Or more often if something happens."

"Don't worry. I will."

She fell silent again, and I could hear her breathing softly.

"And Liam," she said. "Look after yourself."

And she hung up.

* * *

Our mini-compound was becoming unbearable. The screens blocked any breeze but offered no shade from the sun almost directly above us. I could feel the tarmac growing hotter by the minute, burning into the rubber soles of my trainers. It was like being trapped in a small tightly-packed sauna.

Anderson, Simmons, Richards and Blake would move around the space in ever-changing combinations, occasionally joined by officers coming and going with information or questions.

Megan was still sitting with the technician in the van, resting her head against the metal panelling, staring vacantly at one of the control panels.

Nigel and I had watched the hostage release on our toes, peering over the screen. Again, the choreography was slick: two groups of firearms officers emerged from different directions just in time to absorb the hostages into a protective scrum as they came screaming and shouting out of the gym. There were three of them, a woman and two men, all still wearing Lycra and trainers, heads pressed down by the black gloves of their handlers. The scrum had scurried towards two ambulances at the far end of the road where paramedics and Anderson were waiting for them.

"Blake, they're in the manager's office," said Anderson, back now from speaking to the three released hostages, pushing through a gap in the screens. "Driscoll has locked himself in, with Evans tied to a chair. Sounds like he's jumpy and might do anything. One of them thinks he could use the gun on himself."

Anderson glanced towards Megan in the back of the van, who had flinched at Anderson's lack of tact. So had I.

She looked across at me, eyes watery and even more bloodshot, her expression expectant like she thought her coach ought to have some comment to make, but I had nothing to offer. What could I say? It was taking all the composure

I could muster to stay looking calm.

"We have to consider all possibilities," Anderson said in Megan's direction, sounding apologetic.

He turned to Blake who'd been deep in conversation with Richards and Simmons.

"We've lost all contact with him," Blake said, realising Anderson expected an update. "He's not responding to Megan's calls or texts or answering the land line."

"I'll speak to the tech guys," Anderson said. "I want to see if they can run a probe into the roof space above the office." Anderson looked at his watch. "I need to brief Gold Command," he continued. "I'll be back very soon."

Richards looked at Megan, checking that she was out of earshot, and then turned to whisper something to Simmons. All I caught were the words 'Will's flat'. Simmons nodded and jogged across to a nearby police car, its engine running, the driver ready to show-off his car handling abilities. With a three-point turn, and as many screeches, they were gone, the crowd opening up hurriedly to let them pass through a narrow gap in the barriers.

I looked at my watch. It was nearly two o'clock.

A young woman, with black hair and wearing a navy trouser suit and white blouse, had joined Richards and Blake. She was by far the smartest of any of us. She was holding a clipboard and showing them something pinned to it. Richards pointed in my direction. She took the three or four steps needed to cross our little sweatbox.

"Liam?" she said, ignoring Nigel. "I'm Rhian Williams from the Gwent police press office."

"You got my message," I said.

She looked puzzled. I took that as a 'no'.

"You'll need to speak to Mimi," I added. "She looks after this sort of thing."

"Where is she?"

"In London."

Rhian looked surprised. "We've set up a media room in the community centre round the corner," she said, giving me a small piece of paper with a number and an email address on it. "That's how you can get hold of me if you need to."

Megan had climbed out of the van to join us. "Do we need to do this?" she said irritably, looking down at the couple of sentences typed on plain white paper on Rhian's clipboard.

It said about as little as you could say without saying anything. There was 'an incident' involving firearms in Newport; police were at the scene and a further update would be given at 4pm. There was no mention of Megan, Will or the hostages.

"Sky is already broadcasting an amateur video," Rhian said. "We're being inundated. The chief wants something out."

"Call Mimi," I said, showing her the number on my phone, wanting to take the decision-making away from this hothouse.

Nigel was stirring next to me. "If you make any statements mentioning Megan, I want to see them as well," he said.

"And who are you?" Rhian asked.

"I'm Megan's lawyer," Nigel replied.

We stood there in an uneasy deadlock for a moment – Megan looking too washed out to argue, Nigel seeming pleased he finally had a point to make (even if it was a pointless one), and Rhian staring at her announcement like it said something profound.

Richards joined us with Blake and another man tagging along.

"Are you done, Rhian?" Richards said, with a go-away tone. She didn't need any encouraging.

"I'll phone Ms Jacobs," she said, keying the number into her phone and walking off with it held to her ear.

Blake looked at us with a weary smile. "This is Ian Beddows, the tactical firearms officer", he said.

Megan looked at him warily.

"Using force is a last resort," Blake explained, sensing Megan's unease, "but we have to find a way of getting Will talking again. Anyone have any bright ideas?"

He sounded like a teacher inviting his class to solve a problem. I didn't have any ideas at all, bright or otherwise.

Megan was studying her trainers, fingers in her jean pockets, thumbs tapping on the outside. "Graeme…" she mumbled, "why not ask Graeme to try talking some sense into him?"

It didn't seem a bad suggestion to me – anything was worth trying to break the impasse – but Richards was looking sceptical.

"Not so sure about that one myself," he said. "Not at all sure. It could make matters worse. There was a lot of antagonism between Matt and Will, especially in the last couple of weeks before he died."

Megan lifted her head and did a half-turn on her heels, like she was ready to walk off – not that there was anywhere to go.

"How do you know that?" she said, still sideways-on to the circle we'd formed.

"I've spoken to a lot of people, Megan, and take it from me, Matt was pretty angry with Will about something."

"But maybe Will wants to make his peace with Graeme now?" I suggested.

Richards smiled in a smug way, like he thought he knew more about this than we did.

"It's more likely Will is scared of Graeme – or scared of what he might know," Richards said. "I doubt he thinks there's any chance of making his peace with Graeme."

Megan had a surly look now. Richards seemed to be annoying her. "You're talking in riddles," she said.

Blake stepped-in. "Look," he said. "We haven't got time to get into the finer details of all this. Using Graeme sounds too risky. I want to keep things calm, avoid raising the temperature."

On the other side of the compound, Anderson was squeezing sideways between the front of the Range Rover and a screen, back from his tête-à-tête with the Gold Commander, whoever that was.

"The probe's in place," he said with a triumphant smile. "Blake, let's see what we can hear."

The two of them climbed into the van and settled on the bench next to the technician who was fiddling with some buttons and knobs, evidently trying to tune-in to whatever frequency the probe was on.

The rest of us gathered around the back of the vehicle again. Richards and Beddows took up a vantage point that gave them a clear view of the control panel. Megan tucked in next to them, and Nigel and I had to peer over their shoulders as best we could.

The sounds were muffled and disjointed: a door closing; the whirring of a fan; an incomprehensible word or two; a chair scraping; a grunt, like someone was trying to move something. We stood there in complete silence, concentrating on trying to make some sense of the noises.

"Let's try his mobile again," Anderson said, sounding frustrated. He looked at Megan and nodded at the empty seat next to him. She stepped up into the van and sat down.

The technician stroked and tapped Megan's phone. The call sound came up through the speakers in the van and was echoed, via the probe, by the noise of Will's phone ringing in the gym.

The line went dead.

"Fuck her," a voice said, picked up faintly by the probe. I had no idea if it was Will or Gary until I saw Megan's wounded face. She avoided my eyes.

"Try again," Anderson said, oblivious to any sensitivities, or not caring about them. He had a job to do and there was an urgency in his tone.

The sounds went through the same cycle but this time there was an answer.

"What?" the voice said. No question it was Will this time

Blake nodded at Megan and she began reading from a note he'd given her, making a passable attempt at sounding natural.

"Will, thanks for releasing those people. You did a good thing. You should release Gary now and then we can talk…"

"Ha ha! You sound posh," Will said, not letting her finish whatever else was on the paper in front of her. "Who wrote that for you Meg? Police pulling your strings are they?"

Will's voice had an edge to it, a sharpness towards Megan and a tinge of fear. Megan looked at Blake, raising her eyebrows as if asking for guidance.

Blake leaned into the microphone. "It's Ryan here," he said. "Meg's trying to help you. She doesn't want anyone to get hurt. It will only make matters worse."

The phone went dead. Through the probe we could hear a pacing sound and then a door open and close.

Gary shouted, "Where the fuck are you going, you bastard?"

There was no reply. We heard a grinding, metallic sound like a lock turning.

"Fuck you," Gary said.

The noises were mainly heavy breathing and grunting now, like someone lifting weights too heavy for them. It sounded like Gary was trying to move something or was struggling to free himself.

Blake threw his pen down. Anderson picked up a large sheet of paper folded like a map and began opening it up. From what I could see, it was a plan of the building.

"Miss Tomos," he said. "Thank you for your assistance. I think I need to take stock of the situation with my officers. If you don't mind…"

Megan looked from Blake to Richards and realised she was being asked to leave. She stood as near to upright as she could in the van, and put a hand on my shoulder as she stepped down onto the ground. Richards climbed up and took her seat.

Anderson was talking into the mic on his lapel. "Sergeant, take up your positions as agreed and await further orders," he was saying.

Nigel, Megan and I moved away in silence towards the Range Rover. Looking through it, the crowd was now several rows deep behind the steel barriers. Taller people were peering over the heads of those in the front. There were children on shoulders and phones being held high to take photographs.

Beyond the crowd, I could see the tops of gazebos and vans with aerials and satellite dishes. The media circus had evidently made the short journey from the police headquarters and set up camp at the very end of the road.

Megan seemed defeated. She didn't like losing at the best of times. I looked from her drawn and grey face back to the van where Anderson was in animated discussion with Blake, Beddows and Richards. I looked at my watch. It was nearly three-thirty now.

* * *

A young blond woman, hair tied back, looking odd in a sleeve-less orange safety jacket over shorts and a T-shirt, arrived with an open cardboard box full of cans and plastic bottles, packed sandwiches, fruit and cereals bars.

"Where do you want this?" she asked with the matter-of-fact tone of someone delivering the catering for an office party.

"On there," Blake said, pointing towards the back seat of the Range Rover.

The woman dumped the box and smiled at Megan with a nod of recognition, her eyes lingering in the way people do with celebrities, feeling they are entitled to stare.

"Thanks Nia," Richards said, using his go-away tone again.

Nia flushed and looked awkward, not sure which way to turn to leave. Megan gave her a kind, friendly smile and that seemed to make her day. Megan could be good like that.

Blake was first out of the van to check out the refreshments, and for a few minutes there was an atmosphere of almost festive camaraderie as everyone examined the contents of the box and haggled politely over the sandwiches.

About an hour had passed since Anderson's pow-wow with Blake, Beddows and Richards. They'd obviously decided to do nothing for the time being. I presumed the calculation was that hunger, boredom, fear or something would make Will realise there was no point holding-out. I wondered if there was a police textbook on this, a step-by-step guide to sieges.

I also wondered what Megan was thinking: what she thought of Will now; whether she thought he would give up. But it was obvious she didn't want to talk and I left her to pace from screen to screen, while Nigel and I drifted in and out of conversation, making small talk and exchanging uninformed speculation about how the police might handle things, how long their patience would last and whether or not it would make a difference that the only hostage left was a police officer, even if a bent one.

Mimi and I had texted each other a few times. She said the siege was now the 'breaking' story on all the news channels. They were broadcasting live from the end of the road. The chief constable had held a press conference. He'd been questioned about Meg and confirmed she was helping the police.

Mimi had contacted Kelli – introducing herself as my 'colleague', she said. She had wanted to reassure Danny I was alright. And Kelli was friendly and worried and sent her love. For a second, I felt filled-up, moved by the unexpected idea there were people in the outside world looking out for me.

* * *

It was probably nearly six o'clock when it happened, but I don't remember looking at my watch. I must have lost track of time.

Megan's phone rang in the van. It was Will. He wanted to talk to her.

Blake shouted for Megan who was in the Range Rover. I think she must have been asleep. I couldn't see her from where I was, standing next to screen, staring across the entrance to gym.

Megan leapt out of the car, took the width of our compound in two strides and jumped into the van. I winced. It wasn't a routine I'd recommend for an Olympic athlete.

"Will?" she said, speaking before she'd sat down.

Nigel and I had shuffled across and were leaning into the van, listening hard, Richards alongside us. Anderson, Blake and Beddows were sitting with Megan and a new female technician, who had just taken over.

"Megan, I'm in bits," Will said, desperation in his voice.

"Me too," she said. "Let's end this."

It sounded like Will was pacing. "We think he's on his own in the gym," Blake whispered.

Via the probe, Gary could be heard moving around in the office. Beddows frowned at Anderson, as if something was bothering him.

"Sounds like Evans has freed himself," Anderson said.

Through both channels, we heard what sounded like a lock turning and hinges creaking, and then two thuds in quick succession like bodies hitting the floor. There were grunts and groans and more thuds.

And then complete silence.

Evans' voice broke it. "You always were a fucking liability," he said, the menace in his voice so chilling the hairs on my neck reacted instantly.

Beddows was staring hard at Anderson, but the senior man didn't look back at him.

"What are you going to do, boss?" Beddows asked.

Everyone was looking at Anderson now.

"Will!" Megan screamed suddenly. "Get the fuck out of there. Throw the gun away."

But she was answered by the piercing, explosive sound of a shot being fired.

We all recoiled as if hit ourselves.

"Intervene. Go to amber. Amber – shot discharged," Anderson barked, a hand gripping Megan's shoulder firmly.

Beddows had jumped out of the van and was already beyond the screen, standing watching the entrance to the gym. "Can you confirm, sir?" he said through the radio.

"Yes, confirmed," Anderson replied. "Go to amber. Implement the plan. Arrest both targets. We don't know who fired the gun."

"You heard," we could hear Beddows telling his team. "Implement. Go. Yes, go. Both targets."

I had edged towards one of the screens and, pushing up on my toes, I watched four armed officers racing from behind a wall towards the entrance to the gym. One pressed a short, thick shotgun against the door and fired, blowing the lock out. He kicked the door open, and the three other men rushed in past him shouting 'Police! Police!' their voices coming over loudly through the radio in the van, and growing louder as the probe picked them up as well.

"Police, police… Put down your weapon. Now! Put it down… Lie down… On the floor. Lie down."

"Target one injured, sir," one of the officers reported. "Bleeding badly. Severe chest wound."

"Who's that? Is that Will?" Megan asked desperately.

Anderson nodded. "What about target two?" he said, through his mic. "Give me a status on target two?"

"Not injured – under arrest, sir," came the reply.

"Medical attention urgently needed for target one," someone else added.

"On its way," Anderson said, his hand on Megan's shoulder again.

Megan shook herself free. "I want to see Will," she said, starting to get up.

"Miss Tomos," Anderson barked, also rising to his feet. "Sit down! You are not leaving this area until I say so. My officers have a job to do."

"Meg," I said, stepping towards the van, holding a hand out. "Stand with me. They'll have Will out in no time."

Meg looked disorientated like she didn't know me, but she took my hand and stepped down awkwardly from the van like she'd hit a hurdle and couldn't keep her balance. I put an arm around her and held her tight at my side as we watched Beddow jogging towards the entrance, radio in one hand, gun in the other.

As he reached it, an ambulance pulled-up and two paramedics jumped out. Beddows held his arm out, telling them to wait. They checked themselves. He spoke into the radio, then nodded. They rushed into the building, one carrying a bag, the other a stretcher.

Blake and Anderson had left the van too and were pushing the screen blocking our view to one side. They started walking towards the ambulances. Anderson was shouting orders and questions into his lapel as he went.

Richards and Nigel joined Megan and me in a line watching the scene barely forty metres ahead of us. Gary Evans appeared through the entrance first, hands cuffed behind his back, two police officers holding an arm each. He seemed to be trying to appear indignant, outraged at his arrest. He stared at Megan, but she returned his gaze until he looked away. The officers pushed him towards a police car that had pulled-up next to the ambulance.

Anderson went into the building, followed by Blake. Megan pressed closer to me, and Richards gave me a concerned glance. Nigel was tapping messages into his phone.

Behind us, from the van, we could still hear some voices via the probe and the radio. But no one was shouting now and it was difficult to tell what people were saying from where we were. I had an urge to go back there to listen, but Megan seemed calmer and I didn't want to risk her breaking free. So we waited and watched, each second seeming like a minute. The police took Evans away. He threw us a final glare as the car passed. Another police car pulled-up. Finally the paramedics reappeared with Will. He was strapped to their stretcher. They slid him into the ambulance and one of them jumped in with him. The other slammed the rear doors shut and jogged round to the driver's seat. They were gone in seconds, lights flashing, siren blaring.

Megan seemed numbed by it all. I squeezed her to me as the ambulance went by.

Anderson appeared from the gym and started marching towards us.

"Nasty wound, but he should be okay," he said directly to Megan. "Do you want to go to the hospital?"

Megan straightened up, pulling away from me. "Yes," she said, "Yes I would."

"Inspector," Anderson said. "Can you take her?"

It didn't sound like a question and Richards didn't look enthusiastic.

"Of course, sir," he said.

Megan turned to me.

"I'll see you back at the hotel," I said.

Richards smiled at me, and we held each other's look. I sensed we were thinking the same thing: Megan's loyalty to Will defied belief.

23

NIGHT BIRDS

THE CLUES WERE EVERYWHERE. MY watch told me it was 7.50pm. The hotel terrace was packed with people drinking. The sun was casting long shadows. And yet, as I turned the key to the door of my room, it could have been any time, any day. I'd lost track. Eight hours in the surreal bubble of a claustrophobic compound, watching Will's siege unravel, had left me drained and disorientated.

After Megan had gone to the hospital with Richards, I had waited around for Blake, who'd offered to take me back to The Priory. I texted Mimi to tell her I hadn't been in the line of fire, saying I would phone from the hotel. I had watched the police dismantling the paraphernalia of their operation and allowing evacuated residents back into their homes.

I saw them cordon-off the gym, securing it as a crime scene. I witnessed the arrival of a posse in white overalls, carrying their forensic toolkits. I laughed at the sight of the media not really knowing what to do next – whether to stay at the crime scene, chase the ambulance or go to the chief constable's press conference.

Several journalists milled around outside the gym for a while – filming, taking photographs and interviewing local residents. One young reporter, an earnest lad about Megan's age, approached me enthusiastically asking if I'd been affected, wanting a 'vox-pop' from me. I told him I hadn't seen much and suggested he try someone else.

As I entered my hotel room, I felt an overwhelming urge to pack. I started gathering-up my stuff – T-shirts, a tracksuit, underwear, shorts, socks, jeans, trainers – throwing everything onto a bed neatly made while I was out, the normal routine carrying on reassuringly.

I looked at the sorry pile – the wreckage of my week – and felt a sudden sense of euphoria at the prospect of getting out of here. I wanted to bundle everything up and head for the station straight away, but I had promised to go with Megan to see Richards the next morning – Sunday morning, I reminded myself – for what we hoped would be the final interview.

I sat down in the armchair, exactly as I had two days earlier to listen to Megan confess she'd been there when Matt died. That seemed a minor transgression compared to blackmail and hostage-taking, but Richards had made it clear he was still not done with Megan. I doubted he thought Megan was guilty of anything beyond misplaced loyalty and spur-of-the-moment cowardice. I didn't think he seriously believed she'd had a hand – even inadvertently – in Matt's death, or had witnessed a fight or a push that would amount to manslaughter. But he wasn't going to let her off the hook just yet. He was – as he kept saying – doing everything 'by the book', and that meant waiting for the new pathology report. Until then, as long as there was the slightest uncertainty about the cause of death, nothing could be ruled out and Megan would still be 'helping the police with their inquiries'.

The phone started vibrating, and Mimi's name came up on the screen. I smiled and answered.

"Hello, Mimi Jacobs."

"Liam McCarthy. You're alive then?"

"Yes, never in harm's way, but running on empty emotionally."

"I'll see what I can do about that."

"I knew I could depend on you."

We both giggled a little at this point. The relief of normal banter was making me slightly light-headed. The giggling turned, in my case, to laughter – uncontrollable, doubled-up, gasping for breath laughter.

Mimi waited for me to finish.

"Are you okay?" she said.

"Frigging awesome – never better," I said, mimicking her unkindly.

"Fuck off," she said.

I took some deep breaths, trying to calm myself down. Once I thought I could utter some words without laughing again, I started telling her what had happened, filling in the gaps in what she'd seen on TV or been told by the press officer. She knew already about the part Megan played in the freeing the hostages, but she hadn't heard about the probe and she knew nothing about Gary turning the tables on Will.

"Are you saying he meant to shoot him?" Mimi gasped.

"I couldn't really tell from what we were hearing," I said. "There was a struggle, and then Evans says 'You always were a fucking liability'. He didn't know we could hear him. It sounded pretty threatening. Then we heard the shot."

"Oh my God, that sounds intentional to me. But why the fuck would he do that?"

I visualised the two of them in the gym, Gary literally looking down the barrel of a gun for most of the day, and wondered if that would turn you so crazy you might do anything. Or was it more calculating than that? Was it deliberate?

"Who knows? Maybe he was pissed-off he'd been tied up all day?" I said, intending irony but the silence from Mimi suggesting I hadn't pulled it off. "Or maybe he's violent by nature. Or perhaps he actually wants Will dead for some reason?"

"You really think he shot to kill?"

"The bullet hit him in the chest. That doesn't seem like a warning shot to me. But Will could have been rushing him and the gun just went off."

We fell silent.

"Wow," Mimi said finally. "I never thought it would end like this.

"End?"

"Isn't this…? I mean, surely Richards doesn't still think Megan's involved in some way in Matt's death?"

"I've no idea what he thinks, but he wants to see her tomorrow, and there's still the question of the blackmail. As things stands, Meg's a blackmail victim, a manslaughter suspect and a siege hero. Three in one. Not bad, is it?"

Mimi sighed. "So when *are* you coming home?"

The framing of the question took me by surprise. The word 'home' sounded so safe and seductive when she said it – even if she didn't mean it that way.

"The first train I can," I said. "Nothing's going to stop me. Once we've seen Richards, I'll be on my way. Not even a siege would stop me."

"Ha, don't tempt fate," Mimi said. "Danny's desperate to see you. I could bring him to Paddington to meet you."

"Really?" I said, taken aback again. I'd barely got my head round sharing a bed with Mimi, never mind talking like parents. Was this happening too fast? Or was it about time I was dragged from my emotional exile.

"Of course, *really*, you twat!" Mimi said.

I laughed. "Yes, that would be great. Really. Thanks."

We paused for another comfortable silence. I was exhausted, and Mimi seemed to be looking at everything with the fresh perspective that distance brings. I sensed her mind still churning the implications of the day's events.

"So what about the Olympics?" she said. "I can't figure out if this changes things."

"Nor can I," I said, struggling to think straight. "We're still at the mercy of Richards and his pathology report. I don't think he thinks Meg's guilty of anything worse than bad judgement, but that doesn't mean he'll let her off lightly. And then there's Meg herself. The fact she's lost a week's training at this time of year isn't disastrous physically. The work's already in her legs, so she'll be fine if she can get to Bela Horizonte with the others. But I don't know if she's lost the plot mentally. You can't go to an Olympics with your head in a mess."

"Jackie's resigned to it, to her pulling-out I mean," Mimi said. "She's already in damage limitation mode, talking about next year's World Championships, and she thinks the sponsors will love the 'Meg siege hero' thing – that it'll offset their disappointment about the Olympics. She's testing the water with some of them this evening."

It seemed stranger than ever how these commercial calculations – deals worth millions – revolved around a 21-year-old whose life was in turmoil and her ability to get herself to a start line in Brazil for a race that would last just over 12 seconds.

"I wouldn't count on anything after today," I said.

"What do you mean?"

"I really don't know," I said. "Who knows what affect all this will have on Meg? She's not a machine. She seems to be re-evaluating everything. I could even see her giving it all up, and God knows what's going to happen between her and Will."

"Nothing, after today, surely?" Mimi said.

"Well, she's sitting by his bedside now – as we speak."

"It's bonkers. I don't get it… But he has been shot, I suppose. Maybe it's pity?"

"Or she loves him in spite of everything."

Using the word 'love' made me feel unexpectedly awkward. I realised it begged questions about my feelings for Mimi that I had no idea how to answer. I hadn't talked in such intimate terms with anyone for years, and I wanted to say that – to say something about how good it felt – but the words wouldn't come.

"Yep," Mimi said with a laugh, letting me off the hook. "It's amazing what a girl will do for love… I'll see you tomorrow at Paddington."

I looked at the 'Disconnected' message on the screen, and then across at the pile of clothes on the bed. I *really* did want to go home.

* * *

The mindlessness of packing was all I could manage and was such a relief from trying to work out the implications of everything that had happened. I took my time, giving some sort of order to the jumble and trying to fit it all into my bag. It was like everything was in slow motion – so slow that after a while all I could do was lie down, fully clothed, next to my packed bag and drift into sleep.

It was well into the night when Megan woke me. If she'd tried knocking, I hadn't responded, and she was standing over me now, looking down, saying, "Liam, are you okay?"

I jerked into a sitting position, trying to focus on the room and get my bearings, my eyes half-closed to block out the brightness of the lights. I ran my hands through my hair and felt the stubble on my chin.

"I saw the lights were on," Megan said.

Yes, they are on, I thought. That was a mistake. I squinted up at Megan and she sat down on the arm of one of the chairs. I manoeuvred myself into a half-sitting position.

"He's in a bad way," she said. "In intensive care. They operated straight away. Stitched him up and gave him loads of morphine."

I nodded. I didn't think it would be helpful to say, 'I really didn't give a shit right now and please can I go back to sleep'.

"I haven't spoken to him," Megan continued. "I sat with him for a while, but his mother's there now. Oh my God, she's in a state."

His mother? I hadn't really considered the idea of Will having a mother, never mind thought of her rushing to the hospital to sit by his bed.

"So do they think he's going to be okay?" I said, trying to muster a tone of concern for Meg's benefit.

"They think so," she said, sliding off the arm into the chair and, alarmingly, making herself comfortable. "The bullet missed his heart, but they said his lung's damaged."

"Good. I mean, good it wasn't worse," I said. "And what about you?"

Megan looked at me like she didn't know where to begin. What could she say? My boyfriend – if that's what he was – went mad, held innocent hostages at gunpoint and got himself shot. I'm being investigated by the police, a suspect in a possible manslaughter case, and my Olympic ambitions are hanging by a thread.

"I'm holding it together," she said, and looked harder at me like a doctor examining a patient. "But you look a wreck."

"I'm not at my best," I said.

She continued, still studying me intently to a point where I was beginning to squirm.

"Thank you, for everything," she said earnestly.

I smiled, really appreciating the sentiment, if not the timing. I checked my watch. It was just after three-thirty in the morning.

"Thank me when it's over," I said. "We've got another session with Richards in a few hours."

"I know. More questions."

"Especially after today."

"I know, can you believe it?" she said, shaking her head. "I don't know what came over him. Gary must have been putting so much pressure on him…"

I was too tired to start trying to analyse everything again. And most of what I wanted to say about Will would not have gone down very well.

"I've got to go home tomorrow, after we've seen Richards," I said. "I've promised Danny. But I can come back if you need me, and we'll have to have a talk with Jackie about everything – about how this affects Rio. The team leaves on Thursday."

Megan waved a hand dismissively as if the Olympics was the last thing on her mind. "I still can't think straight about that, Li. It's too much, and I can't see myself going anywhere until I know Will's okay."

I cringed inwardly at that but decided that pushing Meg would be counter-productive. "Let's see what tomorrow brings," I said.

"Well, it'll bring my parents for a start," she said. "They're coming down from Cardigan tomorrow. You wouldn't believe what a fuss they're making about all this."

I raised my eyebrows, thinking of saying, 'I wouldn't believe it if they hadn't' but my attention was caught by the sound of a solitary bird singing, anticipating the dawn; repeating two notes over and over again. I'd heard the same birdsong at about the same time all through the week. I'd even become quite fond of it, but I was desperate now for a night without it.

"You realise we're seeing Richards in a few hours?" I reminded her. "Best get some sleep."

"Better had," she said, springing to her feet with extraordinary plyometric bounce. The words of Poetry In Motion came to me again, and I thought what a shame it would be if the Olympics was deprived of her.

24

DEVILS AND DETAILS

I ARRANGED FOR US TO have breakfast in my room. We had managed to avoid the media all week, and I wasn't going to take any chances now.

Megan had been for a workout, much to my surprise, of strides and sprints on the rugby field and wanted her training rations of porridge and fruit. I had the full Welsh – to hell with it, I would worry about my emerging paunch another day.

Breakfast came with a set of Sunday papers, compliments of the owner, who was now a fellow conspirator, actively helping us keep our heads down and shrewd enough to know he'd have a great story to tell or sell later.

The headlines made gratifying reading. It was as if Megan

was another person, re-invented overnight. 'Megan leaps to the rescue' one paper said. Another called her 'the gun siege heroine'. The chief constable said she was "calm and courageous" and played on the sporting connection in describing her as "a winner in a winning team". The freed hostages were even quoted saying they owed their lives to Meg. In one paper, the woman who had been released said she had overheard her on the phone begging Will to release them. They headlined it with an almost Biblical: 'For God's sake, let those people go'.

My involvement in the drama was mentioned by most of them, if only in passing. The chief constable said I had exercised "the calming influence of an experienced coach". And a few papers carried photographs of me peering over the screens, like I was the command centre's lookout.

* * *

Almost every report skated over the background to the siege, missing out the bits that didn't fit their new 'Meg hero' angle. Only a few mentioned that Meg herself was still under investigation in a suspicious death. In some papers, it was almost as if she happened to be passing and stepped in like Wonder Woman to help the police because, by chance, she knew the man who'd gone mad.

Their lurch from villain to heroin was laughable really, but we weren't going to let that spoil our fun. We read the best extracts out to each other. We texted Mimi and Jackie and I took a photograph of a paper that had a picture of me and emailed it to Danny.

"What are you doing?" Meg said.

"Sending it to Danny," I said as if that was obvious.

"Danny, your son?" she said, leaving her mouth open in exaggerated surprise. "So how come I've never seen him?"

The question hit my sore spot, reminding me how much catching up I had to do. "I think you'll see a lot more of him from now on," I replied, but Meg's mind seemed to have moved on. Her eyes were fixed on a piece in one of the sports sections. All I could make out, reading upside down, was the headline saying: *Make up your mind Meg.*

"What's that?" I asked.

Meg silently passed the paper across with a grim look, her lips pursed like she was keeping herself in check. When I read the first sentence I realised why:

> *The uncertainty surrounding the Olympic intentions of Britain's golden girl Megan Tomos are causing growing concern within athletics, with some respected voices saying she is unfairly occupying a place that could go to someone else.*

I looked up at Meg and every trace of sparkle had gone. She'd had only a few hours' sleep and a brutal few days, and it showed now – there was nothing to laugh about.

"Read the rest," she said. "It doesn't get any better."

> *After missing a crucial Diamond League race on Friday against her main Olympic rivals, the 100m hurdler was embroiled yesterday in a bizarre gun siege in Newport involving her former boyfriend Will Driscoll.*

> *Police say Tomos helped them negotiate the release of the hostages held at a local gym by Driscoll, who was banned from rugby for using steroids, but the drama*

has prompted calls from within athletics for Tomos to come clean about her Olympic plans.

With only four days to go before the athletics team leaves for the Olympic holding camp at Belo Horizonte, leading coach Greg Bannister insists she should "make up her mind immediately".

"This is an event in which Britain has an abundance of riches," he said. "We have five athletes with the Olympic qualifying standard, and Meg's sitting on one of only three places. If she pulls out at the last minute, it will be too late for the athlete who replaces her to prepare themselves."

"It had to be Greg, didn't it?" I said. "He's been dying to put the boot into me since I said I couldn't coach his niece. You can't take this seriously, Meg – everyone knows what he's like."

"In athletics maybe," Meg said, "but not *everyone*. It makes me look selfish and irresponsible. Look. Read the next bit."

A fellow athlete who didn't want to be named, added: "It's unfair on the girls who've got the qualifying standard but weren't selected. They don't know where they stand. Meg's messing everyone around."

A spokesperson for UK Athletics said: "We understand the concerns and are trying to contact Megan".

"Great! Nice to see them leaping to our defence," I said with irony. "But there is a simple answer…"

"Yep, fuck 'em!" Meg said, not letting me finish. "Stuff Rio. I'm going to pull out. I'm sick of the whole sodding thing."

"That's not what I meant."

"I know, but it's not you who's in the middle of all this. I can't win. If I go to Rio with Will in intensive care and the Matt investigation still going on, everyone will say I'm selfish and heartless. It'll be, 'Look at her – she left Matt for dead and now she's leaving Will on life support'. Great. That's just the mental prep you need for an Olympics. And then I'll blow it anyway – and they'll say I should have let someone else go. I'm telling you, Li, it's a lost cause, and we both know it."

"But it's only one piece in one newspaper," I said, mainly to Megan's back as she headed for the door, slamming it as she went.

I sat and stared at her empty chair for a few moments and then stood, collected up the newspapers that were scattered everywhere and dropped them in the bin.

* * *

Megan had donned her baseball cap and dark glasses again to go to the police station. As a disguise, it didn't make much sense when she was driving the flashiest car for miles, but at least it hid the sullen look that was tempting me to give her a mouthful about my feelings on the subject of going to Rio.

It wasn't that I didn't have sympathy with her saying she would pull-out – the Olympics isn't something you can tackle when in emotional turmoil – but I thought the decision warranted a bit more input from me.

We arrived early. I'd promised Mimi I would aim for the London train at just after one o'clock, and I was hoping Richards would already be there and we could start right away. He wasn't, and we were shown into the usual interview room to wait.

As we sat down, Meg had a text from Will's mother saying he hadn't woken yet but the doctors were saying his condition was 'stable'. She became even more sullen when that came through, staring at her phone like it was somehow plugged into Will's pulse.

"Are you going to try to see him today?" I said, attempting to empathise.

Megan shrugged. "The trouble is, I don't really get on with his mother. Another one who blames me for everything."

"But she texted you," I said.

"Yep, but only because she's seen the papers and thinks she'll be a celebrity too. Sad cow. She doesn't actually give a shit about Will. That's why he left home as soon as he had the chance."

Richards arrived at ten o'clock, prompt as ever, with Simmons in tow. Both had the careworn look of people for whom this wasn't the first meeting of the day and wouldn't be the last. Simmons had about half a dozen files under his arm this time, and he nearly spilled them all onto the floor as he manoeuvred into his seat.

"I have to tell you it's been a bit hectic," Richards said, nodding at the files. "You could say we've had a busy night."

He looked across at Simmons, evidently self-satisfied but making a point of sharing the moment in a fatherly way with his young colleague.

"Well, here we are again then," he continued. "Let's hope we don't have any more interruptions. Where's Mr Winters?"

"On his way, I expect," I said.

"Have you both had a chance to recover from yesterday's nonsense?"

"Megan spent most of the night at the hospital," I replied,

sensing Megan next to me tightening with irritation at his slightly patronising tone.

"Yes – how is Will?" Richards said.

"I'm sure you're more up to date than me," Megan said, "but he's stable, last I heard from his Mum."

"Good, yes – you're right," Richards said. "I have had a very recent report, and my understanding is he's awake and they're happy with his progress. We're hoping to interview him later today."

I was conscious we hadn't been through the ritual of the recorder and was about to point this out when a flustered Nigel barged in apologising for his lateness and saying he hoped we hadn't started.

Megan and I shuffled our chairs along to allow him to pull-up one for himself on our side of the table. He sat down and put this hands together on the table as if saying 'I've arrived so get on with it'.

Richards nodded to Simmons to press the record button and ran through the date, time and location and then asked all of us to state our names again.

"Well, now we're all here, let me start by bringing you up to date," Richards said. "We've charged the owner of the gym, a Mr Michael Samuels, with trafficking illegal drugs. Do you know him?"

Megan shook her head.

"He owns a garage in Cwmbran and a couple of other businesses: a respectable pillar of the community by some accounts. Of course, 'innocent until proven guilty' as they say, but there were enough syringes in that gym to supply the Royal Gwent for a month. Samuels is in custody and will go before a magistrate in the morning."

"That's very interesting, inspector," Nigel said, "but what exactly has it got to do with my client?"

Richards looked at Nigel for a minute as if he was deciding whether to jump down his throat or to treat him like a child who was slow on the uptake. He went for the latter.

"Nothing at all, Mr Winters, in terms of the Matt Davies case, nothing whatsoever," Richards said, wearily, "but I thought as Miss Tomos had kindly been so helpful yesterday, she'd be interested to know how our enquiries had gone since."

Megan nodded but in an abrupt 'cut-to-the-chase' way.

"So turning to the question of Sergeant Evans," Richards said, "he's been suspended of course. But we've also charged him with possession with intent to supply a Class C drug – anabolic steroids."

"Yeees!" Megan said, giving a half-punch in the air, and looking as if she wanted to start dancing round the room.

Richards allowed Megan her moment, but he was smiling smugly, exuding a sense that there was more to come.

"That's for starters," he said. "We have enough evidence from searching his house to cover that charge and keep him in custody, but as regards the more serious matter of the shooting, we can't do much until we've interviewed Will and had reports from the pathologist and the ballistics people. We need to know how far that bullet travelled. At the moment Evans is saying the gun went off accidentally when they were struggling, but we'll see if that stacks-up when we get the reports. This is all confidential in the meantime of course. You understand?"

"Of course," Nigel said, sounding contrite after his earlier surliness. "We appreciate your candour."

Richards knotted his brow and gave a sombre nod. I suspected what Nigel did or didn't appreciate meant nothing to him.

"Which brings us to the matter of Mr Driscoll himself," he said, turning to Simmons. "Megan, we appreciate you're worried and upset about Will, and of course we all hope he makes a full recovery, but we can't allow the fact he's been injured – serious though his condition is – to stand in the way of our enquiries." He turned to Nigel, repeating his stern look. "And, yes, Mr Winters, for the record, this is relevant and necessary. Despite what happened yesterday, much as we appreciate the help Miss Tomos gave us, we still have to get to the bottom of what happened the night Matt Davies died, and we still need to clarify some matters concerning the relationship between Megan and Will Driscoll."

Nigel seemed about to interrupt, but Richards held up a hand. "DC Simmons," he said, "you have a few questions for Megan."

Simmons cleared his throat and started rifling through the files in front of him until he found the one he wanted and took out a sheet of paper. He looked nervous at finding himself in the spotlight.

"Right, Miss Tomos," he began tentatively, glancing first at Megan and then studying the notes on the paper, which – from my angle – looked like a minute by minute countdown to Matt being declared dead. "Let's start with Matt, on the night in question."

Megan wriggled, her euphoria over Gary being charged completely deflated now.

"You said on Friday that you thought Matt arrived at Will's flat between two- and two-thirty in the morning."

Megan nodded.

"We know that a 999 call from Driscoll was logged at 4.10am and that the ambulance arrived at 4.34am. You also said Matt collapsed about half an hour after he'd arrived."

"If that," Megan interrupted.

"Thank you," Simmons said, writing a note at the bottom of the sheet and then looking up earnestly at Megan. "And you left immediately afterwards, thinking Matt was dead?"

"Yes," Megan whispered, sounding embarrassed at having to confirm her callous desertion of Matt yet again.

"You told us on Friday about Matt arriving and the state he was in," Simmons said, business-like, no hint of sentiment, only occasionally looking up from the timeline in front of him. "And you said Will gave him a glass of water. You're sure it was water?"

Megan nodded.

"Could you confirm please: you're certain it was water?"

Megan recoiled slightly and frowned in my direction. "Not certain…" she said, turning back to Simmons. "I suppose I assumed it was water."

"But you can't remember seeing Driscoll pour the drink?" Simmons said.

"No – well, I suppose he would have had his back to me, facing the sink, when he was pouring it."

"But were other drinks there, on the counter?"

Megan took a moment, squinting slightly as if trying to remember.

"Yes, there were a few bottles left from the party – vodka and stuff."

"So the drink Will offered Matt could have been something else – vodka, for all you knew?" Simmons said, allowing himself a self-satisfied smile.

"It could, but why… why would…?"

"I don't know," interrupted Simmons. "I want to be clear that's all – about what you actually remember or know, not what you *think* happened."

Megan looked down at her hands, fingers splayed out flat on the table. It looked like she might be counting them, just to be sure.

Simmons jotted something else on his timeline.

"Okay, don't worry. I'm not going to go over everything you told us on Friday again, but there's one part of it I need to clarify: you said Matt grabbed his chest – and 'suddenly crumpled' were the words you used. You said that you reached out to try to stop him falling, but you couldn't. Now, let's leave aside how badly he bumped his head on the way down: I want to concentrate on what happened once he'd collapsed. There he was, laid out on the floor. Tell us exactly what happened next."

Megan was rigid next to me. Her back was straight. Her hands were still laid flat on the table. She was staring at Simmons but seemed to be looking through him.

"What happened next?" she repeated. "What happened was…" Megan clenched her hands and closed her eyes… "I stepped towards him. I remember that, and I remember his face – his face had no colour. And I remember the vomit. He was on his side, and Will knelt down and tried to lift him up. But Matt was writhing around, and Will couldn't…"

"So he was still moving at that point?" Simmons persisted.

Megan shook her head. "I think he'd stopped. Will let him drop so he could take his pulse."

Simmons pulled another piece of paper from the file and scanned it until his eyes settled about halfway down the hand written notes.

"You have a clear memory of Will taking his pulse?" he said.

Nigel and I both turned towards Megan at the same to time, from either side of her, our eyes meeting. I had no idea what Nigel was thinking, but my sympathies at this point were with Simmons. His precision was as exacting as I tried to be when dissecting one of Megan's races, only this was a matter of life and death.

Simmons waited, his eyes fixed on Megan who was

motionless, looking down at the file.

"No," she said finally. "To be honest, I don't actually. It's a blur. I think I was about to bend down and do it myself, and then Will suddenly stood up. He nearly knocked me over. He said, 'He's dead… you've got to get out of here.' But…"

"But what, Megan?" Simmons said.

Megan's eyes danced from Simmons to Richards and then, half-turning her torso, settled on me. "But I don't actually remember seeing Will take his pulse," she said, as if confiding in me. "I remember wanting to touch him, to see for myself how he was, but I didn't. Will said I should go. And I did. I panicked."

"So you can't be absolutely sure he was dead?" Richards interjected, sounding harsh and judgemental.

"No. No, I can't," Megan said, "but why would Will say he was if he wasn't?"

Simmons shrugged. I thought I detected a smirk forming, but he turned serious and started rifling through his file for another piece of paper, this time retrieving a photocopy of a form headed with the name of a taxi company.

"You left and went home by taxi?" Simmons said.

Megan nodded.

"You got a taxi from town?" Simmons said, his eyes directing Megan to the recorder.

"Yes," she said.

"The taxi records appear to confirm the timings you gave us," Simmons said. "There's a record of a taxi going from the rank at the railway station to your parents' address, just after three. We've spoken to the driver, and the description he gives suggests it was you."

"Inspector," Nigel said. "My client had a difficult day yesterday, to say the least. Where's all this leading?"

Simmons turned to Richards as if asking for permission to

continue. "Mr Winters," he said, taking the inspector's silence as his cue. "We want to confirm – for the record – that, firstly, Miss Tomos can't be sure Matt was dead when she left – she only has Driscoll's word for it – and secondly, assuming it took Megan ten minutes to reach the taxi rank, and that's admittedly less than we'd allow for a person of average fitness," Simmons smiled as if to emphasise he was trying to pay Megan a compliment, "there was more than an hour between Megan leaving the flat and Driscoll calling for help."

"I don't believe it – that can't be right!" Megan said.

Richards raised his eyebrows. Involuntarily, and with my usual insensitivity, I looked at my watch. It was nearly eleven. With the magnitude of Simmons's statement hanging in the air, I began to wonder how much else was in those files and whether or not I would make the train I'd promised Mimi I'd catch at one o'clock.

Megan and Nigel both seemed about to say something to break the silence, but Simmons was already plucking more papers from his file, eager to move on.

"I'd like you to cast your mind back over the last couple of years," he said, "and tell me how many times you've given Will Driscoll money, and what the reasons were? If you would."

Megan flinched and straightened her back again. Her breathing was level and calm, but she was as taut as she'd be at the start of a race. I sensed, beyond her, that Nigel was having a mini-panic and about to intervene again.

Megan beat him to it. "What the fuck has that got to do with anything?" she said, looking antagonistically at Simmons across the table.

"We're not sure yet, Miss Tomos," Richards said firmly before Simmons could reply, "but may I remind you, you're still under caution. As I said earlier, your help yesterday was greatly appreciated, but it doesn't give you any special privileges. We still have a job to do, and part of it is to deal with your allegation that Evans was blackmailing you."

"So why don't you ask Evans about it?" Megan said.

"Because there are things we want to clarify with you first," Simmons replied, assertively, encouraged now by his boss's tone.

"Is there anything you want to discuss with me before continuing?" Nigel said to Megan, his concern obviously growing at the possibility of yet another Megan surprise. "I'm sure the inspector will allow us a break."

"No, it's okay. I can answer the question, but I can't see why it matters."

Simmons leaned forward, and picked-up the pile of papers he'd taken from the file. They looked like bank statements.

"We found these in Mr Driscoll's flat yesterday," he said. "We had a search warrant of course. As far as I can tell, you transferred money to Driscoll on at least eight separate occasions over an eighteen-month period. Does that sound about right?"

Megan shrugged. "Yes, at least that," she admitted.

Nigel's face was in his hands. Part of me was seething at the way Megan had, for some reason or another, continued to hide aspects of her relationship with Will. But I also felt relief that we seemed to be nearing the end of the journey Simmons and Richards were taking us on, step by meticulous step, towards the truth. I thought the least I could do was make an effort to stay calm.

"You paid him," Simmons continued, "amounts ranging from £250 to the two payments of £10,000 you mentioned yesterday? A total of £25,650?"

Megan nodded.

"Could you confirm that verbally please?"

"Yes," she said sounding truculent now.

"And why *was* that?" Simmons queried.

Megan sighed, but I felt like telling her: 'He's got a bloody point!'

"You're mixing-up different things," she said. "I gave Will money a few times to help him out. He was always skint. The jobs he had didn't pay very well, and his mother never had enough money to help him. So he asked me."

She turned in my direction, as if feeling a need to justify herself to me.

"He couldn't have afforded that flat without the money I gave him, and I didn't mind. I didn't mind at all. I wanted to help him. I had plenty – more than I could spend on myself."

"He seems to have come to you more and more often, asking for bigger and bigger amounts," Simmons said.

"I didn't really notice," Megan replied. "But what does it matter? I suddenly had all this money: it was like I'd won the lottery, so why not help him? He needed money to buy stuff, furnish the flat, whatever – I can't remember the details – but some of it was supposed to be a loan. He was going to pay me back."

"So he told you he was broke?"

"Yes, completely skint," Megan said, like it was a stupid question. "He had a debt on his credit card – I had to help him pay it off."

"Yes, well – we found some of Will's credit card statements too," Simmons said, pulling them out of the same file. "They don't cover the whole of that period, but there's no sign of any ongoing debt. He was running up big bills and paying them off every month."

Megan picked up one of the statements, holding it with just a thumb and forefinger like it was contaminated. It was clear – even from my angle – that Will enjoyed spending money. The list of entries filled the page, but he had also paid-off the full amount from the previous month.

Megan tossed the statement down on the table. Simmons retrieved it and placed it neatly on top of the credit card pile.

"Megan," Simmons said, a hand on each pile. "What these show is someone with plenty of cash. His account had balances in the thousands, and a high turnover, not just the transfer from your account and his own pay going in, but also other cash he was depositing. He was never short of money."

"No, no – I'm telling you, you've got this wrong. That's not what he told me," Megan said, brittle anger in her voice.

But I was finding it harder to tell where the anger was directed. She sounded desperate, still clinging to her faith in Will – hoping he hadn't been a shameless sponger as well as everything else – yet unable to square her loyalty with the evidence being laid, literally, before her.

"Okay," Simmons continued. "Let's turn specifically to the blackmail money. Tell us what happened?"

Megan fidgeted in her chair and rested her forearms on the table. She looked at the recorder and seemed to be composing herself, realising her every word would be examined forensically.

"Will phoned me," she said. "I think it was a few weeks after the Worlds last year, and about a day or so after I'd come back from Brussels. I'd run in the Diamond League final, so it must have been the middle of September. He was angry... He said Gary had found out about the blood sample and told Will he could make trouble. He said it would give them – you – a reason to reopen the investigation."

"That was the first time," Simmons said, "and then the second time was about six weeks ago, yes?"

Megan nodded.

"Yes – by then I was going mental. I didn't know what to do. I was so ashamed of what I'd done – of being exposed as completely heartless – but I was thinking, 'I can't go on keeping this to myself'. But then Will said if they tested the blood and found it was Matt's, it would look like there'd been a fight and he could be done for manslaughter and me for running away and lying about it. Will said I'd be charged with perverting the course of justice."

Megan paused and took a long, deep breath.

"So that's why didn't you come to us?" Richards asked. "But if you'd admitted you were there, you would have been able to tell us there wasn't a fight – if there wasn't."

"I know, but I was scared. I wasn't thinking straight. I suppose I was worried no one would believe me after I'd lied in the first place." Megan looked down at her hands, now clasped together. "And I kept thinking about Graeme and what he would think of me – how disappointed he'd be. I wanted to see him to apologise but, and I know it's pathetic, to be honest I couldn't face the shame of it."

Megan lifted a hand and wiped the tears forming in each eye with the tip of her forefinger. She was calm and seemed relieved now to finally be telling the whole story. I put an arm round her shoulder.

"And you didn't doubt what Will was saying at all?" Simmons asked. "You believed him when he said Gary was threatening to expose you?"

Megan looked at Simmons like it was a silly question.

"Of course I did," she said. "Why would Will lie to me about a thing like that?"

"You didn't think he might be setting you up?" Richards said.

Megan jerked her head back and shook it firmly.

"Miss Tomos has confirmed she didn't think Will had set her up."

"Why would he? What do you mean?" Megan said,

looking horrified. I squeezed her shoulder and she turned and smiled at me appreciatively.

"And you didn't hear directly from Gary? No phone calls from him?" Simmons said.

"No, no way," Megan said. "I wouldn't speak to that shit anyway."

"Megan, I think you should look closely at these," Simmons said softly, pushing the pile of bank statements across the table. "Especially the one on the top for last September."

Megan picked up the top sheet from the pile with the same wariness and suspicion she'd shown with the credit card statement. But this time she put it down on the table in front of her and went through it line by line, her forefinger running down the date column and then across to the description of each transaction, the amount withdrawn or paid in, and the balance.

My eyes followed her finger down and across the page. The statement had bigger numbers on it than any I'd ever seen for my own account. The balance was rarely less than five figures.

Megan stopped at the entry with her name on it, about halfway down. The £10,000 was shown as paid in on 16th September, taking the balance to £21,463. She carried on down the page until she reached an entry on 23rd September saying Online Transaction G Evans. The sum transferred was £5,000. Megan stopped and looked at me and then across at Simmons.

"Five - thousand - pounds..." she said, each word pronounced distinctly, horror in her voice. "Only five thousand? Oh my God."

Simmons nodded. "We've been through the subsequent months," Simmons said, "and we can't see another transfer for that amount. There are two other transfers to Evans, but they are for smaller amounts and add up to a lot less than five thousand. Until six weeks ago, that is, when you paid Driscoll the second ten thousand pounds and he transferred five thousand straight to Evans."

Simmons pulled another statement from the pile and slid it in front of Megan, pointing to the entry.

"They were in it together," she said, like she was talking to herself, needing to say it out loud for her own benefit.

"It certainly looks like it," Richards said.

Megan was shaking her head, sprinkling tears on the table.

"But we need to do some more work before we charge them," Simmons continued. "We're obtaining a court order for Evans's bank information, and we'll have to interview both of them and speak to the Crown Prosecution Service. We will also need a full statement from you, of course, before we charge them. Mr Winters will explain the procedure and help with that, I'm sure."

Nigel nodded, looking chastened by the gravity of Simmons' revelations.

Megan stared blankly past Richards and Simmons. Her cheeks were wet. A tear was hanging from her chin, ready to fall. She had a tissue in her hand but didn't seem to have the energy to use it. I squeezed her shoulder again.

"I can't believe it," she said, sounding empty and exhausted. "The bastard."

25

NEGOTIATING THE MINEFIELD

"WHAT A STUPID BITCH," MEGAN said, standing up and pacing along the other side of the table in the interview room.

We were on our own. Nigel had disappeared with Richards and Simmons to talk 'procedure'.

"I can't believe it," Megan continued, turning and striding back, not looking at me. "He's been using me. All this fucking time – and I fell for it."

Countless possible comments came to mind, but I took it she wasn't asking for my opinion. I let her vent. My questions could wait. I wasn't even sure they were that important now.

"I've only seen Will a couple of times since I moved to London," Megan said, second-guessing one of my thoughts; still pacing, talking like she was playing it back in her head. "He phoned me occasionally, and we texted, but after my parents moved, I hardly ever came back to Newport. I didn't want to, couldn't face it, after what had happened."

Megan sat down opposite me, her eyes locked into my face but not really seeing it, still seeing the playback.

"All I could think about was, 'What if people found out?' Oh my God, I'm telling you, the thought of people finding out... I was terrified. And Will was making out he was on my side: 'No one will ever know – trust me.' That's what he used to say, Liam, 'Trust me'. Bastard."

Megan stood up, starting to pace again, her back to me. "And I actually felt grateful. Un-fucking believable. Can you believe that? I was grateful and I was still fond of him – and all the time, the bastard was using me like a cash machine, making out he was my friend when he was up to his neck in this shit with Gary."

She turned to me, shaking her head. "I'll tell you what, Liam – the longer it went on and the more successful I became, the more *scared* I was. And he knew it. He knew I was panic-stricken about, you know, being *exposed* for doing something so..."

Megan stopped and sat down opposite me, elbows on the table, her lips quivering, the words coming out through gritted teeth, "...for being such a heartless bitch," she said, almost in a whisper, talking more to herself than me. "Running away like that, like all I cared about was myself and my fucking career and enjoying the glory and the celebrity. But actually, I was scared shitless the truth would come out. And I was angry with Matt. Angry? How bizarre is that? Everything got so twisted... And all the time I couldn't bring myself to face Graeme. I didn't even have the guts to do that."

I reached out across the table and put a hand on Megan's forearm.

"You have now though," I said.

We sat there for a moment, Megan sobbing quietly, and me way beyond anger, thinking how much I wanted to see Mimi and Danny and how tired I was of police stations and hotels and Newport and the clothes I'd been wearing since the trials.

Nigel walked in.

"Right," he said, jauntily, rubbing his hands – and it struck me how much he must be enjoying this high-profile case, paid on the clock at God-knows-what hourly rate.

He stopped when he saw the state Megan was in, hunched at the table, shielding her eyes with one hand and producing a tissue from her track suit pocket with the other. He walked to the far end of the table, sat down with his hands clasped together, looking priest-like, and waited for Megan to compose herself.

"We've had an 'off-the-record' chat – me and Inspector Richards," he said slowly and calmly. "I'm clearer now about the lie of the land, and you'll be pleased to hear our friend Driscoll is dead meat. No surprises there, with the siege and the blackmail and the steroid ring, but they don't think they can nail him for Matt's death. The vodka thing is only a theory and the delay in calling the ambulance isn't enough. They don't really have any hard evidence, especially if the pathology report comes back saying Matt only had a minor bump on his head, and it wasn't the cause of death – and that's what they're expecting. But Matt's death was certainly convenient for Will – and Gary – because he'd become a loose cannon. They'd used him for some low-level dealing – around schoolmates, that sort of thing – but his drink problem, and his dabbling in coke and meth, along with the steroids, made him a liability. So the thinking is that Will was quick-witted enough to see his chance to get rid of Matt by – put it this way – not busting-a-gut to save him. But whether or not, at that time, he also realised it would give him leverage over you – sending you off like that – well, that's another matter. We'll probably never know."

Megan was no longer a heap on the table. She'd pulled herself upright and was listening intently to Nigel. I sensed a steely resolve coming over her.

"But it didn't take them long to work it out, to spot an opportunity, did it?" she said.

"No, not at all. You were off in London. Will didn't have to put a show on for you, or worry about you finding out about his extra-curricular activities. And when you started doing well, they saw their chance to put the squeeze on you."

"So why did Gary and Will fall out?" I asked.

Nigel looked at me as if he thought that was fairly obvious. "Thieves do, I suppose, when the pressure builds-up," he said. "We've probably got Matt's mother to thank, mainly. When she started kicking-up about the first police inquiry not being thorough, they put Richards on the case and he went through the file again and found they'd overlooked things, not least the blood sample. The original investigation was sloppy; they'd just assumed it was a typical misadventure. But Mr Meticulous left no stone unturned and Will and Gary realised they were in trouble."

Megan was switched on now. You could sense her churning everything over, starting to look at things from every angle, the fog of her loyalty to Will having finally cleared.

"So why the tweet?" she said. "You know, Will's tweet just before the trials."

Nigel looked bemused. "That was before my time," he said.

"It was odd, when you think about it now," Megan said. "He mentioned my name. He was replying to other tweets, accusing him of all sorts, but he didn't need to say, 'Don't bring Megan into it'. By saying that, it was him who was dragging me in."

"It worked then," I said.

Nigel had pulled out a tablet and was busy tapping and stroking it to find the tweet. "I see what you mean," he said. "Yes, I reckon that was desperation on his part. He had to drag you in because you admitting to being there gave him a witness. He was banking on you to help him wriggle out of the manslaughter accusation. But then it all unravelled with Gary, and it was every man for himself."

Megan was nodding to herself. " I owe Julie an apology," she said.

"Hold on. all in good time," Nigel said. "Julie's probably still gunning for you, and you're not completely out of the woods with the police enquiry. Technically, you're under caution until the pathology report eliminates the possibility of Matt being pushed. They made it fairly obvious to me that they believe you on that point, but that's not official yet…"

"Yes, yes, I get it," Megan said, sounding impatient and frustrated.

"Well, not entirely you don't," Nigel replied. "This is not only about you and Matt's death now. The arrest of Driscoll and Evans, and all that's come to light about their activities has widened this into a major drugs enquiry. Richards wouldn't give too much away, but put it this way, I wouldn't be at all surprised if there are raids and arrests all over the place in the next few days. This steroids network stretches far and wide – there's millions changing hands. Driscoll and Evans are small fry."

* * *

Megan was still deep in thought as she drove me the short distance to the railway station. I didn't try to talk. There was so much to take in. Over breakfast she'd been worrying about Will lying in a hospital bed. Now she wanted him behind bars as soon as possible. Only a few hours ago, Julie Davies had seemed a troublemaker. Now she was on Megan's apology list. And what started as a few steroid pills being dished out at a gym was beginning to look like a national epidemic.

As we pulled up in a large, almost empty car park behind the station, Megan took a call on her mobile.

"Hello. I'm okay… Where are you? I'm dropping Liam off… At the railway station. I'll be there soon… Wait, I'm doing it… See you in a minute… Bye."

Megan flicked the phone off.

"My mother," she explained. "My parents are at Graeme's. He's done the shopping and I'm cooking lunch."

Megan seemed to radiate pleasure at the prospect of a simple family event.

"So, what about the Olympics?" she said after a moment.

I waited for her to answer her own question. No one – not even the best coach on the planet – can tell an athlete whether or not they're in the right shape, physically and mentally, for the ultimate test.

"I've got to pull-out," she said. "We don't know when I'll be off the hook with Richards. And Bannister was right – it isn't fair on the others with the qualifying standard to keep them waiting until the last minute. I've got enough to be ashamed of without acting like a prima donna. Li, I want to do the right thing."

I couldn't contest her logic. With the plane leaving on Thursday, it was beginning to look bad that she was still embroiled in this mess and not able to say unequivocally that she would be at the airport – and I worried if she could mentally get herself back to the sharp focus needed to reach – never mind win – an Olympic final.

"Meg, I'll support you whatever you decide," I said, not as a cop-out but because I really believed that if there was one thing she had to learn from all this it was not to rely entirely on the judgement of others – to trust herself.

"I want to get back in control, to bow-out gracefully," she said. "I'm only 21 – there's the Worlds next year and at least two more Olympics before I'm over the hill."

She looked at me, but I think it was more to say, 'I mean it', than to seek my approval.

I smiled.

"Okay," I said. "I'll talk to Jackie and we'll work out how to handle it."

I felt there was a finality about it now. We had been dancing around the issue for days. I'd had time to adjust to the idea of my own vicarious Olympic dream going down the pan. It didn't at this point seem so earth-shattering – not in the great scheme of things.

I looked at my watch. Twenty minutes until my train. Megan didn't seem in any hurry. We sat there in silence for a couple of minutes, and my mind drifted to Rio and what it might have been like. I imagined Megan on the start line, favourite to win, composed, toned, focused, ready to execute everything we'd been working on for two years.

Megan was watching me, perhaps guessing my thoughts, possibly sharing them. She looked exhausted, grey around the eyes, her complexion drawn and mottled, but she was wearing that charming smile, her eyes sparkling.

"It would have been great," she said.

"It would," I said, squeezing her hand and pushing the door open with my shoulder. "But there'll be other great days – you know where to find me."

* * *

The train crawled to London, struggling to get going after each stop like it had a Sunday hangover. It was nothing compared to mine, though. I'd hardly touched alcohol all week, but I felt like I needed to sleep off the worst binge of my life.

My carriage was – mercifully – nearly empty; a smattering of people and no one showing a flicker of interest in me, oblivious to my face being in most of the newspapers lying around.

Mimi phoned to check I'd made the train, and I tried – in a hushed and coded way – to tell her the revelations of the morning. Losing the signal every other sentence meant my version probably didn't match the forensic clarity of Simmons and Richards, but she got the general idea of it judging by the intakes of breath as I peeled away the layers of duplicity and betrayal.

"Wow. How's Megan?" she asked.

"Beating herself up mostly," I whispered, conscious the carriage seemed to have gone very quiet. "And she's decided not to go."

"Rio? Definitely? You're kidding."

"That report this morning clinched it – the Bannister one. Tell Jackie we need a meeting."

* * *

The train drew painfully slowly into Paddington, metal screeching against metal, my head angled through the half-opened door window, one arm dangling on the outside, hand ready to open the door.

I spotted Danny at the far end of the empty platform, running in my direction. I clocked the good knee lift and arm action before seeing Mimi, some distance behind, struggling to catch up, handicapped by a slim-fitting cotton dress and sandals she kept losing.

I wrestled the door open and stepped onto the platform just as Danny reached me. We collided into the warmest hug I'd ever had from him. Over Danny's shoulder, my eyes met Mimi's as she arrived breathlessly, laughing at herself.

"Dad – are you alright?" he gasped.

"I'm fine," I said, standing back. "Not a wound on my body."

"But it must have been scary," he said, sounding like he wanted me to big-up the hero thing.

"I'll tell you everything when we get home," I said, buying time, thinking I might need some advice from my personal PR consultant on the risks of exaggerated tales being spread across Sussex by my newfound fan.

Keeping one arm round Danny's shoulder, I leaned forward to kiss Mimi, intending only a peck on the cheek – conscious we hadn't kissed with anyone else around before – but Mimi put a hand to my chin and directed my lips to hers and then nestled her head into my shoulder like she was as relieved to see me in one piece as Danny.

"Is she your girlfriend?" Danny asked.

We both laughed, though mine was more of an

embarrassed chuckle. I was about to say, 'That's personal', but Mimi stepped in without hesitation.

"I suppose I am," she said.

* * *

Mimi drove us from Paddington to Hendon, while Danny – leaning forward from the back seat – quizzed me relentlessly on the siege. Watching Mimi for guidance, I gave him a version that didn't add much to what had been in the media.

"I've spoken to Jackie," Mimi said, when Danny was having a rare pause for breath. "She's meeting us at your place."

My flat isn't homely, never mind stylish. My standards have slipped in the years of living alone, but we walked in to a welcoming smell of spicy odours drifting our way from the kitchen.

"Eat now?" Mimi said. "It's a Thai thing."

I nodded, too choked to speak. You wouldn't think a curry could do that, but it was a long time since anyone had cooked a meal for me in my own home.

So we ate, the three of us, plates on our laps in the living room, me and Danny on the settee, Mimi in an armchair, watching cricket on TV.

Danny was silent now, except when he was talking about the cricket, displaying a knowledge of the Pakistan and England players that made me realise how much homework I had to do to get this father-thing back on track.

When Jackie arrived, Danny had gathered our plates and was heading for the kitchen. She breezed past him into the living room, mobile pressed to one ear, finishing a call with a, 'Catch you later'. After pecking the cheeks of Mimi and me, she registered Danny's return to the living room with a look of slight surprise.

"Who have we here?" she said.

"This is Danny," I said, but she still seemed confused. "My son," I added.

"Oh right, great – you've got a son. Yes, I knew that," she said.

"Danny," I said. "You can stay while we talk but turn the volume down."

"Right, let's do this," Jackie said in brusque but sombre business mode, sitting down on the spare armchair and pulling a tablet out of her bag. She was facing Danny and me on the settee with Mimi on the other armchair to her right and the TV to her left silently showing Pakistan piling up the runs.

"We've had a chat," she continued, meaning with Mimi, "and I've spoken to Megan and Nigel. So I've got the picture: Will's a blackmailer or worse; Meg isn't quite off the hook with the police – but it looks like they know she's been stupid not criminal; and Rio's a lost cause. Meg's dug her heels in after that nasty piece in the paper this morning. I've tried talking her into delaying an announcement for a few days, but she's adamant she has to give them time to pick someone else and because she's a wreck, mentally – her head's all over the place. So somehow we've got to spin her pulling out as positively as we can to keep the sponsors on board. Is that about right?"

Mimi and I looked at each other, nodding in unison.

"So, Liam," Jackie continued. "You're the expert – how should we pitch it so the athletics fraternity doesn't react badly and the media doesn't bury us?"

Mimi let out a noise that sounded like a bird being throttled.

"You're kidding, right?" she said. "They're going to bury us whatever we say. They're bound to. The team's losing one of its best medal hopes at the last minute because, let's face it, she did a really bad thing. I mean, I sympathise with her, but – however you dress it up – you can't escape the fact she abandoned a dead or dying friend."

"But no one knows that yet," I said.

"Enough people know it for there to be a leak," Jackie said, and both of us looked at Mimi.

"Oddly, the Bannister piece helps," she said, absently, like she was running through it in her mind. "Meg can say she accepts that the uncertainty about her position is unfair on other athletes with the qualifying standard. She's pulling out now, so they have time to pack their bags for the flight on Thursday."

"I like that – giving them time to pack – make sure you get that in," Jackie said "And as for the Matt thing, can't we stick to the line it's a police matter and we can't comment?"

"Yes, it won't stop people gossiping on social media," Mimi said, "but the fact the police have charged Gary should help shut the media up. They'll have to be very careful what they say about anything to do with the case."

Mimi fell silent again, and we waited, sensing there was something else on her mind.

"I've spoken to the police press office this afternoon and they say the chief constable is making a statement at ten tomorrow morning. I'm not sure what it's about exactly but they were hinting something big's happening and there could be more arrests."

"That would be very helpful," Jackie said, a smile forming now as the path through the minefield became clearer. "Then we can have our press conference while they're all getting excited about that."

"I'll work on a statement, and you can check it later," Mimi said.

"Just make sure it reminds everyone about Meg helping to free the hostages," Jackie said. "The sponsors loved that – it averted a complete meltdown – and it's bought us some time. I think we can keep most of them on board as long as there's a sense Meg will be back. Mimi, you must mention the Worlds next year. Make sure Meg's quote says something about that, and, Liam – you'll be there tomorrow?"

My mind had wandered to the cricket. Pakistan were all out for an outrageous total, and Danny was slumped against me as we watched their batsmen leave the field.

"Sorry, where?" I said.

"Newport, Liam. We'll have to do it in Newport, don't you think? I can't see Megan coming down here."

This hadn't occurred to me. I looked at Mimi. She looked at Danny.

"He can't," Mimi said.

Jackie raised her eyebrows.

"Can't? Excuse me, this is Megan withdrawing from the Olympics, and Liam's her coach."

"I'm sorry Jackie, but I've got commitments," I said.

"Commitments?" Jackie said incredulously, as if nothing could be more important.

"Yes. I'm going for a bike ride with Danny for a start." Danny looked up at me, and I gave him a 'keep-your-mouth-shut' glare, not wanting him to give away the fact that we hadn't made any such plans.

"We don't need Liam to be there anyway," Mimi said. "If it's just a statement and some photos, Liam wouldn't be saying anything or answering any questions anyway. It's better if he isn't around. I can handle it."

Jackie's seemed unconvinced, but she started typing onto her tablet as if she was already moving on.

"Okay," she said. "Let's nail this down. I'll do a round-robin email and copy Meg and Nigel. So, the police will do their press conference at ten. We'll do ours later – in the afternoon at three o'clock. Will that give you enough time to get down there and set things up?"

Mimi nodded.

"Hold it at The Priory?"

Mimi nodded again.

"You'll do the statement tonight. Nigel to legal, me to check, then to the police for vetting. I'll warn UK Athletics.

"And you'll be on standby tomorrow if Mimi needs you?" Jackie said to me.

Mimi lost a battle to stop herself giggling. Jackie frowned at her like a teacher disgruntled by a childish pupil.

"Is there something I'm missing?" she said, turning to me.

"She's his girlfriend," Danny said helpfully.

26

THE STATEMENTS

"Nineteen people have been arrested in raids across England and Wales by police targeting a steroid cartel allegedly responsible for supplying drugs with a street value of more than £100m…"

The words entered a troubling dream I was having about Simmons interrogating Megan like she was a hard-core gangster. They swirled around in my semi-conscious paranoia for a few seconds until I realised I wasn't in a dark cell at Maindee police station.

It was the radio alarm, and I was now hearing that a reporter – I missed the name – 'had the details'. And the next voice said:

THE STATEMENTS

"Nineteen people were held after officers from the National Crime Squad and several police forces carried out early morning raids in South Wales, Bristol, Manchester, Nottingham and Leeds.

"The sixteen men and three women are thought to be involved in a drugs cartel supplying steroids to young people in dozens of gyms and schools for bodybuilding.

"A police spokesman said steroid use among male teenagers had reached epidemic levels, causing a number of deaths from infected needles and heart failure.

"The police are refusing to comment on whether or not the raids are connected with two arrests made over the weekend following a siege at a gym in Newport, during which Olympic gold medal hope Megan Tomos helped negotiators free three hostages.

"The chief constable of Gwent is holding a press conference later this morning. The BBC understands the Home Secretary will be making a statement on the police raids in the House of Commons this afternoon."

I was sitting up on the edge of the bed now. The alarm said it was 8.03. I switched the radio off and looked over my shoulder at the bed. Mimi wasn't in it. I wasn't sure what day it was, but the Watford Way roaring outside told me I was in London and it wasn't Sunday. I opened the curtains and watched a few people below walking down to the tube station at Hendon Central. Some of them were familiar, which was not surprising as I'd lived in the flat for ten years and in Hendon for most of my adult life. It felt good to be back in my home territory, and I had an urge to let out a few ape-whoops to let the neighbours know I was around.

But the phone rang.

"Oh my God," Mimi said, sounding like she'd swallowed helium. "Have you heard the news? I was expecting something big – I spoke to Nigel last night – but, oh my God – not this big… Not nineteen arrests, not… Liam?"

Part of me was still somewhere in the depths of Maindee police station and another part was thinking about apes and what nice, peaceful vegetarians most of them are.

"Yeah, yeah, I heard," I said. "Just now, on the news."

"Are you okay?" Mimi said.

"Slept really heavily, that's all. Haven't woken up properly yet."

"You sound rough."

"Yeah. I feel a bit groggy. What day is it by the way?"

"Liam, get your act together. It's Monday, and I'm on a train to – guess where? – Newport. Meg's pulling out of the Olympics today, and you're going out on your bike with Danny."

"Right, got it now," I replied, stretching and letting out a half-yawn. "So what time did you leave?"

"I didn't stay Liam. I left you and Danny to it."

"Right, right – yes, I'd forgotten," I said. "But you're coming here tonight, right?"

"Yes, Liam, with my toothbrush and clean knicks." Mimi gave me a mischievous giggle. "I've got to go now," she said. "Work to do."

* * *

I gave Danny an hour or so to lie in. It was, after all, the first Monday of the school holidays, and besides, I wanted to check all the drug raid stories online to see what they were saying about Megan.

I booted-up my old PC on a makeshift desk in the corner of the living room and searched through all the news about the raids, the siege and Megan. They were all much the same as the radio report, except longer and with more of the background rehashed. There were innuendos about Megan's links with Will and mentions of her 'helping the police with their enquiries', but most of the media were – like the Sunday papers – still portraying her as the heroine of the siege.

I imagined Mimi on the train going through them too, adjusting Megan's statement for anything new, as far as she could. She had emailed me a copy of the draft, with a note saying she'd 'tickle' it in the morning if there were 'developments'.

I couldn't work out how the raids would affect the way people would see Megan. Would they think she was linked to this drugs cartel and had turned snitch? Or would they see her as innocently caught up in it all? The sooner the police made a statement saying Megan was no longer part of their enquiries the better. But even then – as Mimi had pointed out – she wouldn't be able to admit her mistakes publicly and move on because she would be a witness at the trial of Gary and Will. That would be when the whole truth about the night Matt died and everything since would – or should – come out.

I felt a sense of emptiness in the pit of my stomach. The reality of Meg actually pulling-out of the Olympics was kicking-in. For two years, my life had been divided between things I had to do now and things that could wait until after Rio. I hadn't had a proper holiday – that was for 'after Rio'. I hadn't paid much attention to my day job – work on the new curriculum could wait until after Rio. And I'd spent even less time with Danny – if that was possible – because Meg had a Diamond League meeting or a vital training session.

Even the satisfaction of playing a part in bringing Will and Gary and nineteen others like them to justice didn't feel complete. These people were probably small fry, foot soldiers. Running a multi-million pound cartel was way beyond the capabilities of the likes of Will and Gary. So who was behind it? Who really raked in the profits? And how did the peddling of steroids tie-in with the culture of bodybuilding, with Action Man having ever-bigger dimensions and magazines full of males with ludicrously toned bodies? It all seemed oddly orchestrated, too convenient, and it left me fearing for Danny and the pressures he would face.

* * *

Danny was sleeping heavily, lying diagonally across the narrow bed in his room, when I walked in. His head was over the edge of one side, and one foot was dangling from the other. I put a glass of milk down on a wonky DIY unit I'd put together in a hurry when I was decorating the room a few years ago – an earlier attempt at trying to show Kelli I was serious about being Danny's father.

Danny was wearing boxers, and I was surprised how

broad his bare shoulders seemed in the half-light coming through the thin curtains. His voice hadn't broken yet, but he was looking more and more like a teenager every day. I was running out of time.

"Dan," I said. "There's some milk there for you."

He groaned and wriggled a little, pulling the duvet over himself in a tangled heap.

"You still up for this bike ride?" I said.

He groaned some more.

"Okay, we need to go soon, because I have to get back to see Meg's press conference on TV."

"Daaaad," he said.

I left him to it, but he did surface about half an hour later, staggering into the kitchen, rubbing his wiry black hair with one hand, his other hand shoved down his boxers.

"Have a shower and I'll do some breakfast," I said, with a cheery tone that was probably physically painful to the ears of a 12-year-old.

He gave me a jerky, silent nod and shuffled into the bathroom.

* * *

Our bike ride took in all my favourite Hendon spots: the Burroughs field where cows used to graze in my childhood; St Mary's church and the old church farmhouse; the top path through Sunnyhill Park, and over to Copthall playing fields, stretching out with Mill Hill rising behind.

We pedalled through my territory, Dan chatting about the cricket and his school, and me telling a few childhood stories. When it was my turn, Dan would listen and ask questions, his bright-eyed curiosity not yet suppressed by adolescent sullenness.

As Copthall athletics stadium came into view, I felt a spasm of emotion. It's a ramshackle place. The facelifts given to the fifty-year-old concrete stand on the home straight can't hide its age and inadequacies. And the new seating on the back straight - built for recent intruders Saracens rugby club - would never win a design award. But Copthall was my addiction, and I still got a buzz out of seeing the place full.

Danny and I stopped at an entrance near the finish line, where you could peer in through steel gates at the track and the stands. I could visualise Megan on the track, grimacing as she pushed herself to the limit, all that effort, all those sessions not now being taken to their natural conclusion in Rio.

"Do you think that's good, Dad?" Danny said.

He was reading a plaque I had never noticed before, the club motto of the Saracens: Honesty, Work Rate, Humility, Discipline.

"It'll do for starters," I said.

* * *

We arrived back at the flat and switched the TV on just in time to catch Megan's announcement. The news channel presenter was saying, *"We're going live now to Newport for an update on the breaking story that Megan Tomos, widely considered Britain's best hope for an Olympic track medal, will not be going to Rio".*

The face of a male reporter came up on screen. He was

on the lawn at The Priory with dozens of people milling around behind.

"Chris, what's the latest?" the presenter said.

"Well, this looks set to be an unusual press conference," he said, gesturing to the scene behind him. *"It seems this hotel in Caerleon has been Tomos's hideaway for the last week. This is the first time she's spoken to the media since before the Olympic trials, and of course there's been mounting speculation she might pull out of the Olympics…"*

"And we understand she's going to confirm that today," the presenter said.

"Yes, we haven't been issued with a press release yet, which is a bit odd, and there seems to be some delay, but the spin from her team earlier was that she's pulling-out because her situation is so uncertain and she wants to give the selectors a chance to pick someone else…"

"There seems to be some activity behind you," the presenter said, and the reporter looked over his shoulder as the camera zoomed-in on Megan, striding across the lawn with Mimi on one side and Graeme on the other.

"Graeme? What the hell..?" I said to Danny and slumped on settee.

The three of them lined-up, standing in front of a single microphone with the photographers gathering into a semi-circle, crouching with cameras whirring.

Megan stepped forward, holding a single sheet of paper and looking nervous and pale in the unforgiving mid-afternoon sun.

"There has been a great deal of speculation about whether or not I'm going to be taking part in the Olympic Games in Rio," she said, obviously reading from a statement. *"As you know, on Saturday, I was involved in helping the police free three hostages taken by a former friend who has now been charged and is in police custody.*

"You also know that the police have made a number of other arrests relating to a steroids cartel operating across the country and that the police are separately investigating the death of my friend Matthew Davies, whose father Graeme is here today.

"I can't comment on any of this – that's a matter for the police – but I'm pleased to say that I have been cleared of any wrongdoing and that I have now given a witness statement to the police to help them with their enquiries."

Megan smiled in an earnest, diffident way and then seemed to swallow on her next words, bowing her head as if she was struggling to continue.

Mimi and Graeme stepped forward, each holding one of Megan's arms.

"Dad, what's going on?" Danny said

"I haven't a clue – where's my phone? Can you have a look in the kitchen? I think it's in there," I said, not wanting to miss anything.

Mimi was whispering something in Meg's ear, but Meg was shaking her head, and she looked up and started speaking again.

"But I have made mistakes," she continued, *"and I regret some of the decisions I've made and the people I've trusted. But my family and friends, and especially Mr Davies, have urged me to put those things behind me and go to Rio to do my best for the team and for them and for the memory of Matt."*

At those words, I was as close to passing-out as I've been since drinking a bottle of vodka on my 18th birthday.

I looked up, and Danny was standing over me holding out my phone.

"So she's going after all!" he said.

"So it seems," I said, grabbing the phone. It was showing six missed calls and three messages from Mimi.

```
Call me
Where the fuck are you?
Meg's going to Rio. x
```

* * *

As I was still digesting this, the phone went, and Mimi's name came up on the screen. I looked up at the TV and could see her walking away from the camera with Megan and Graeme and with the phone to her ear.

"What the hell's going on?" I said, practically hyperventilating with excitement.

"You saw it," Mimi said. "She's going!"

"So what happened? How come?"

"Graeme. It was Graeme. Apparently, he was furious when he found out she'd decided not to go and went to see Richards this morning, and it's been bedlam ever since. The chief constable intervened. Suddenly, the frigging pathology report could be turned round in an hour! Meg was off the hook, and I was tearing up my press release and going mad trying to contact you and write that statement. But didn't she do well?"

I was too choked to speak.

"Liam – are you okay," Mimi said.

Danny sat down next to me and put an arm round my shoulder.

"Yes," I said. "She did very well indeed."

EPILOGUE

FOUR WEEKS LATER

MY PHONE PINGED WITH A text:

Enjoy this Liam. You've definitely earned it!
Love Mimi and Danny Xx

I was sitting in the Maracana Stadium with about seventy-five thousand other people watching Megan and seven other 100m hurdles finalists peeling-off their tracksuits ready to be introduced to the crowd.

While I was waiting for Megan to appear, I had been pondering how many double-decker buses all these people would fill, thinking this was indeed a far cry from cold winter nights at Copthall, or even a packed Alexander Stadium.

I had been to three previous Olympics – London, Sydney and Athens – but I had never had an athlete in a final and nothing had prepared me for the mix of euphoria and nausea I was feeling.

As usual, the other coaches and I had been allocated seats just beyond the finish line, allowing us to look down the home straight across the tops of the perfectly-aligned rows of hurdles that seemed from this angle far too close together for athletes racing at such speed.

Mimi and Danny were going to watch the race on the TV in our hotel room. Tickets were scarce – we knew that before we came – but Megan and Kelli had insisted on paying for Danny to come, haggling with each other to do the honours. The upshot was that Danny was having the time of his life: Kelli had paid for the flights and his spending money, while Megan told Jackie to fix us up with a palatial suite in one of the best hotels in Rio and a post-Olympic boat trip up the Amazon.

Megan, meanwhile, was staying in the Olympic Village, protected from the paparazzi, some of whom were on a mission to grab any shot that could portray her in some pre-determined negative light – as 'troubled' or 'tearful' – you name it.

After the siege and the press conference, numerous, often anonymous 'friends' had popped up with fantastic stories about her. She hardly seemed to be off the front pages of some tabloids, fuelling a build-up of anticipation for the final that was alarmingly disproportionate and often poisonous.

I had been receiving daily reports from Mimi while we were at Belo Horizonte but, thankfully, Megan was largely oblivious to all this. We had left for the holding camp only three days after the press conference, and Meg had become intensely focused on making-up for the time she had lost. We had broken the event down into all its components, polished each and every one of them and pieced them back together meticulously like a highly-tuned machine.

And it seemed to be working. Megan had sailed through the rounds, looking as sharp and confident as her main rivals: the American, Debbie Masters, and the Russian, Natasha Sholokhova. But Masters had edged the faster time in winning her semi-final and was being talked about by almost every pundit – except the British ones – as the favourite.

As I looked at Megan now, walking back after rehearsing her start, I knew she was capable of winning and I knew, equally, that she could stumble and come last. It was in the nature of this event that something could go dramatically wrong; that years of work could be undone by a split-second miscalculation, a slightly misjudged stride pattern or a spike coming unscrewed.

And it was in the nature of coaching that there was nothing more you could do once you had said good-bye to your athlete at the entrance to the long walkway to the pre-race holding area. On this occasion, for the first time, I had kissed Megan on the cheek, attracting surprised looks from the other finalists passing by. It may not be in the coach's handbook, but it seemed so natural after what we'd been through to get here.

The athletes were lining up now and being introduced to the crowd and a global TV audience running to billions. When Megan's turn came, she lifted both arms to give a two-handed wave turning in a half-circle to take in most of the stadium. On my virtual clap-o-meter – otherwise known as my ears – she had the biggest reception of any of the finalists, but it could have been that I was clapping very loudly myself.

Another text from Mimi pinged:

She's looking good

I was too nervous to reply, and – my superstitious streak surfacing – I didn't want to tempt fate by agreeing. It was too late anyway because the starter had them under orders and the crowd was falling silent.

The athletes settled into their blocks. The screen above the Start was showing a close-up of Megan. She looked twitchy but seemed to find the right spot for her fingers and thumbs on the line just as the starter said, 'Set'.

The athletes rose as one and burst into a sprint before the delayed sound of the gun had reached my ears.

Megan, Natasha and Debbie reached the first hurdle together, but Debbie was more upright at take-off and brought her trail leg down faster. By the second hurdle, she had taken a slight lead, which she held through the middle part of the race. But Megan and Natasha were both running well and seemed to be pulling level as they approached the final hurdle. They rose together, their technique perfect, and there was next-to-nothing separating them as they sprinted and dipped for the line.

I had no idea who'd won. The judges were examining the photo finish.

Megan was wide-eyed and euphoric, bouncing up and down and then linking arms in a circle with Natasha and Debbie like footballers in a team huddle after a match.

Meg broke away from the others, her eyes going first to the judges, who still hadn't made a decision, and then to the section of the stand where I was, on my feet, hemmed-in by all the other cheering spectators.

She started scanning the rows, trying to pick me out, knowing from my ticket I would be about halfway back near the middle. I waved furiously, and she seemed to look in my direction without seeing me.

Finally our eyes met, and hers were sparkling as she smiled that charming smile, and we held that look for a fraction of a moment until the screaming erupted and Meg buried her face in her hands, and I knew the result must have flashed onto the screens, but I couldn't bear to look.

ABOUT THE AUTHOR

STEVE HOWELL WAS BORN ON Merseyside, and brought up in Hendon, north London. He went to university in Sheffield, where he stayed for more than a decade working in the steel industry and local government. He has lived in Newport, South Wales, since 1993 with his Welsh wife, Kim, and their three (now grown-up) children.

Steve has been passionate about athletics since competing as a junior and for his school's highly successful team. He subsequently competed at club level and ran for Wales as a veteran. For a number of years, he was in the same training group as Olympic athletes Christian Malcolm and Jamie Baulch, and both remain good friends.

Steve's professional career spans local government,

journalism, PR and business. In the 1990s, he worked in print journalism (including for *Athletics Weekly*, *Today's Runner* and *Runner's World*, *The Argus*, *The Independent* and *The Guardian*, and was a member of the Athletics Writers' Association) and as a *BBC* radio and TV news reporter (among other things covering sieges and suspicious deaths). In 1997, he set up a PR agency, Freshwater UK, which grew to become one of the UK's largest independent consultancies. Steve appears on Radio Wales in panel discussions and as a newspaper reviewer, on programmes such as *Sunday Edition*, *Wales At Work* and *The Jamie Owen Show*.

For a number of years, Steve has been writing short stories and working on this novel and is now in a position to concentrate on writing fiction more fully. In addition to fiction, he writes a business column for the *Western Mail* and occasional pieces for other publications. ***Over The Line*** is his first novel. It draws from his experience as a parent, journalist and athlete and from first-hand knowledge of steroid abuse for body-building in South Wales.

Twitter @fromstevehowell

ACKNOWLEDGEMENTS

THIS BOOK GREW OUT OF conversations with people who have direct – and, in one case, tragic – experience of steroid abuse. Some of them cannot be named but they know I am grateful for their insights.

My thanks also to numerous other people who have helped and who I can name. I spent several enjoyable evenings discussing the plot and police procedures with Martyn Jones, a former police superintendent who was deputy head of crime in South Wales. Another friend, consultant epidemiologist Professor John Watkins, shared his knowledge of the steroid scene and acted as a sounding board for my ideas, as well as being my athletics training partner when I was still competing. And I am grateful to Nigel Walker, the former Olympic hurdler and current National Director of the English Institute of Sport, for finding time to answer my questions on the lifestyle of an elite athlete and the preparations for Rio.

I am lucky my family has been so unstinting in their support through all the ups and downs of this project and so willing to take time to help and share their thoughts. My daughter Cerys and her partner Sion read an early draft and gave invaluable feedback. My son Josh answered my endless questions on the youth scene in Newport – any failures in authenticity on that score are entirely mine. My eldest, Gareth, and his partner Cynthia put up with me writing at all hours when I was visiting them in Long Beach, California. And my wife Kim deployed a red pen extensively on the very first draft and has been a sounding board – as well as source of encouragement – from start to finish.

I am grateful to my friend Steve Hoselitz, who was my editor at the South Wales *Argus* in the mid-nineties, and to his wife, Virginia, for reading an early draft and giving me numerous useful comments.

I also sought professional literary advice from Lorna Howarth of The Write Factor to whom I'm indebted for providing a thorough manuscript review and then undertaking the task of editing and proofing the final draft.

My thanks to the directors of Freshwater UK for their support and to my colleagues, Louise Harris and Elinor Evans, for providing the Welsh translation in Chapter 15.

The excellent cover design is the work of Peter Reynolds, and the rest of the book design and lay-out was undertaken by The Write Factor.

My re-acquaintance with Hendon (where I was brought up) was aided by the helpful and friendly staff of the University of Middlesex library, Copthall Stadium and Forever Flowers (coffee shop and florist).

The book was written mainly at home in Caerleon, Newport and while visiting Long Beach. However, I also had very productive writing breaks at a cottage overlooking Llangollen and The Green Man Inn at Fownhope, Herefordshire.

While all the people mentioned have been hugely helpful, I am ultimately the author of every word in the book – any errors are entirely my responsibility.

And, finally, a special thanks to my two-year-old grand-daughter Ilana Megan Howell for being an inspiration.